"Go," Beckham said. He twisted the doorknob with a click and stepped out into the humid night.

Wind whipped against his body armor as he moved with calculated steps. Beckham pushed his scarf farther over his face until it was just below his eyes. He charged forward with his jaw clenched shut, breathing into the cotton.

His eyes darted from the abandoned vehicles to the gas station at the end of the lot. His gut told him they weren't being watched, that they were in the clear, and his eyes revealed nothing but the rustling of tree branches and swirling wrappers.

Then a guttural screech sent him running for the nearest vehicle. Beckham slid onto his knees and propped his back against the passenger's-side door. Horn took up position behind a pickup.

"One o'clock," Horn said, his voice cold and tense.

Beckham swept his rifle toward the roof of the Kangaroo Express. Two of the creatures were perched on the ledge, their pale, naked skin shimmering under the moonlight.

The shattering of glass pulled Beckham's gaze to the entrance of the building, where a male and female emerged from the broken front door. Their bodies were twisted and grotesque, their joints snapping as they turned in place, looking for their prey.

Horn made a dash to the car and took a knee next to Beckham.

"They know we're here," he said.

"If we take them out, we'll draw others."

"I'm not sure we can outrun them," Horn said. "I don't think we have a choice."

Books by Nicholas Sansbury Smith

The Extinction Cycle

Extinction Horizon
Extinction Edge
Extinction Age
Extinction Evolution
Extinction End
Extinction Aftermath
"Extinction Lost" (An Extinction Cycle Short Story)
Extinction War (Fall 2017)

Trackers: A Post-Apocalyptic EMP Series

Trackers
Trackers 2: The Hunted (Spring 2017)
Trackers 3: The Storm (Winter 2017)

The Hell Divers Trilogy

Hell Divers
Hell Divers 2: Ghosts (Summer 2017)
Hell Divers 3: Deliverance (Summer 2018)

The Orbs Series

"Solar Storms" (An Orbs Prequel)
"White Sands" (An Orbs Prequel)
"Red Sands" (An Orbs Prequel)
Orbs
Orbs 2: Stranded
Orbs 3: Redemption

The Extinction Cycle
Book Two

NICHOLAS SANSBURY SMITH

www.orbitbooks.net

Orbit
Hachette Book Group
1290 Avenue of the Americas
New York, NY 10104
orbitbooks.net

Originally published in ebook by Orbit in February 2017
First Mass Market Edition: June 2017

Orbit is an imprint of Hachette Book Group.
The Orbit name and logo are trademarks of Little, Brown Book Group Limited.

ISBNs: 978-0-316-55803-7 (mass market), 978-0-316-55890-7 (ebook)

Printed in the United States of America

OPM

10 9 8 7 6 5 4 3 2 1

For my nephew Noah James Angaran Smith.

"Biological diversity is messy. It walks, it crawls, it swims, it swoops, it buzzes. But extinction is silent, and it has no voice other than our own."

—*Paul Hawken*

Prologue

The popping of distant gunfire startled Meg Pratt awake. She jolted upright, wondering at first if she was still dreaming.

The stillness of the night closed in on her like a vise. Reality slowly set in as she remembered, bringing with it a wave of despair and anxiety that worked its way from her gut to her pounding heart. Several fuzzy minutes passed before she came to her senses.

She had awoken from one nightmare only to enter another. Over two weeks had passed since the hemorrhage virus swept across the nation. Honking horns, blaring sirens, and shouts from noisy neighbors were absent now. New York City was a dead zone. No more neon lights, no more blinking advertisements.

The old world was gone, and no one could bring it back.

After rubbing her eyes, she scanned the room. Jed and Rex slept in the adjacent beds, their silhouettes frozen in the rays of moonlight seeping through the gaps in the boarded-up windows.

Meg examined the two-by-fours she and the other firefighters had hastily nailed across the windows. So much had happened in a short time. As her gaze fell upon the empty beds neatly lined up throughout the rest of the room, her mind and heart ached.

The agony was brief, ripped away by more gunshots. She held a breath in her chest, listening, trying to pinpoint a location, but once again the noise slipped away. It was the first sign of a military presence since the jets had swooped in twelve hours ago.

The next round of gunfire came a moment later, the crack of fully automatic weapons. The noise reverberated through the derelict city streets. It had to be military. There had been only a few civilians who could get their hands on that type of firepower, and they were all dead.

"You hear that?" asked a voice a few feet away. It was Jed, the quiet marine with a Southern accent. Meg's crew had taken him in days earlier when his platoon had been wiped out ten blocks away.

Jed swung his feet over the side of his bed and crossed the room on his toes. The creaking of floorboards woke up Rex. All three hundred pounds of him shot upright. "What's going on? Did they find us?" He ran a hand through his thick red hair.

"Shhh," Meg said, holding a finger to her mouth. She'd always found Rex to be a bit paranoid for a man of his size. But she couldn't fault him for that now, especially after the unthinkable things they'd seen. The three of them were all that was left now. Every other civilian and firefighter that had sheltered here had died. Their families and friends were dead. Everyone they ever knew was gone.

Meg closed her eyes at the thought of her husband, infected and crazed. She'd watched him kill a neighbor before a soldier gunned him down. No matter how many times she told herself it wasn't her husband who died that day, she still couldn't bring herself to believe it.

Some small part of him had remained when the bullets tore through his body. She had seen it in his dying eyes.

Grabbing her axe, Meg joined Jed at the window.

"See anything?" she asked.

"Not yet."

Pressing her right eye against a crack in the boards, Meg scanned the rooftops for motion. She flinched when the gunshots came again. They were getting closer.

Meg continued to probe the darkness, her gaze stopping on the gargoyles that protruded off the stone ledges two buildings down. There was something else too, something moving in the shadows.

"You see that?" Meg asked.

Jed squinted. "I can't really see anything."

Another round of automatic gunfire broke out. Muzzle flashes flickered on the rooftop, illuminating the silhouettes of soldiers. They fired as they ran. And although Meg couldn't see the ravenous creatures chasing them, she knew they were out there.

"Soldiers," Jed whispered. "And..."

Meg pressed her eye closer, scratching her forehead on the coarse wood. Moonlight spilled from the clouds and lit up the rooftops.

A chill spiked through Meg's body when she saw the dozens of infected chasing the soldiers. The pack skittered across the rooftop and along the exterior walls of the building like human-sized insects.

The gunfire couldn't mask the noises the creatures made—the scratching, the clicking joints, and their primal screams. These no longer seemed like men and women; they were the predators of the new world. Humans were transformed into monsters through the hemorrhage virus. People like her best friend, Eric, a man she'd known her entire life. Turning her axe on him had been the hardest thing Meg had ever done. She could still hear the crunch of bone and the screams of agony.

Meg brushed a lock of brown hair from her face and pressed her eye closer to the crack in the wood, following the soldiers as they jumped from ledge to ledge. They were fast, but the creatures were faster.

She remembered her own narrow escape from a pack of the monsters when they'd rescued Jed. She could outrun almost every firefighter she had worked with. She was a three-time Ironman triathlete. But it wasn't the endurance or speed she'd gained from swimming, biking, and running over 140 miles in a day that had secured her escape. It was the adrenaline that only pure fear could produce.

She imagined the soldiers were experiencing that same adrenaline rush. They eased to a stop on the next rooftop; a thirty-foot-tall billboard loomed over their bulky frames.

"They're out of room," Meg whispered. She strained to see the creatures trailing the team. Shadowy shapes dashed across the buildings, apparitions in the night.

More flashes lit up the scene. The three soldiers stood close together, firing at the horde of infected racing toward them. The deformed creatures twitched and jerked, dropping one by one as bullets riddled their bodies. It was over in a few seconds.

The moon vanished, the sky swallowing the light like a brooding storm.

Meg pulled away from the boards at the sound of heavy footfalls. Rex had finally decided to get out of bed. The man walked hesitantly toward the window.

"I think we should try to get to that rooftop," Jed whispered.

"Are you insane?" Rex said. "We won't make it for more than two minutes outside."

The distant thump of a helicopter pulled Meg back to the window. Her eyes roved across the skyline, searching for the aircraft.

"Hear that? That's our ticket out of this hellhole." Meg gripped her axe tighter. "I'm with Jed. We need to get to that rooftop."

"We don't have much time; we need to move," Jed added.

"But—no—we..." Rex trailed off.

"What's that?" Infected were climbing the back of the billboard now. There were a half dozen of them, maybe more.

"Shit," Meg said. She scanned the roof for the soldiers and spotted them on the east and south ledge. For a moment they looked like the gargoyles, frozen as they waited for extraction, oblivious to the approaching threat.

"Those things are going to sneak up on them!" Jed said in a voice just shy of a shout. "We have to warn them."

Rex grabbed the marine by his arm. "Keep it down. Are you crazy? They'll hear you."

Meg watched with gritted teeth. "There isn't anything we can do. Not from here." Rex was right. He was a paranoid son of a bitch, but he was right. The infected were drawn to noises—and the scent of flesh. From the safety of the boarded-up room, she'd seen the creatures sniffing the air, hunting other survivors. And here she was again, helplessly watching the three unsuspecting soldiers as the monsters advanced. There was no running from them. No escape. Hiding was the only option.

Blinking red lights on the skyline pulled her gaze away from the roof. The sleek outline of a Black Hawk descended over the building. There was no way Meg and the others would make it to the rooftop, even if they tried. They were stranded.

Jed pulled out of Rex's grip and moved back to the two-by-fours. "Oh my God," he whispered.

The creatures spilled over the top of the billboard. They slid down the other side, and then Meg lost sight of them. Gunfire lit up the south ledge as the soldiers opened fire.

Adrenaline flooded Meg's system with each shot. She was used to running into fires. It was almost worse being on the opposite side of the fence. She had joined the Fire Department of New York City to help people, not watch them die.

The chopper hovered low, and tracer rounds streaked through the night, each one hitting its target as the soldiers fought back the infected swarm. Meg strained to see, but the gunfire ceased almost as fast as it started. The chopper pulled to the right and then flew away over the skyline. Just like that it was gone, the red lights blinking one last time before there was only darkness.

Meg cursed their luck. They hadn't seen a chopper in days, let alone one so close.

"Great," Jed said. "That's fucking great." He scratched his closely trimmed crew cut and then slammed his hand into the boards.

Meg glared at the marine. "Keep it down."

Jed shrugged and muttered an apology. He had turned away and started walking back to his bunk when the sound of shattering glass came from below.

The three of them froze.

A guttural screech ripped through the building. Pounding followed. The walls shook from the impact. It sounded as though a wild animal was loose on the first floor.

Rex grabbed Meg's arm as she stepped away from the window.

"Don't go down there," he said.

Meg shook free and exchanged nods with Jed. Together, they crossed the room cautiously. She eyed the empty M16 on Jed's bunk. Without a gun, Meg felt naked. Her axe slowed the creatures down, but bullets were much more effective.

A second scream echoed through the fire station, the sound lingering in the night. Meg gritted her teeth and stopped. The axe slipped in her grip, sweat bleeding off her palm.

"Guys," Rex said. "Guys, come back."

Meg held up a hand to silence him. Then she heard the clicking. It was the sound of cracking joints, and it wasn't coming from inside the building. It was coming from the street, as if they were surrounded by hundreds of oversized crickets. Rex stood with his eye pressed against one of the gaps at the windows.

"Oh no," he said.

Meg scanned the bookshelves and boxes in front of the door. If the monsters found them, the barricade wouldn't hold for long.

"Let me see," Meg said. She tapped Rex on the shoulder. The man's thick arms were trembling.

She pressed her eye against the crack in the boards, waiting for her eyes to adjust to the dark. Movement flickered across the rooftops, but how—

"Holy shit," Meg gasped. She had never seen so many infected in one spot. The entire street and even the walls of the buildings had come alive with a blur of flesh.

"They must have been drawn to the gunfire," Jed said.

"What do we do?" Rex asked, his words a panicked slur.

Meg shook her head. "We pray."

1

Two Days Later . . .

The room erupted with applause as Dr. Kate Lovato entered the mess hall. Uniformed men and women from every branch of the military stood and clapped, cheering as she walked past.

The sound took Kate's breath away. Ever since her bioweapon, VariantX9H9, had been deployed, she had been hailed as the "savior" of the world, the woman who had stopped the hemorrhage virus in its tracks. But there were others in the audience who glared at her with resentment. She knew what they were thinking: She wasn't a savior, she was a monster. And she felt like one. The burden of so much death rested solely on her shoulders. The weight made it difficult to breathe.

Her gaze gravitated to the commander of Plum Island, Lieutenant Colonel Ray Jensen. The African American commander narrowed his eyes as she approached. He clapped with the others, but he was sizing her up too, seeing if she was mentally fit to address the crowd. They had let her out of quarantine only a day earlier, and she was still a bit groggy.

"Good morning, everyone," Jensen said, bringing a mic

to his mouth. "I think all of you know Doctor Kate Lovato, with the CDC."

More cheering rang through the room. Kate scanned the faces for someone familiar, but soon realized she was alone. Her friends were all working. Dr. Pat Ellis was in the lab, and Master Sergeant Reed Beckham and Staff Sergeant Parker Horn were in the hospital with their injured teammate, Staff Sergeant Alex Riley. The kid had come back from New York with two shattered legs. He was evidence that her weapon hadn't killed all of the monsters—a new threat had emerged in the blood-soaked streets.

The Variants.

Kate shivered at the thought. The memory of the Variant that had attacked her two days ago was fresh on her mind. She could still hear the creature's claws skittering across the ceiling. It was an experience she would never forget.

"Thank you for coming, Doctor," Jensen said. He handed Kate the mic and gestured toward a podium with the Medical Corps insignia on the front.

Kate knew what he wanted from her. He wanted her to reassure the staff on Plum Island that there was still hope, that the Variants could be defeated.

Clearing her throat, she said, "Good morning, everyone. I was told to give you all a sitrep on what's happening outside. There is good news and bad news. The good news is that VariantX9H9 is still being deployed in every major city. Ninety percent of the infected are dying. The weapon attacks their endothelial cells and causes massive internal bleeding. It's a relatively quick death."

Kate paused and scanned the crowd, focusing on a woman in the front row. She was dressed in a neatly pressed navy uniform. The officer couldn't have been more than twenty-five years old. When she saw Kate looking at her, she stiffened her back and smiled. Her eyes pleaded with Kate to say something encouraging, to tell them that things were going to be okay.

But Kate couldn't lie. She couldn't feed these people false hope. After a brief pause, she continued. "The bad news is that the other ten percent of the infected are recovering from the Ebola virus, but not the effects of VX-99. Those epigenetic changes seem to be irreversible at this point."

The word hung in the air, and nervous voices broke from the crowd. A familiar feeling of dread crept into her thoughts and caused her mind to drift. It threatened to steal her sanity, to break her.

Closing her eyes, she said, "I don't believe there is anything we can do to bring these people back." She shook her head. As she handed the mic back to Jensen, she muttered two final words: "I'm sorry."

She rushed out of the room with her eyes downcast, avoiding every single glare. No one stopped her or protested her departure. They were still digesting what she had just told them. Learning that VariantX9H9 had only delayed the inevitable was difficult to stomach, even for the most hardened of soldiers.

A Medical Corps guard opened the door, and Kate stumbled out into the blinding morning sunlight. Shielding her eyes with a hand, she looked out over the island.

Kate wasn't the type of person to leave others behind. She never ran from a fight. But the death toll from her bioweapon had taken a piece of her. The numbers were hard to fathom, with billions of losses that produced a constant ache that wouldn't go away.

She walked aimlessly across the island and paused to study the ocean, wondering what was on the other side. In the end, she'd done her job. She had stopped the spread of the virus, though she'd fallen short in eradicating the monsters. Now she could only wonder what the world looked like beyond the safety of the island.

The American military had shared the recipe for VariantX9H9 with the nation's European allies, but the strike on foreign soil had come days after the US operation. Kate hoped it hadn't been too late to save her parents, living in Italy.

Exhaling a sigh, she continued through the hexagonal campus. The white, domed buildings rose above her. She wasn't sure where she was headed; her thoughts were muddied with guilt and regrets. They drifted from Javier, her brother, to her mentor, Dr. Michael Allen. They'd been dead even before the missiles descended on Atlanta and Chicago, but if they hadn't, they would have died from VariantX9H9. From *her* bioweapon.

Kate choked on the thought.

She didn't fight the tears that streaked down her cheeks. Everyone had a breaking point, a moment where everything came crashing down. Kate had finally reached hers.

There was only one person left in the world who could make her feel better, and he was in the medical building nearby. For the first time that morning, Kate felt a sudden burst of energy. She finally knew where she was going.

Staff Sergeant Alex Riley couldn't believe his fate. He'd built a career on his speed and his ability to sneak in and out of some of the most secure locations in the world. Now he lay in a hospital bed, staring at his shattered legs and wondering if he would ever run again.

If it weren't for Beckham and Horn, he would never have made it off that rooftop. Then again, he would never have made it out of Building 8 at San Nicolas Island without them either. What were the odds?

Riley let out a sad laugh.

The noise woke Horn and Beckham. They stirred in stiff-looking chairs facing the foot of his bed.

"Feeling better?" Beckham asked.

Riley eyed his casts. "I'm happy to be alive. But my legs, man."

"They'll heal," Beckham said.

"I thought you were toast, Kid," Horn said, his voice scratchy.

"Me too," Beckham said.

"Shit. It's going to take a lot more than some crazed shithead to take me out." Riley laughed. "I would have been fine without you guys."

Horn rolled his eyes. "Right. You had the situation under *complete* control."

"Damn straight," Riley said.

The three men chuckled. It was the first time in weeks that they'd all had a good laugh. It was like old times, but they knew that things would never be the same.

A rap on the door pulled them back to the grim reality of the status quo, where old times were nothing but memories. Kate waited outside, waving from the other side of the small window in the door.

"Beckham, it's your girlfriend," Riley said, jerking his chin toward Kate.

Beckham shot him an angry glare but didn't respond. His narrowed, dark eyes were enough to silence Riley. He knew what Beckham was thinking: *Keep your trap shut or you're going to stay in that bed even longer.*

"It's open," Horn mumbled, scooting his chair to the side.

"Morning," Kate said.

Riley picked up a hint of sadness in her soft voice. He

watched her walk into the room and stand a few feet away from Beckham. The shadows of the dimly lit space couldn't conceal her swollen, red eyes. It wasn't surprising, Riley thought, considering she had killed most of the world's population.

"How are you doing, Alex?" Kate asked. She hardly made eye contact with the men.

Riley forced a smile. He wasn't used to people calling him by his first name. "I'm feeling much better. The pain meds here are killer."

Kate nodded. "You can thank Colonel Gibson for that."

"How's that piece of shit doing?" Horn asked.

"He's awaiting trial," Kate said. "I noticed Lieutenant Colonel Jensen posted another guard outside his room. Must be worried about the man's safety."

Beckham stood and stretched. "I would be too, if I were him."

"There aren't enough soldiers on this island to protect Gibson from what's comin' to him." Horn snorted.

Riley shuddered. His friends were right. The colonel was partially responsible for the end of the world. He had earned a spot at the top of the list of the biggest assholes in the history of the human species.

"Any developments?" Beckham asked.

Kate shook her head. "Not really. We have reports coming in from Europe that VariantX9H9 has destroyed around ninety percent of those infected with the hemorrhage virus."

"And the ones it didn't work on?" Beckham asked.

Kate's brittle voice cracked. "Variants."

"How many do you think there are worldwide?" Riley asked.

Kate rubbed her forehead. "The last projections I put together were from old numbers, but that's all we have to go on. I estimate about seventy-five to eighty percent of the world's population has been infected with the hemorrhage virus."

Silence washed over them. No one spoke. Riley did the math in his head—if five and a half billion people had been infected, and now 10 percent of them were Variants...

"Holy shit," Riley said. "Five hundred and fifty million Variants? There's one of those things for every three human survivors." He let out a low whistle.

Kate cupped her hands over her head. "You don't need to remind me."

"Sorry," Riley said. He reached for a pillow and propped it behind his back, wincing in pain.

"You did what you had to do, Kate," Beckham said. He stood and put a hand on her shoulder. "You saved the human race."

Kate glanced up, tears sparkling in her eyes. "I stalled the inevitable."

"What's that mean?" Riley asked. "We all know the world will never be the same. But even after we kill all of those things, we'll still have people left to rebuild society, the economy, food production..."

Riley searched Kate's face for confirmation, but she pivoted away to stare out the window. She parted the blinds with a finger, letting the sun leak through. "The human race might be the next species on the extinction list after all," she said, with her back still to Riley, Horn, and Beckham.

Sandra Hickman and Ralph Benzing looked exhausted. They sat in front of a wall of communications equipment in the command center, quietly skimming the channels for intel.

Lieutenant Colonel Ray Jensen paced behind them anxiously. Both communications officers were in the twelfth hour of their shift, and he could tell that the coffee was finally starting to wear off.

Chatter was coming in from around the country. Jensen hadn't even started filtering the info streaming in from Europe. There was so much to process, but his priority was Plum Island and keeping his people safe. There was also a larger mission—a mission that Central Command was still piecing together.

"Here we go," Benzing said, cupping his hands over his headset. "I'm picking something up."

Jensen chewed the inside of his lip. The phantom taste of tobacco made his stomach growl. Four days without it and he was already going through withdrawals. Digging into his pocket, he felt for a piece of chewing gum.

"Patch it over the speakers," Jensen said, preparing himself for the worst. He'd never been much of a deep thinker; taking things too seriously caused unnecessary stress. Now that he was acting commander of one of humanity's last strongholds, all of that had changed. The fate of so many rested in his hands. Every single soul on the island was invaluable. Whatever Command was cooking up was likely to put many of his own in harm's way, and he wasn't looking forward to it.

"It's an automated message," Hickman said. "I'm picking it up on several frequencies."

"Switching," Benzing said. "Mine just cut out."

The speakers coughed static and then went silent for several seconds.

"What happened?" Jensen asked. He leaned over Benzing's shoulder as a voice suddenly crackled from the speakers.

"This is General Richard Kennor, broadcasting from Offutt Air Force Base. This mission might be the most important in the history of the United States military. Our species has been divided. Operation Depletion was a success, but now we face a new enemy. I have seen with my own eyes what these creatures are capable of. Our brave men and women in the armed services are vastly outnumbered. But we have something these monsters do not." He paused for a moment and then said, "We have the weapons of the twenty-first century."

Goose bumps popped up on Jensen's skin as the general's voice grew louder. That was the effect legendary commanders had on those under their command. They could convince young men to run into enemy fire and politicians to fund wars based on lies.

"With these weapons at our disposal, I am confident that we *will* retake our streets. America will once again be a free nation," Kennor said.

There was a break in the transmission. The general came back online a moment later. "In ninety-six hours we will embark on Operation Liberty, a massive coordinated attack that will send our remaining troops into every major city to destroy the enemy. Stand by for specific orders to be relayed to individual bases and outposts in the coming hours."

Jensen caught Hickman's worried gaze. He stood strong, his arms folded. Managing his emotions was key to reassuring those under his command. With more at stake than ever before, it was imperative he retain his composure.

Giving Hickman a strong nod, Jensen walked to the observation window. "Get Major Smith on the line. Tell him to get here ASAP. We have a war to plan."

Beckham shoveled a spoonful of slop into his mouth. He wasn't even sure what he was eating. It tasted a bit like fish but had the texture of chicken. He forced the food down and looked over at Kate.

She cringed. "What is this?"

"Better get used to it," Beckham said in between bites. "We're going to be eating reserve supplies. Riley was right when he mentioned food production. The world economy has shut down, which means..."

Kate answered with an exaggerated sigh. "No more hamburgers."

Beckham chuckled. "I thought you were going to say 'no more margaritas' or something."

"We still have tequila," she said with a wink.

Beckham held his spoon in front of his lips and ran his tongue along the roof of his mouth as he studied the doctor. She wasn't exactly his type, definitely not the kind of woman that he normally dated—when he dated, anyway, he reminded himself. The last woman he'd dated had been a yoga instructor. That had ended when he walked in on her banging a college football player half his age.

He'd have kicked the guy's ass if he had cared enough. Beckham had always been loyal to his team first. He had yet to meet a woman who could hang with him on a ten-mile run or three-mile swim. And that was okay. His career had taken precedence over finding a partner. His men were his family.

But he couldn't deny there was something about Kate. She carried herself in a graceful way. Strong, intelligent, and striking, she was the type of woman his mother would have wanted him to marry. He shook his head. There was no place for those thoughts in this new world. Everyone was dead or dying outside the safety of their little island. He refused to be the asshole who made a move on a woman at such a vulnerable time. But he couldn't deny he was attracted to her. More than that, he cared about her. Looking at Kate made him realize, for the first time in a very long time, that he *could* care.

Horn walked briskly toward their table. His eyebrows were scrunched together, his strawberry-blond hair sticking out in all directions as if he'd been running his hands over his skull.

"What's wrong?" Beckham asked.

"Lieutenant Colonel Jensen and Major Smith want to see us," Horn said. He turned to Kate. "Wants to see you too."

Kate finished off her plastic cup of juice and raised a brow. "About what?"

"Sounds like Central Command is planning something big."

Beckham dropped his spoon into the mush on his tray. He had known another operation was in the works. If he were in charge, he'd be planning one himself.

Kate and Beckham stood at the same time, grabbing their trays and following Horn between the packed tables. Several uniformed men and women glanced up from their food as they walked by. For once they weren't looking at him or Horn. They were looking at Kate.

"There goes the savior of the world," an African American marine sneered. Beckham recognized him from weeks before. He paused in his tracks and took a step back, shooting the man an angry glare.

"You have a problem, Johnson?" Beckham asked. His nostrils flared.

"No," Johnson said. "Sorry."

Beckham nodded and held the man's gaze for several seconds before following Kate and Horn outside. When they reached the door, she leaned over and whispered, "Thank you, Master Sergeant."

2

The horizon warned of another storm. Swollen clouds, the color of fresh bruises, crept across the skyline. Beckham needed more men—trained soldiers. He'd made the decision he should have made a long time ago. He'd obeyed every order Colonel Gibson and Lieutenant Colonel Jensen had thrown at him since Team Ghost arrived at Plum Island. Now it was his turn to make a request. He and Horn needed to go back to Fort Bragg to search for Horn's family and any surviving Delta Force operators.

He followed Kate and Horn to Building 1 in silence, using the time to consider the situation from a tactical standpoint. The war was entering a new stage, and as in any war, the problem was resources. The US military was strained. They had the firepower and the aircraft, but they lacked pilots and boots. His request to return to Bragg would likely fall on deaf ears, but he had to try.

A streak of lightning ripped through the gray sky. The scent of rain mixed with the salt-tinged wind blowing off the ocean. It was beautiful here, but the serenity of the island was a cruel deception. Beckham knew better than anyone just how bad things were out there. And as they reached Building 1, he had the sinking feeling that they were about to get worse.

The minty smell of the lab replaced the salty breeze as they entered the facility. Two guards sealed the doors behind them, shutting out the distant clap of thunder.

"This way," Kate said, gesturing with her chin toward the hallway.

Beckham took a sidelong glance at the windows along the left-hand wall of the passage. Scientists in CBRN suits worked tirelessly on the other side. The spotless facility glimmered under banks of fluorescent lights. It was all so... clean.

"So this is where you created the bioweapon?" Horn asked.

Kate nodded and paused in front of a panel of glass. "They're still studying the virus."

Horn approached the window. "What's the point?"

Kate smiled politely. "The epigenetic changes that the hemorrhage virus—"

"In layman's terms," Horn said.

"Sorry. Before scientists mapped the human genome, they believed there were a hundred thousand or more protein-coding genes. In reality there are closer to twenty or twenty-five thousand. But approximately thirteen thousand of those genes are what we call *pseudogenes*. In other words, they're protein-coding genes that we inherited from our ancestors, but they're 'turned off,'" she said, using her fingers to trace quotation marks through the air.

"Let me guess: VX-99 turned on a bunch of those genes," Horn said.

"You got it," Kate replied. "The nastiest ones too. The ones that date back to the primordial ooze, when life was just starting. Think of parasites or spiders—that's why we see the epigenetic changes in the Variants."

"And that's what makes them violent?" Beckham asked.

Kate focused her concentration on the lab through

the window. "These are genes dating back all the way through our evolutionary history—to a time where we were just like wild animals with predatory instincts."

"Like the State of Nature," Beckham replied.

Horn raised a brow. "Like what?"

"Thomas Hobbes wrote about it in *Leviathan* in the seventeenth century. He deduced there was a time before civilization when man lived by the sword, relying on predatory instincts to survive."

Kate turned from the window and gave Beckham elevator eyes. "I didn't know you studied philosophy."

"We don't just put bullets in bad guys."

"I know," Kate said. "I was—never mind." She turned back to the observation windows.

Horn placed a hand on the glass, his jaw clenched. Wrinkles formed around his eyes as he squinted and then dropped his gaze to the floor. Beckham knew he was thinking of his wife and two daughters.

A blur of motion caught Beckham's eye. Several of the scientists had moved to the center of the first chamber. They huddled around a monitor and pointed at the display. Under other circumstances, the view would have fascinated Beckham, but something about the end of the world made science seem less important to him. He had other concerns now, and two of them were right next to him.

"We better get moving," Kate said. "We're already late."

Beckham waited for Horn to move away from the glass. Placing a hand on his friend's shoulder, he whispered in a voice low enough that Kate couldn't hear him. "We're going back to Fort Bragg."

Horn stiffened. "You serious?"

Beckham ran a hand over his facial scruff and winked.

"Hell yeah," Horn said. He slapped Beckham on the back, and they walked side by side down the hallway.

Beckham's heart swelled with pride. The moment of camaraderie reminded him that he had the best job in the world. His philosophy was simple: He was only as good as the man standing next to him. And he was standing next to some damn good men.

The momentary rush vanished when they entered the conference room. Its weak lighting matched the darkened features of both Lieutenant Colonel Jensen and Major Sean Smith's faces.

"Take a seat," Jensen said. He gestured at the chairs across the table and rolled up both of his sleeves. "General Kennor, with Central Command, has issued a message to all remaining military assets across the country." Jensen regarded each of them in turn. "I wanted to personally inform you of Operation Liberty before anyone else hears about it. In approximately ninety hours, the military is sending boots into every major city. The first objective is to defeat the Variant threat. The second is to rescue any survivors."

"Do you have numbers?" Kate asked.

"Of survivors?"

"No, Variants."

"Hundreds of millions," Jensen replied grimly.

Kate's eyes darted toward the ceiling as if she were mentally double-checking the math.

"That's why we invited you here, Doctor," Smith said. "Command has asked us to research the Variants. We want you to head the team."

"Absolutely," Kate said. "Whatever you need."

"Excellent," Jensen said.

"So why are *we* here?" Horn asked.

"Because we have also been asked to provide military support," Jensen replied. He crossed his arms and exhaled. "Command wants us to send teams to New York to join a marine company of five platoons pieced together from surviving units. Each platoon has been assigned a borough. We have been asked to support First Platoon in Manhattan. They're a mechanized unit with at least two Bradleys and multiple Humvees. The air force will provide support too."

Beckham could feel Horn studying him. He held Jensen's gaze, anticipating what came next.

"We want you to lead a team," the lieutenant colonel said. "It breaks every rule in the book, but I don't give a shit. You've been out there. You two know better than anyone."

"Half of the men and women stationed at this island haven't even seen combat," Major Smith added. "We need you two."

Beckham considered his next words carefully. He still didn't trust Jensen. He wasn't Colonel Gibson, but he had worked with the disgraced man for years. Sure, Jensen talked a good game, but he had yet to prove himself. Beckham knew from experience that evil was most dangerous when it was hard to see. Gibson was the perfect example of that. Unfortunately, the new commander controlled the aircraft on Plum Island. Beckham needed him, just as he'd needed Gibson.

"I can give you some time to consider," Jensen said.

Beckham exchanged a glance with Horn. He could see the pain in the man's eyes. Horn needed resolution. Horn deserved to know. One way or another, Beckham and Horn were going back to Fort Bragg.

"I'll lead a team back into New York," Beckham finally said, "but there's something I need to do first. Something we need to do."

Jensen formed a triangle with his hands, concentrating. "You want a ride to Fort Bragg?"

Beckham nodded; the man was smarter than he gave him credit for. "And a ride back, with any survivors we find."

Smith shook his head. "No fucking way. We can't risk a chopper." He looked up for support from Jensen. The lieutenant colonel held up a hand.

Jensen scanned Beckham and then Horn. "I know what you all must think of me. But I am *not* Colonel Gibson. I'm not going to make the asshole excuse and say I was just following orders, but I did not know the complete truth behind the development of the hemorrhage virus." He bowed his head. "If I had known, I would have stopped the project, I swear to you." His eyes pleaded with Beckham for a response, but Beckham remained silent, listening and sizing up the commander as he spoke.

"You have thirty-six hours," Jensen said after a pause. "That enough time?"

"Plenty of time," Beckham said. He reached across the table and secured his second deal since arriving at the island with a firm handshake. He was finally going back home to Fort Bragg.

The sunset lit up the horizon like a fire raging on the water. The beauty lost its appeal as Beckham's watch ticked. He could feel every second passing. Each one potentially represented another life lost.

"Where is she?" Horn grumbled.

Beckham stared at the cluster of dome-shaped buildings. "She'll be here," Beckham said. He dropped his rucksack on the edge of the tarmac and adjusted the strap of his M4 carbine. He'd elected to carry a different weapon after facing the Variants in New York; 9-millimeter rounds no longer cut it. He had upgraded to 5.56-millimeter NATO rounds. The air-cooled, gas-operated carbine with mounted advanced combat optical gunsight would do the trick.

"You look like you're about to rob a bank," Horn said.

Beckham glanced down at the extra magazines tucked into his tactical vest's pouches. "Can't afford another situation like New York, man. Riley's legs wouldn't be broken if I hadn't run out of ammo."

Horn nodded and glared at the skyline. The skull bandanna tied around his neck rustled in the wind. He turned back to Beckham and squinted as if he was in pain. The freckles on his nose crunched together.

"You think my family is still out there, boss?"

"If they are, we're going to find them. Jensen had his comm team run through the last radio transmissions from Bragg. There were survivors holed up in the Special Warfare Center and School building, so that's where we're headed." Beckham pulled out a map and pointed at the facility he'd circled in red.

"I remember that place," Horn said. He reached inside his vest and retrieved a cigarette. Wedging it between his lips, he cupped a hand over his Zippo as he lit the tip. He closed his eyes and took one long drag. "Thank you, Reed," Horn said, smoke trailing out of his nostrils. "Thank you for doing this. I can't tell you—"

Beckham held up a gloved hand. "Don't, man. You don't need to say anything. If Sheila, Tasha, and Jenny are out there, I stand by the promise I made to you on the rooftop in New York."

Jamming the cigarette back between his lips, Horn placed both hands on Beckham's shoulders. They locked eyes, neither of them flinching.

"We'll find them," Beckham said. "One way or another."

Horn gave a solemn nod and then turned toward the sound of approaching voices. Two figures rounded Building 1. They strode toward the concrete barricade and stepped into the sunlight.

"Here she comes," Horn said. "Finally."

"Sorry we're late," Kate said. She dropped two duffel bags on the ground and bent down to unzip them. A crew chief and pilots hurried past them, all three men eyeing Horn's cigarette without uttering a word.

"What's in the bags, Doc?" Horn asked, taking another drag.

Kate pulled out a CBRN suit and handed it to Beckham.

"I thought you said there's no risk of infection anymore." He hesitated and then grabbed the white suit.

"That's mostly true," Kate said. "But there might be infected that were outside the primary and secondary drop zones."

"People with the hemorrhage virus?" Beckham asked.

Kate nodded. "The bioweapon is still being deployed in remote areas outside the cities. The virus has mostly been eradicated, according to reports from Central Command. Fort Bragg was part of the initial drop. But I don't want to take any chances."

"I'll let you two hash this out," Horn said. He swung his M249 Squad Automatic Weapon across his back and walked over to the pilot and crew chief, discussing something that Beckham couldn't hear.

"Kate, I don't think we need them. We didn't use them in Atlanta. Besides, I'm already bogged down with all of this extra ammunition." He patted his vest and ran a finger over the pocket containing a picture of his mother.

"But—"

"I'm more concerned about the Variants than the remote chance of contracting what's left of the hemorrhage virus."

Her eyes darted to the ground.

"We'll be fine, Kate. These things are only going to slow us down," he said, handing the suit back to her.

Kate dropped it onto the bag and wrapped her arms around Beckham. He let out a short gasp of surprise. She hugged him tighter before finally letting go. "Fine. You can make up your own mind."

Horn whistled. "Gotta go, boss!"

Beckham bent down to scoop up his gear. "I'll be back in thirty-six hours."

"Be safe," she said.

"Always am."

The blades of the chopper whooshed through their first pass. Beckham jogged across the tarmac, ducking as he approached the craft. Grabbing a handhold, he climbed inside and waved one final time as the bird ascended into the air.

Beckham and Horn stood at the edge of the troop hold. They flew in complete darkness; not a single light flickered below as the chopper raced over the landscape.

Flipping up his night-vision goggles, Beckham stared over the side. A veil of black consumed him, and all sense of motion vanished. For a moment he felt as though he were suspended in space. Then his eyes adjusted. He could vaguely make out the outline of a city in the distance. Never in his life had he seen a landscape so dark. The entire grid was down. No one was left to run critical facilities. The chopper passed over an abandoned water treatment plant, the stink of sewage rising to meet them. It was the smell of the new world.

For two hours they flew over crumbling buildings and scorched urban areas, the scars from Operation Depletion present even in the darkness. No city had been spared. Outside the cities, the acres of lush crops would never see harvest. The destruction was numbing.

The promise Beckham had made to his team years ago flashed across his mind. He could picture that day in Iraq vividly: Insurgents had his six-man team pinned down behind a wall in the filthy streets of Fallujah. Spinoza, Edwards, Riley, Horn, and Tenor had been crouched behind the stone, waiting for air support as a hundred hostiles had crept closer. Brass had fed him some bullshit intel, claiming they could help take back the city. Instead, Beckham had led Team Ghost into a trap.

"Six against a hundred," he muttered.

Horn spat over the edge of the chopper. "Fallujah?"

Beckham nodded. "Never thought we'd make it out of there."

"If it weren't for Panda, we never would have."

Beckham chuckled at the memory of the gigantic man breaking through the ten-foot stone wall. Spinoza had rammed it three times with a shoulder before the stones toppled, allowing the team a chance to escape into an alleyway. He had also taken four shots to his flak jacket that had put him out of commission for a month. And now he was dead, along with Edwards and Tenor.

"Goddamn," Beckham said, shaking his head. He would have traded places with any of them. The pain of seeing a fallen brother was worse than the idea of death itself. He was barely managing the losses, motivated only by the mission ahead of them.

Horn reached over and nudged Beckham in the side. "We all should have died a long time ago, bro."

He didn't want to admit it, but Horn was right. Maybe fate had finally caught up to them. Thousands of hours of training and experience meant nothing when it was your time. Somehow Beckham had always come out unscathed. The other men had joked that someone was looking out for him. And maybe there was. He liked to think that his mother was keeping an eye on him.

"Holy shit," Horn said. "Take a look at that."

"What?" Beckham flipped his NVGs back down and saw the vivid outline of a highway cluttered with vehicles. Not just any vehicles—tanks.

Beckham examined the abandoned M1 Abramses as the chopper flew closer. The expensive symbols of American military muscle were now just graveyards of metal.

"Wonder what happened," Horn said.

"Probably got trapped."

A flash of movement pulled his gaze to the adjacent ditch. Something lurked in the darkness. Several somethings, human sized.

Beckham reflexively gripped the handle of his M4 tighter when he caught a glimpse of four Variants. They galloped into the forest, escaping as the chopper whipped overhead.

"You see that?" Horn asked.

"Yeah," Beckham said. He turned toward the cockpit. "You picking up any sign of survivors down there?"

The lead pilot shook his head. "Negative."

Closing his eyes, Beckham scooted away from the door and rested his back against the wall of the chopper. "Wake me up when we get to Bragg," he said. "I'm going to snag a few minutes of sleep."

"No problem," Horn said.

Beckham tried to rest, but the ghosts of his past kept him awake. He had tried to leave them behind, but the flashbacks ambushed him whenever he closed his eyes. There was Spinoza lying on the floor in Building 8, a human bone jammed deep into his skull. There was the infected child they'd found in Niantic, and there was Riley, his legs smashed, screaming on a New York rooftop. No matter what he did, his mind returned to those moments. Each time the dread caught him in his gut. He tried to do what operators were taught to do:

compartmentalize and suppress emotions. Pain, both mental and physical, was a distraction that could result in death.

Crackling static in his earpiece yanked him back to the present. "Landing zone in five," said the primary pilot's voice. Beckham scanned the skyline. A dense cloud hovered over Fort Bragg to the east.

"Jesus," Horn said. "I thought it wasn't supposed to storm."

"That's no storm," Beckham said. "That's smoke."

Horn shook his head. "Nah, man, can't be..."

"Where's it coming from?" Beckham asked.

The comm channel crackled. "Uh," the pilot said, "I think that's the Womack Army Medical Center."

Horn and Beckham sat in silence, watching the vortex of smoke swirling above the north quadrant.

"Never thought I'd see the day when we bombed our own fucking posts," Horn said.

The words lingered in the air like the black haze above Fort Bragg. The country Beckham had fought for, bled for, sacrificed everything for, had dropped bombs on her own men and women, the same soldiers who had sworn to defend her against enemies foreign and domestic. He understood that they were trying to stop the hemorrhage virus, but this?

"Western wind at fifteen miles per hour, would advise insertion south of the post," the pilot said.

They circled for several minutes until Beckham found a suitable insertion point.

"Put us down in that field," Beckham said into the comm. He grabbed a handhold and scanned the area. The knee-high grass whipped back and forth as the chopper descended.

"You ready to find your family, Big Horn?" Beckham asked.

There was a flicker of fear in Horn's eyes that disappeared as he flipped his NVGs into position. "Ready, boss."

Beckham slapped him on the back. Horn jumped first, bolting away from the chopper as soon as his boots hit the dirt. With a breath, Beckham followed his best friend into the darkness, as he had so many times before.

Data rolled across Kate's computer screen. She studied every single line, searching for abnormalities in the blood samples from Patient 12, the Variant that had attacked her several days earlier. The hours passed, leaving Kate more frustrated than she wanted to admit.

Colonel Gibson had been right about one thing: In order for her to learn more about the Variants, she needed a living, breathing patient. The mere thought of the colonel still made Kate angry. They were in this situation because of him. He'd ordered the development of the hemorrhage virus.

Kate massaged her temples and then reached for her empty coffee mug. A clock in the corner of the office read 9:45 p.m. If she was going to squeeze any more work out of her brain, she needed a refill.

She cracked her neck from side to side and got up to leave. The door to the office squeaked open, and Dr. Pat Ellis peeked in.

"You're still working?" he asked.

Kate sighed. "I keep thinking that I missed something in today's tests."

"Mind if I join you?"

"Not at all," Kate said with a smile. She was happy to have the company.

Ellis plopped down at his station. "I've been working

on identifying the genes that VX-99 turned on. Maybe if we can figure out exactly which ones mutated, we can find a way to bring them back."

With a few keystrokes he logged in to his terminal and brought up a myriad of data streams. Slipping on his glasses, he pointed to the screen.

"Take a look."

"Ellis," Kate said, "we've been through this."

He didn't reply. His fingers danced across the keyboard, and then he punched the Enter key. A new image filled half of the screen. "Maybe this will interest you then."

Curious, Kate stepped closer to his display.

"This is Marine Lieutenant Trevor Brett. His platoon was given doses of VX-99 in 1968. Every last one of those marines died, except for this lucky lieutenant." He glanced up, his brows arched. "Or unlucky."

Ellis moused over to another image, enlarging it so it filled the other half of the screen. A picture of a pale, gaunt man popped onto the display. "He was found ten years later and over one hundred miles from his platoon's insertion point."

"Is that—?"

"Yup. Same guy."

Kate nodded. "You have my attention. Where did you find these images?"

"Beckham told me about the guy. It was part of the briefing they watched on their way to Building Eight. Colonel Gibson had known about Brett for years. But what Beckham didn't know is this." Ellis hit the Enter key again. A grainy video popped onto the screen.

The camera angle provided a view of the inside of a prison cell. A frail, naked man was stretched into an *x* supported by chains attached to the ceiling and floor. His chin slumped against his chest, his eyes downcast. The cameraman took a step back and swept the lens over the three military officers studying the man from the other side of the bars. One of them glanced at the camera, and Kate instantly recognized the young man.

"Colonel Gibson," she said with a shiver.

"Yup," Ellis said, turning up the audio.

"Lieutenant Trevor Brett," Gibson said, his voice distorted by the old video footage, "can you hear us?"

The camera moved again and fell on the prisoner. He slowly raised his head as he became aware of his observers, his eyes roving, scanning. In another instant they centered on the soldiers. Rattling chains filled the audio as Brett thrashed against his restraints. Joints cracked and popped. The man's body twisted in a way that would have broken the spine of a normal person.

"Calm down, Lieutenant," another voice said. "You're only going to hurt yourself."

Kate didn't need to see or hear what would come next: a snarl, followed by a high-pitched shriek. Inhuman rage. She'd seen it many times before.

Only Brett didn't scream or snarl.

He spoke.

The words weren't much more than a growl, distorted by his malformed lips, but Kate could understand him.

"I will—" Droplets of saliva burst from his mouth. "I will *kill*."

The soldiers flanking the colonel stepped away from the cell. The camera panned to the profile of a stone-faced Gibson walking closer. Gripping one of the bars, he asked, "What did you say, Lieutenant?"

"I WILL KILL YOU ALL!"

"My God," Kate said. "He can talk."

Ellis brought a finger to his lips. "Keep watching."

Gibson tightened his grip on the bars as Brett fought his chains.

"It's a shame," Gibson said. "You were supposed to be a supersoldier."

The video fizzled out a moment later, leaving Kate in a state of shock. She ran a finger over her lips, trying to process what she had seen.

"Why didn't you show this to me earlier?" she asked.

Ellis shrugged defensively. "I just discovered it this morning."

Kate stared blankly at the dark screen. "What's the date of the video?"

"One second." Ellis fidgeted with his glasses and then drilled down on the keyboard. "That can't be right."

"What's it say?"

"March fifteenth, 1988."

"Twenty years after Brett's mission?"

Kate exchanged a glance with Ellis as they considered the dates. She suddenly felt light-headed. Brett was a glimpse of the future: Given time, Variants could evolve. They were more than wild animals. They could think. That meant they could also strategize.

And maybe even speak.

"This discovery could change everything," Ellis said. "But we can't jump to conclusions just yet. We have to remember Brett was never infected with Ebola. Doctor Medford altered VX-99 after Brett's platoon took the initial doses. We need to perform tests on the Variants. We don't know if Brett is an accurate example of what the creatures are capable of."

"Maybe not," Kate replied. "But Brett does prove the effects of VX-99 are truly irreversible. The only way to end this nightmare is to kill every last one of the monsters."

3

The wind howled outside the dark hotel room, gusts rattling the window with every pass. Inside, the air was sultry and stale, carrying with it the stink of sweat and mold. With his eyes narrowed and his breathing slow, Beckham studied every flash of movement through the filthy glass. He knelt under a pair of ragged drapes and raked his M4 across the empty parking lot, searching for any sign of hostiles.

Trash and pieces of newspaper flew past. One of them slapped against the pane. His muscles tensed as he spotted something else moving in the darkness.

Horn fidgeted. He saw it too.

Beckham listened, still expecting to hear noises of the old world. But the hum of civilization had long since vanished. Instead, Beckham heard new sounds, automatically identifying them to create a sonic map of his surroundings. He didn't need to see the open car door grinding against the concrete to know someone had hastily abandoned the vehicle. He didn't need to see the downed power line to know it was the source of the whining in the distance.

As a Delta Force operator, Beckham had made a career of using his senses to get him out of hot zones, to succeed where other men failed. But things had changed. There were new rules now, and they required constant focus and attention. Ignore them and you would end up a rotting corpse, like the majority of the world's population.

Beckham zoomed in on the Kangaroo Express gas station beyond the parking lot and then the tree line across the street. He heard a faint clicking, but he saw no other sign of motion. Variants were out there somewhere. Images of their swollen lips, distorted bodies, and reptilian eyes were tattooed on his memory.

Back at Plum Island, Kate had explained that the creatures had undergone epigenetic changes. He had tuned out most of the science but understood the fundamentals. The Variants weren't just insane, deformed humans; they possessed superior strength, speed, and predatory senses. And they moved like insects, scaling walls and hanging from ceilings. Beckham missed the days of fighting enemies that moved on two legs.

A distant screech ripped through the night.

Beckham ducked under the window ledge. He caught Horn's gaze and pointed at the curtains. They were used to being the hunters, not the hunted. He took a measured breath, trying not to focus on the awful stench of rancid fruit and rotting flesh. He never thought he would miss the smell of plastic inside a biohazard suit.

Pulling his scarf over his nose, he waited a few more beats before moving back to the window. He slowly peeled back the curtain with his right hand. White rays of moonlight spilled across the parking lot. It was just enough to light up the abandoned vehicles. Flipping up his night-vision goggles, Beckham peered through the glass without the aid of his optics.

Nothing.

The lot was empty—no sign of the creatures. Beckham

scoped the blacktop one more time just to be certain, noting the sagging power line and open car door he'd heard before. Under normal circumstances, he would have grinned at being right, but this wasn't normal. They were deep in enemy territory and a few miles away from Fort Bragg.

A lot was at stake on this mission. Horn's wife and daughters were basically Beckham's family too, the only family he'd had since his mother and father had both died of cancer. And there was the possibility of finding more Delta Force operators. If anyone had survived out here for this long, it would be his brothers-in-arms.

"Clear," he finally whispered.

Crouching, Beckham spread his crinkled map on the stained carpet and studied it one last time. The plan was to move north along the All American Expressway and then take Gruber Road west to the John F. Kennedy Special Warfare Center and School building.

Beckham grabbed the doorknob as Horn fell in behind him. "We move on three," Beckham whispered. He held up his fingers as they waited and mentally counted.

One.

Two.

"Go," Beckham said. He twisted the doorknob with a click and stepped out into the humid night. Wind whipped against his body armor as he moved with calculated steps. Beckham pushed his scarf farther over his face until it was just below his eyes. He charged forward with his jaw clenched shut, breathing into the cotton.

His eyes darted from the abandoned vehicles to the gas station at the end of the lot. His gut told him they weren't being watched, that they were in the clear, and his eyes revealed nothing but the rustling of tree branches and swirling wrappers.

Then a guttural screech sent him running for the

nearest vehicle. Beckham slid onto his knees and propped his back against the passenger's-side door. Horn took up position behind a pickup.

"One o'clock," Horn said, his voice cold and tense.

Beckham swept his rifle toward the roof of the Kangaroo Express. Two of the creatures were perched on the ledge, their pale, naked skin shimmering under the moonlight.

The shattering of glass pulled Beckham's gaze to the entrance of the building, where a male and female emerged from the broken front door. Their bodies were twisted and grotesque, their joints snapping as they turned in place, looking for their prey.

Horn made a dash to the car and took a knee next to Beckham.

"They know we're here," he said.

"If we take them out, we'll draw others."

"I'm not sure we can outrun them," Horn said. "I don't think we have a choice."

The clacking of joints grew closer, claws scratching across the concrete. Beckham snuck a look through the car's windows.

Neither of the creatures wore much of anything, their clothing torn away from constant scratching and biting. Bushy, tangled hair hung over the side of the woman's face. A reptilian eye probed the parking lot as she shambled forward. She stopped abruptly and tilted her head to scratch a bloody bald spot. When she was finished she clamped down on her arm with her sucker lips and tore away a piece of flesh.

The two on the roof remained still, while the male on the edge of the parking lot sniffed the muggy air. It was an odd feeling, Beckham thought, knowing they were smelling for him.

Before Beckham could duck, the woman stared in his

direction. Hunger radiated from her eyes. She let out a roar.

"Shit," Beckham said. "You take the top. I'll take out the other two. Then we run."

Horn's response came as the heavy crack from his SAW. Fire flashed from the muzzle and cut into the roof's awning. The creatures perched there dropped to all fours and disappeared over the back side of the building while the two on the ground loped forward.

Beckham's shots were more accurate. With every squeeze of the trigger, he felt the rage of war building inside of him. It wasn't bloodlust; it was his internal processor. As though he were a computer, his military training had been programmed into his every movement. He knew what to do by instinct, and his body simply took over. His movements were automatic, robotic.

The first shots caught the female by surprise. The bullets tore into her stomach and sent her wailing into the darkness. He whirled to the right and fired on the male galloping toward him. The bullets peppered the side of a Jeep Cherokee as the creature dashed for cover.

Horn was already on the move, his M249 leveled at the vehicle. Both men opened fire at the same moment. Dust and shrapnel exploded into the air as the bullets chipped away at the concrete. The Variant zigzagged between the rounds. Using its back legs, it sprang into the air. With hands morphed into claws, the creature flew toward Beckham. He sidestepped and squeezed the trigger without hesitation.

Gore plastered his clear shooting glasses, but he didn't flinch. He wiped the slime away and watched the monster flopping on the pavement, the large holes in its chest gushing blood.

"Got 'em," Horn said. "You good, boss?"

Beckham nodded. He let out a breath, remembering

there was only a remote chance of X9H9 infection. Still he waited in anticipation for the hallucinations to set in. A flashback to Building 8 raced across his anxious mind. He vividly remembered finding Sergeant Will Tenor's broken body as the hemorrhage virus rapidly took control of it. He had turned in just minutes.

"You're fine. Kate said this area was part of the first drop zone," Horn reassured him.

"I'm good, let's move."

Beckham fell into a run and changed his magazine in midstride. The rap of his footfalls was the only response Horn needed. Together, they advanced through the empty streets, navigating around vehicles until they came to the on-ramp of the All American Expressway.

Magnolia trees lined the right side of the ramp. Even in the dim moonlight, Beckham could see their beautiful blossoms, and the breeze carried their sweet candy scent. He took a moment to soak it in, enjoying the ability to breathe freely.

"Looks clear," Horn whispered.

Beckham checked the skyline. The moon vanished behind dense clouds, and darkness reclaimed the road. Both men snapped their night-vision goggles into position and sprinted up the ramp. They were completely exposed amongst the abandoned vehicles. It was a goddamn minefield of places the Variants could hide.

Beckham flashed a signal toward the shoulder of the road, and the operators melted into the shadows. The depression provided them a vantage of both the road to the left and the hillside, thick with trees, to the right. They were still visible, but this way they weren't forced to clear every vehicle. Beckham took a moment to scan the road crowded with FEMA trucks, Humvees, police cruisers, and civilian cars.

Not everyone had made it out. Beckham's gaze locked

onto a minivan with its doors still closed. Three small bodies were curled up in the back seat.

The numbness returned. The loss of innocent life was difficult to understand, even for a Delta Force operator. He'd seen war most of his life. He'd lived it, breathed it. He'd killed in order to keep the war machine going. But never had he seen this much death. These children were only three amongst billions.

Billions, he thought. How was that even possible? How could billions of people have lost their lives?

Horn stood a few feet away, staring at the dusty windows of the minivan. Beckham saw the tear crawling down Horn's face. He gave the man a moment as he swept the area for contacts.

"Those aren't your girls," Beckham said. "Let's keep moving."

After a few minutes of jogging at a brisk pace, Beckham saw the checkpoints on the highway. Barbwire fences and the metal rooftops of buildings protruded over the dense ridgeline to the right. He didn't need to read the wooden sign up ahead to know what it said:

FORT BRAGG. HOME OF THE AIRBORNE AND SPECIAL OPERATIONS FORCES.

They were home, and dead or alive, they *would* find Horn's family.

"I'm coming," Horn whispered. He shouldered his rifle and continued jogging toward the post.

Beckham eyed the skyline again. The dense cloud he had seen earlier was actually a cloud of smoke that was coming from behind the trees, rising up like a wall somewhere in the base.

"Shit," Beckham said, pointing to the north. "You see that?"

"Yeah. Do you think that's the Womack?"

"I don't know, but the wind is changing course."

Horn sniffed the air. "Yeah, I can smell it. What's your point?"

"I don't want to get caught out here if the wind shifts the smoke toward us."

Horn nodded. "You're right."

A rustling sound from the forest shocked both men into action. They spun simultaneously to scope the trees on top of the hillside. Branches rattled in the wind, but otherwise, they saw nothing.

"You got anything?"

"Negative," Horn replied.

More rustling and snapping twigs pulled Beckham's gaze up to the canopy.

"Contacts," Beckham said, realizing how crazy it sounded. The movement had to be from something else. Variants weren't monkeys. They didn't swing from branches or climb trees.

Did they?

"Holy shit," Beckham muttered as the treetops rustled to life. The canopy swayed as if in a torrential wind. Leaves and twigs cartwheeled to the forest floor. And then he saw them. His heart rate went into overdrive. There were dozens of Variants scaling the trees on all fours. Jumping from tree to tree, the pale creatures swarmed toward Beckham and Horn.

"Run," Beckham choked. "Jesus Christ! Run!"

"You can't see him. I'm sorry," Lieutenant Colonel Jensen said.

Major Smith nodded. "Sorry, Doctor."

Kate knit her brows as she responded. "Listen to me very carefully. Colonel Gibson has information that I believe can help my research."

Crossing his arms, Jensen frowned. "What kind of information?"

"She's right," Ellis said. He stepped forward to stand beside Kate. "I'm sure you've heard of Lieutenant Trevor Brett?"

Jensen's features remained unchanged. If he had heard of the man, he wasn't giving any clues.

"Even if I wanted to let you see Colonel Gibson, I wouldn't be able to," Jensen said. "He's been admitted to the ICU."

"What?" Kate asked.

"Turns out the bastard has degenerative heart disease. Been a smoker his entire life. Doubt he'll even make it to stand trial."

Kate stared at the ceiling, wrestling with her anger. If Gibson died, then the secrets of VX-99 would go to the grave with him. She wasn't going to let that happen.

"Sir," Kate said, in her most businesslike tone, "Colonel Gibson has been studying VX-99 for decades. We have to know more about his research."

Jensen's right eye twitched. The man was nervous, and if her suspicions were correct, he already felt guilty for the part he had played in all of this. She would use that to her advantage.

After a short pause to let her words sink in, she continued. "You are a natural leader. I can see that. Master Sergeant Beckham sees that. But you were part of Colonel Gibson's entourage—his confidant. You played a role in the end of the world, even if you didn't know exactly what was going on."

Jensen dropped his arms to his sides. "Doctor Lovato—"

"Please let me finish," she said. "All I need is a few minutes of Colonel Gibson's time. He may have information that could help us find a way to fight the Variants." She looked over at Ellis and added, "Or possibly bring them back."

Jensen's eyes widened. He looked down at his watch. "Can't this wait until the morning? It's late."

Kate bit the inside of her lip. "Every second we wait, more people will die outside of this island."

"Fine," Jensen said. "But do *not* get him riled up."

"I won't," Kate said, unsure if she could live up to her promise.

Jensen glanced at his watch again. "Meet us at the ICU in thirty minutes." He glared at Kate and then walked past her, leaving the room.

"That went well," Ellis said.

"Yeah. But that was the easy part." She placed a hand on Ellis's shoulder. "Wait till we talk to that son of a bitch. I doubt he's going to tell us anything."

"Too bad Beckham's not here. He'd get it out of Gibson."

Kate's gut sank at the thought of Reed out there somewhere being a hero, facing danger to help save what was still worth saving. It was what he did, and it was the reason she was falling for him. She hoped they'd both survive long enough for her to tell him.

4

Beckham darted toward a convoy of army trucks and tankers. They had been abandoned in a hurry. Open doors swayed in the breeze, their metal creaking eerily.

The soldiers had inadvertently blocked the southbound ramp connecting to the expressway, or maybe they had done it on purpose. He wasn't sure. One of the semitankers stretched across the road, blocking the view of the street on the other side.

Beckham kneeled in a defensive position a few feet from the tanker.

"Shit!" Horn shouted. "They're coming from the east too!" He pointed to the ridgeline. There was movement across Beckham's entire line of sight. The Variants were coming from the south and the east. They were trapped. There was only one way forward—under the trucks.

"Let's move!" Beckham shouted. He dropped to his stomach and began crawling.

"Right behind you," Horn said.

Beckham squirmed across the concrete, his impact armor dragging and scratching as he struggled forward. The noise didn't bother him. The Variants knew where they were, so stealth was no longer a concern.

He emerged from under the first truck to see a second

tanker blocking the road. It was obvious then that the soldiers had created a roadblock on purpose. With no way to climb over the top, Beckham dropped back to his stomach and crawled under the second vehicle.

With a final push he burst from under the tanker and pulled himself to his feet. A gust of wind caught him as soon as he stood. The strange smell of barbecue and sour fruit filled his lungs. Beckham pulled the scarf over his face. He checked the right side of the road: all clear.

Then he looked to the left and froze. Horn squirmed out from under the final truck and stood next to Beckham, staring at the surreal scene the trucks had hidden from their view—the source of the awful smell.

Through the shifting smoke they could see bodies lining Gruber Road. Hundreds of them, some charred beyond recognition. With the changing wind, the stench of death filled the night.

"Holy shit," Horn said. "What the hell happened here?"

"I don't know, but we need to move!"

The primal shrieks from the Variants grew louder.

As soon as Beckham turned, he saw the sandbags and the M240 set up on the far side of the road. A single soldier in a CBRN suit lay draped over the bags, his body limp. The man had mowed down the refugees trying to escape to the expressway in a desperate maneuver that was probably aimed at stopping one infected.

Beckham swallowed hard at the sight. Was Horn's family amongst them? There was no time to find out. Together, the men moved west along the road, passing familiar landmarks. Beckham always assumed every mission would be difficult, but with a horde of flesh-eating monsters trailing them and a lingering wall of smoke ahead, he felt grossly underprepared. If the smoke shifted any farther, they would have to make a stand.

"Is this the turn?" Horn yelled.

"Negative. Keep moving!" Beckham said. "One more to go until we get to Reilly Road."

Beckham rounded the corner at breakneck speed. His boots slipped across a stretch of wet concrete. The body of a US Army Ranger lay on the curb. Blood oozed from his shattered skull. The fresh scarlet puddle meant the man had been killed recently.

Other survivors, Beckham thought, running harder.

The sound of Horn's heavy footfalls pounded the concrete. They were only a few blocks away from the building now. The smoke grew closer with every step.

Beckham coughed violently into his scarf and wiped away the tears blurring his vision.

"Twelve o'clock," Horn shouted.

Ahead, a single figure crouched over another dead Ranger, its shiny skull buried in the soldier's chest.

There was more motion to the right. Three shirtless men emerged from behind a Humvee. They moved slowly, catlike, their backs hunched and their heads tilting as they caught sight of Beckham and Horn. Tremors shook their pale skin as they cautiously inched forward. Their suckers puckered in the air, popping.

Beckham shivered. They'd run out of blacktop. The only thing between them and the monsters now were bullets. No more running.

"Boss," Horn said.

"I see 'em."

The operators stood back-to-back. The group of creatures to the north halted in the middle of the street. They crouched silently, sniffing the air and licking their bulging lips with swollen tongues.

Beckham glanced over his shoulder. The pack from the south had caught up with them. Their distorted bodies clogged the road, slowing as they closed in. Several of the creatures were moving too fast and plowed through the front of the crowd. The monsters tumbled and skidded across the concrete.

Guttural howls followed.

Beckham raised his M4 and readied himself.

"Open fire!" he cried. Gritting his teeth, Beckham fired on the four to the north.

The crack of gunfire drowned out the sound of the creatures. Bullet casings pinged off the concrete. Beckham cut down the entire pack before they could react. The creatures dropped to the pavement, limbs flailing. But more came, swarming from the tree line. The dark wall of smoke swirled behind the creatures.

"Changing," Beckham yelled. He reached for another magazine and palmed it into his gun with a click. He shouldered the gun and sprayed the street with short bursts. More Variants dropped to the concrete, blood oozing from gaping wounds.

Yet they kept coming.

Within seconds, Beckham and Horn were completely surrounded.

"Conserve your ammo, aim for the head!" Beckham yelled. He dropped to one knee and drew down on the closest creature. Squeezing the trigger, he then pivoted to the next target, hardly noticing the bloody mist that exploded from the first Variant's skull. The second shot caught another in the forehead, and the third did the same. He continued firing, dropping the enemy until his magazine was dry.

He reloaded and finished off another wave. Never had the killing felt so simple. It was as though something inside of him knew what was at stake and an internal strength had taken control. But the men only had so many bullets. And after fifteen minutes of keeping the Variants at bay, both ran out of ammo. They switched to their pistols as the pile of dead bodies grew around them.

More of the creatures flocked to the street. The gunfire had attracted every single Variant in the area.

With a final shot, the slide of Beckham's pistol locked open.

"I'm out!" he yelled. He dropped the pistol and fumbled for his knife.

"Me too."

The operators rose to their feet as the creatures formed a perimeter around them. Beckham couldn't remember a time when he'd been so fucked. He'd left himself no outs—broken his cardinal rule. There was nowhere to run. No more bullets to fire.

Gripping his knife, Beckham studied the subhuman faces of the enemy. Deformed mouths snarled and vertical pupils stared back at him.

The creatures surged forward in a distorted wave. His body tingled from the adrenaline coursing through his system. A hundred thoughts drifted across his mind, and none of them made any sense. His brain was working in overdrive, unable to focus in the face of inexorable death.

A flash from the west pulled Beckham's gaze away from the creatures.

Crack, crack, crack.

Beckham knew that sound. Only an MK11 sniper rifle made that particular war cry.

More flashes lit up the rooftops of several buildings west of the road. Bodies dropped to the concrete, bones and gore splattering the pavement. Beckham kicked at a hand that came rolling toward him.

"Yeah!" Horn cheered.

Beckham watched the street fill with blood. The sight was surreal. Surely there were men and women he'd known amongst the dead, but he couldn't bring himself to look. He wasn't sure how long the gunfire lasted. When the sound of the last shot waned away, he took a guarded step forward.

"Jesus," Beckham muttered. He sidestepped around the corpses, jumping over some that were piled on top of one another.

"Freeze!" came a raspy voice.

A trio of silhouettes stood at the edge of the swirling smoke. They wore gas masks and the same "four-eye" NVGs as the two operators. All three men were covered in impact armor similar to Horn and Beckham's.

"Get on the ground!" the leader yelled. He pointed an M4 in their direction.

"Boss?" Horn said.

"Do it," Beckham said.

Both of them dropped to their knees and put their hands on their heads. In the distance, Beckham spotted three more figures standing on a rooftop with their rifles aimed at his chest.

"We're friendly!" Horn protested.

The soldiers didn't reply. They walked cautiously, heel to toe. Beckham recognized their calculated movements and their equipment. These were no grunts. These were well-trained killers. And if their sharpshooting skills were any indication, they were probably Army Rangers.

A smile dawned on Beckham's face. He didn't mind being rescued.

"Don't move," the leader said. His voice was stifled by the gas mask, but it sounded familiar.

"What the hell are you doing out here?" the man said.

"Rescue mission," Horn said.

The two men behind the leader exchanged looks and the one on the right said, "Just the two of you?"

"Not just any two," the other man said. He slowly slipped off his gas mask and leaned forward. "Delta Force operators."

Beckham blinked away the burn of the smoke and focused on a Chinese American man with strands of black hair stuck to his forehead.

"Chow? Is that you, man?" Jay Chow was a staff sergeant with another Delta team, code-named Titanium. Beckham had assumed Chow and Staff Sergeant Drew "Jinx" Abbas were dead, but here they were, standing right in front of him.

"Hell yeah, brother!" Chow said. He lowered his rifle and reached out with open arms, bending to pull Beckham into a strong hug.

"Damn good to see you guys," Jinx said. He flashed a smile and rubbed a streak of dirt off his tanned face before looking behind Horn and Beckham, who had clambered to their feet. "Where's the rest of Team Ghost?"

Beckham pulled away from Chow and shook his head. "Only Riley made it."

Chow's eyes darted to the ground. "There aren't many of us left either. Just me and Jinx." He pointed to the rooftop. "Everyone else was infected or killed. We teamed up with a squad of Rangers."

"What about my family? Have you seen my family?" Horn asked.

Beckham's heart stuttered when Chow hesitated.

"I'm sorry," Chow said, finding Horn's eyes. "Sheila didn't make it."

Horn sucked in a deep breath as if he'd had the wind knocked out of him. He took a step backward, his hands clutching his chest. A deep groan erupted from his mouth.

Beckham felt the churning dread in his stomach. A powerful wave of anxiety took hold of his fatigued body. Sheila was gone. It was real now: They couldn't save her.

He walked over and put a hand on his friend's shoulder. "I'm—"

"What about my girls?" Horn said, shaking. He pulled away from Beckham's grasp.

"Alive," Chow said. "Back in the tunnels with the others."

"We don't have much time," one of the Rangers said. "Those things will come back. They always do."

Jinx eyed the skyline. "That smoke is getting worse. The hospital is still burning."

Chow nodded. He reached in his pack and tossed two gas masks to Horn and Beckham. Eyeing their weapons, he dug through his supplies again for magazines.

"You're lucky, Beckham. I got some extra mags," Chow said. He pushed three of them toward Beckham. "You can thank me later." Then he pulled several M249 magazines from his bag and turned to Horn.

Chow held out the ammo and said, "Follow me. I'll take you to your girls, brother."

A lone soldier stood guard outside the medical ward. He stiffened when he saw Kate and Ellis approaching.

"Good evening, Doctors," the man said, glancing at their badges. "Lieutenant Colonel Jensen is waiting for you at the front desk." He pulled the left door open and ushered Kate and Ellis inside.

They walked into the shadows of a sparsely lit hallway. A loud metallic click followed as the guard sealed them inside. Kate hustled down the passage, anxious to get started. Every room they passed was dark, save for the one at the end of the north quadrant. That was where she was headed. Jensen stood behind a desk on the right side of the hallway, his arms crossed, staring at the locked door to Gibson's room.

Kate rehearsed the questions she would ask the colonel over and over as she walked. The goal was to keep them simple. She wasn't interested in linking him further to VX-99—that wasn't her job. Some hotshot prosecutor would take care of that. Her job was to find out what had happened to Lieutenant Brett in that prison cell almost thirty years ago.

Jensen stepped out from behind the desk when they arrived. "We have to make this quick," he said, tapping his watch. "The colonel's primary doctor threw a fit about your visit."

"Understood," Kate said.

"He's awake and knows you're here to see him. But *please*, Doctors, don't get him agitated," Jensen said.

"I won't," Kate said.

"Me neither," Ellis added.

The lieutenant colonel glanced at them in turn and then pushed the door open. "You have five minutes."

Kate hesitated, suddenly unsure if they were making the right decision. She had no idea what to expect from Gibson.

Ellis nudged her. "Kate..."

"Sorry," she replied, stepping into the room. The colonel lay in his bed, staring at the ceiling, his blue eyes fixated on the white panels. Multiple tubes snaked under his sheets. A biomonitor displaying his vitals chirped in the corner of the room.

"Colonel Gibson?" Kate whispered.

The man's eyes remained locked in place.

"It's Doctor Kate Lovato. I'm here to ask you a few questions."

Jensen strode to the corner of the room as she inched closer to Gibson's bedside. He didn't seem to react to her presence. Hopefully he wasn't too far gone to speak with her.

"I would really appreciate your help, sir," Kate said.

Gibson tilted his head in her direction at last. "Good job on the bioweapon, Doctor."

Kate was taken aback. She hadn't expected such a direct response. "I'd like to ask you…uh…"

"We're here to talk to you about Lieutenant Trevor Brett," Ellis cut in when she fumbled.

Gibson lifted his head off his pillow and looked at Ellis. He coughed deeply, fluid crackling in his chest.

Kate softened her voice. "We know he was given a dose of VX-99. And we know he was taken to a maximum-security military prison after he was found, ten years later."

Gibson squirmed in his bed. The biomonitor chirped louder.

"Yes. This is all true," the colonel said.

"We know that the lieutenant…evolved. Both physically and—" Kate began to say, but Gibson interrupted her.

"That was the point of VX-99."

"How do you mean?"

Gibson returned his gaze to the ceiling. "Isn't it obvious by now?"

Kate didn't reply.

"VX-99 started off as a serum that was supposed to turn men into supersoldiers. Lieutenant Trevor Brett was one of the first ever to be exposed to the chemicals. The result was horrific. His entire platoon died in some rotting jungle, along with a hillside of VC. He was the only survivor. Spent ten years wandering that godforsaken jungle."

"And he changed over that time, didn't he?" Ellis asked.

Gibson coughed again and wiped an arm, attached to cords, across his face. "Yes," he said. "He became a monster. Those—what do you call them, Variants? They aren't much different." He held up a finger and said, "The Ebola virus would have caused brain damage, so I doubt any of them can speak like he did. There may be some, however, that display higher levels of intelligence."

Kate pursed her lips, wanting to ask more questions, but she waited. Gibson clearly had more to say.

"During the lieutenant's isolation we ran hundreds of tests on that poor bastard," he continued. "He was an animal. Rabid, deadly, and forever changed. We couldn't control him. It was then that my vision changed from creating the perfect soldier to creating the perfect weapon—a bioweapon that could be dropped over foreign soil, do its job, and fizzle out. Efficient. Untraceable. And no more American soldiers—our men and women, our *sons and daughters*—would need to die in hellholes halfway around the world."

Gibson blinked several times. If Kate didn't know better, she'd think he was crying. "But that's not what happened, Colonel," Kate said.

The biomonitor chirped again. His heart rate was elevating. Jensen strolled over and nudged Kate's arm.

"Help me understand," Kate pleaded. She began to speak more rapidly. "I'm not sure you realize how dire the situation is outside Plum Island. The world is dying. The human species could very well plummet into extinction if we don't stop the Variant threat. I need to know how Brett evolved. I need to know what these things are capable of."

Gibson tilted his head in her direction. She held his gaze for several seconds, but his blue eyes had gone dull. They were the eyes of a broken soldier.

"Like Lieutenant Brett, the Variants will change," he said grimly. "Doctor Medford was supposed to solve that by creating a weapon that would kill its host. That's why he used Ebola. But instead he created something that was too contagious, something that *didn't* kill the host. That's why I sent in a team to get a sample of his research, and that's why I wanted to bring Doctor Michael Allen to Plum Island."

Kate held back her anger. She spoke just loud enough for everyone around her to hear. "Doctor Medford created a monster. Void of emotion. Void of *humanity*. I need to know how to stop them."

"How do we bring them back?" Ellis asked.

Gibson laughed at that. "Bring them back? You can't bring them back."

"Do you understand what you've done?" asked a voice full of anger. At first Kate thought it was Ellis, but then Jensen approached the bed and leaned close.

Gibson glanced at the man who had replaced him. "I'm sorry."

"You tried to play God."

"I wanted to save our soldiers!" Gibson snapped. "I didn't want other fathers to go through what I did when I lost *my* son."

Kate and Ellis exchanged glances. The biomonitor beeped again, faster and louder this time.

"Congratulations. You killed billions of people instead," Jensen said.

Gibson closed his eyes, agony filling his features as he burst into another coughing fit. The nurse rushed into the room. Kate took a step back to let the woman through.

"He needs to rest," the nurse insisted.

"Yeah," Jensen replied. "Rest up, Colonel. You'll have to answer for your sins soon."

5

Beckham took a long, deep breath. The plastic of his gas mask had never smelled so good. Hours of taking in smoke and the stench of the decaying world had numbed his senses.

He concentrated on his breathing as he struggled to keep up with the rest of the group. The smoke and the battle minutes before had left him unsteady, groggy. A fog latched onto his brain. He couldn't seem to shake it.

Palming his helmet, he blinked away the stars floating before his vision, and the team that had saved his ass came into focus. Chow and Jinx took point, and the four Ranger snipers fell in line behind them. Horn was a few steps ahead, fueled by the determination of a father who knew his daughters were still alive.

Just when Beckham thought the mental cloud was beginning to pass, he saw a female in the middle of the street. She stood there under the moonlight, her arms at her sides.

"Sheila," he whispered. He squinted and slowed as he approached yet another ghost. And then she was gone, blowing away like a cloud of dust.

Beckham smacked his head harder. He was hallucinating, no doubt the effect of smoke inhalation. Pushing on, he wondered if he was still seeing things when Chow flashed a hand movement north toward the gray wall of smoke along Zabitosky Road. Beckham followed the group around the turn. The cloud swirled through the streets, coming from all directions, not just the hospital.

Chow balled his hand into a fist and stopped a hundred feet away from the hospital. Jinx and the Rangers took up positions nearby. Horn seemed ready to keep moving by himself, but he settled against an overturned Humvee and watched the area. The thick black vortex they'd seen from the sky was coming from Womack, but there were other fires licking the skyline.

"How long have they been burning?" Beckham asked.

"A few days," Chow said. "The hospital wasn't the only thing the bombs hit. They also took out the ammunition depots, the fuel station, and a few admin buildings. The fires have been burning out of control ever since." Adjusting his gas mask, Chow asked, "Want the bad news or good news first?"

"Bad," Beckham replied.

Chow pointed to the smoke. "Tunnels are through there."

"What's the good news?" Horn asked.

"Those things won't follow us," Jinx said.

Beckham understood now. There had always been rumors about Cold War–era tunnels that ran beneath parts of the post. He'd even seen pictures of the damp concrete corridors under the Womack Army Medical Center. The army had spent millions of dollars on supplies in the event that the post was ever bombed.

Chow waved the team forward and vanished into the smoke, the dense cloud swallowing him. Jinx and the Rangers followed.

Horn approached the cloud and then turned to look at Beckham. "Let's find my girls," he said.

Beckham nodded, flipped his NVGs down over his

visor, and took the plunge into the green-hued darkness. The world changed drastically inside the cloud. He'd only trained in smoky conditions with the "four-eyes" a handful of times and had forgotten how eerie the experience was. They ran for what seemed like an hour, following Zabitosky Road under the expressway. The fires at Womack raged in the distance, flickering in the sky. Without anyone to put them out, they would continue until the entire area was consumed.

Chow jogged ahead, leading the team off the street and toward a three-story building with a partially collapsed roof. Several bodies lay on the lawn; puddles of now dried blood had formed in the grass around them. Bullet casings littered the sidewalk.

Another slaughter.

Jinx dragged a body out of the way, and Chow kicked in the door.

"Let's move! Get inside!" Jinx said.

Two of the Rangers trailed him into the dark building. The other two stayed outside, monitoring the perimeter with their MK11s.

"Clear!" came a voice from inside the building.

Chow, Horn, and the other Rangers hustled inside, but Beckham hung back to stare at a magnolia tree towering over the one-story building. Half of the branches were twisted and burned. Ashes and charred leaves littered the grass. The other half of the tree was still healthy, the blossoms vibrant.

Half dead and half alive, he thought as he followed the team inside.

Jensen stood with his back to the makeshift war table and stared out of the observation window. He watched the sapphire waves below, wondering how it had come to this. Colonel Gibson, the man he'd followed for a decade, had deceived him. The truth behind his actions was heartbreaking. He had succeeded where Adolf Hitler, Joseph Stalin, Genghis Khan, Xerxes, and so many other men had failed—he'd created a new world, albeit a world of monsters and death. Gibson had been obsessed with saving young soldiers like his son, but in the end he'd doomed them all.

The revelation was like a knife to the gut. Jensen's body burned with anger. Every muscle flexed and tightened as he approached the window. He wanted to scream, to jump through the glass and drop into the cool water below. But he had responsibilities—men and women under his command to protect. Good men like Master Sergeant Reed Beckham and Staff Sergeant Parker Horn, and good women like Dr. Kate Lovato. At the end of the world, they were the most valuable assets the military and the country could have at their disposal.

With a deep breath, he cleared his mind and mastered his temper. He took a seat and swiped the monitor on the table. A map of the country emerged on the display. Central Command was sending him projections of the Variant populations every few hours. Red blotches covered every metropolitan area.

He scooted the chair closer. The images had changed since he had looked earlier that morning. Hundreds of reconnaissance units were set up in cities across the United States, watching and monitoring the Variants. Every single satellite the military had orbiting the planet was now focused on tracking the new enemy. Analysts in bunkers buried deep beneath the surface were studying the data, looking for trends and sending the intel out to remaining posts like Plum Island.

Surely they'd seen what he had. The Variants seemed

to be gathering—forming clusters, hunting in packs. That would help Operation Liberty run much more smoothly, he imagined. The air force would weaken the enemy, and the troops would clean up the rest. No matter how cunning or strong the Variants were, they were no match for missiles, tanks, and good old-fashioned bullets. Even if they *had* evolved, as Dr. Lovato thought they would.

The door slid open and Smith walked into the combat information center. "You get the updated projections?"

Jensen nodded. "Find me any chew?"

Smith chuckled. "I don't think there's a single can on this island. Maybe Beckham will bring some back from Fort Bragg."

"Can't get a message through to him," Jensen said. "Must have turned his comm off for stealth."

Smith pulled a chair up to the table. "I hope that's the reason. Losing those guys would—"

Raising a hand, Jensen cut off his second. "They're Delta Force operators, and Beckham has proven he can survive out there. Besides, there's still another twenty hours before extraction. I'm not going to worry yet.

"Talk to me," Jensen said, changing the subject. "What do you make of this?" He swiveled the monitor closer to Smith.

Smith slipped on a pair of reading glasses. "Looks like the Variants are gathering in clumps. But why?"

"Hell if I know," Jensen responded.

Smith put a thumb under his chin and scratched at his skin. "Seems odd, don't ya think? Maybe there's a reason the Variants are flocking to these areas."

Jensen sighed. He zoomed in the map onto New York and enlarged the image, focusing on a red blotch of Variants in the Bronx. For several minutes he stared blankly, trying to make sense of their migration. But no matter how hard he tried, he just didn't get it. Why would these creatures swarm? And where were the rest of them?

The team rushed down the first-floor hallway. Emergency lights flickered, casting an intermittent red glow over the corridor.

Chow took a knee. "Beckham, get up here."

Jogging past two Rangers, Beckham crouched next to the operator.

"There's a tunnel entrance through there." Chow pointed to a set of double doors at the end of the hallway. "Thing is, we haven't been using this access point. The other one is about a mile to the north. I didn't want to risk it."

The roof groaned, and several ceiling tiles fell to the floor, where they shattered. Chow bowed his head as dust rained down. When it cleared, he brushed the powder off his shoulders and helmet. "You hold rank, Beckham. It's your show now."

Beckham adjusted the strap of his carbine and checked on the team. Horn, Jinx, and the Rangers hung back in the shadows. The flickering red light illuminated their armored bodies. Covered in ash and smoke, they looked as though they'd just survived a nuclear holocaust.

"You said the other access point is through those doors?" Beckham asked.

Chow nodded.

After a brief pause, Beckham said, "Okay. We proceed through the tunnels." He stood and walked toward the doors with his M9 aimed in front. The team fell into position, and Beckham flashed an advance signal to Horn, who approached at a careful trot. At the double doors, Horn snapped his night-vision goggles back into place.

They exchanged a nod, and Beckham nudged the right door open for Horn. He strode into the darkness with his M249, and Beckham followed. The passage curved, and a sloped floor ran to a pair of doors so far away he could hardly make them out. Horn had already covered a good chunk of the hallway.

Shit, Beckham thought. The man wasn't thinking with his head. His only concern was for his daughters.

Increasing his pace, Beckham flicked the mini-mic on his headset closer to his lips. "Hold up."

No reply. Either Horn was ignoring him or the channel wasn't working.

Grunting, Beckham fell into a run. The noises of equipment mixed with the sound of footfalls reverberated through the passage. The sound would let any Variants know they were coming, but the time for a gear check was behind them.

By the time the team reached the other end of the hallway, it felt as though they had descended a couple floors underground. The concrete leveled off at two heavy steel doors. Horn waited there, panting. Beckham shot him an angry glare. This time he nodded at Chow to take the lead. Horn fell into position behind the Rangers.

As Chow slowly pulled the door open, Beckham heard a click. But it wasn't the locking mechanism. Quickly, he grabbed Chow's flak jacket and yanked him away from the door. Then he dropped to one knee and aimed his pistol through the gap. Wide yellow eyes stared back at him. The creature coiled, ready to spring.

Beckham squeezed the trigger before it could move. One of the rounds found a home in its right eye socket. The other took off the bottom of its chin. The monster screeched and retreated.

The bank of emergency lights flickered on the other side of the open door. A dozen of the nightmarish creatures skittered across the walls and the ceiling, their joints clicking as they powered forward.

"Fall back!" Beckham yelled. "Get away from the doors!" Horn, Jinx, and the Rangers formed a wall, standing shoulder to shoulder in the middle of the hallway, where they opened fire on the Variants.

Beckham's senses amplified as he dove for the ground. Every movement the creatures made resounded in his ears. He could see the sweat and blood trickling down their pale skin, could smell the scent of rotting fruit bleeding from their pores. His processor was working at full capacity, his body once again a killing machine.

He hit the deck and continued firing as his mind went into overdrive too. He saw his mom, his dad, Spinoza, Edwards, Tenor, and Sheila. Every shot was for them. The animalistic screams of the Variants waned under the heavy pop of gunfire. Flashes of red and orange crisscrossed the corridor. Chunks of concrete exploded from the walls and ceiling, raining debris on the floor.

Beckham reloaded, closed an eye, and aimed from his prone position. A female Variant leaned around the open door. *Big mistake*, Beckham thought as he squeezed off a shot.

The creature grabbed her stomach, squealing in pain. It was just a flesh wound. Beckham fired again, this time aiming for her throat. The Variant slumped forward, blood gurgling from its mouth.

In seconds, the passage clogged with twitching bodies, but more of the creatures came, leaping from the darkness and through the door. One Variant, still dressed in a ragged janitorial outfit, managed to make it through the gunfire. He had lost an arm, but he was still moving. He growled and leaped into the air.

Two voices called out simultaneously. "Changing!"

Beckham kept firing, watching the ex-janitor's hands

curl into claws. He fired off the rest of his magazine into the man's mutilated body. Blood splattered across Beckham's visor as the creature collided with him, knocking him on the ground with a thud.

"Boss!" Horn yelled.

"I'm fine," Beckham replied, pushing the corpse off him. He jumped to his feet, ran back to the blockade, and slid through a gap between Jinx and Chow.

Empty shells rained down, pinging off the concrete. The gunfire was so loud he could hardly think. Beckham had trained in conditions like this, but the effects of the smoke inhalation had screwed with his senses. A minute earlier he could hear every agonizing movement, now he couldn't even focus.

Beckham caught a glimpse of movement at the team's rear. He changed his magazine and angled his night-vision goggles toward the far end of the hallway, the same way they'd come in.

"Contacts on our six!" Beckham shouted.

Chow turned, while the others kept firing at the Variants coming through the doorway.

"Rich, Timbo, Jinx, cover our asses," Beckham said. "Chow, Horn, Steve, Ryan, you're with me."

The men repositioned themselves in the center of the hallway, their backs together. Both ends of the hallway were crowded with half-naked monsters.

"I thought you said they wouldn't follow us into the smoke!" Horn screamed in between bursts.

"They never have before!" Chow yelled back.

Beckham winced. If the Variants were swarming the tunnels, then how the hell were the others supposed to hold them back? "Are there more guards protecting the survivors?"

Chow hesitated between shots. "Only a few. They've never come in this far!"

Beckham gritted his teeth. He knew what Horn was thinking as his fire became stronger, less controlled. Blood coated the floor, empty bullet casings falling into the slimy red pool.

The Variants were getting closer now, many of them hurtling from wall to ceiling and back to the floor. It made finding a target incredibly difficult, even in the narrow space. Beckham counted a dozen of the creatures coming from his side of the corridor. They were using one another as shields, streaming forward en masse.

"Changing!" Chow shouted.

Beckham concentrated on the lead Variant and fired off two shots. The first caught the monster in the kneecap, the second in its chest. It slid down the wall, blood tattooing the concrete scarlet. Another clawed its way across the ceiling like some demented spider. Beckham stared, wondering if he was in some sort of suspended nightmare, as if he would wake up suddenly and find himself on a beach in the Florida Keys.

The creature dropped from the ceiling and dashed down the hall. It didn't make it very far before it was torn apart by bullets, blood splattering the walls. Beckham regained his stature and reached for another magazine. *Last one*, he thought as he eyed the rest of the pack.

He got off three shots before it was all over. Chow moved ahead of him as soon as the gunfire stopped. He kicked several twitching bodies and double-tapped every one with his rifle.

"Clear," Chow said, nonchalantly.

Beckham held his M9 by his side and could almost feel the heat radiating from the muzzle. He wondered how many lives he'd taken over the past few weeks. Looking at the dozens of bodies and the pooling blood, he wasn't sure he wanted to know the answer. His gaze fell on the face of one of the creatures. Its features were hardly recognizable, so deformed by the bulging, sucker-like lips and transformed eyes that it no longer looked quite human. Yet he saw a trace of a person he remembered. Beckham couldn't recall his name, but he had seen this man around the post several times.

Beckham shivered and ran a sleeve across his visor to remove the blood. This wasn't the type of war he was used to fighting. These enemies had once been their friends and family. He pushed past the corpses with the rest of the team. He didn't want to know who they'd killed.

Chow paused in the doorway ahead.

"How far to the others?" Horn asked.

Chow pulled out a tattered map. He studied it for several minutes.

"A right, a left, and another right," Chow said, tapping the sheet with a gloved finger.

"Then let's move," Horn said.

"Hold up," Beckham replied. "How do we know the other tunnels aren't full of hostiles?"

"We don't," Jinx said.

"You guys better have sealed the doors to the place where my girls are hiding," Horn said. His voice was just shy of a growl. His chest surged with each exhale. Beckham knew he was about to blow a gasket.

"Don't worry. Your girls are safe. Only one way forward," Chow said, pointing down the hall. "Unless you guys want to go back outside."

Horn jammed a fresh magazine into his SAW. "We've already wasted enough time."

"Check your ammo and take a drink," Beckham said. "We move in two minutes." He walked over to Horn and pulled the man to the side.

"Look," Beckham said. "I have no idea how you're feeling right now."

Horn glared at him, his breathing fast and raspy through his mask.

"But you can only help your daughters if you're alive. Get it together, Big Horn!" Beckham smacked the wall with his palm. "We made it this far. You need to slow down and do things the right way. The way we were trained."

The man sucked in a breath, his shoulders dropping as he calmed down. "You're right, boss. Wasn't thinking back there. It's just..." He formed a fist as the anger returned. Shaking his head, he said, "Fuck! Sheila's dead."

Beckham patted the armor above Horn's heart. "But your girls are *alive*. And we're almost there, man. Almost fucking there."

They embraced. For the first time that day Beckham felt a sense of pride, of friendship. The small act reminded him, again, that he was only as good as the man next to him. Horn was his best friend, his brother. And they were going to find his daughters.

Together they trailed Chow and the rest of the team into the next hallway, moving cautiously this time. Moving as one.

6

Meg Pratt felt piss running down her legs. Instant relief washed over her. She'd held it for two days, in the same stinking closet that she shared with Rex and Jed. Their makeshift hiding place in the firehouse had been built to hold outdated gear—small items like helmets, suits, and boots, *not* oversized firefighters.

The closet stank of more than bodily fluids—it stank of death. They'd escaped the Variants that had infiltrated the station by hiding under a pile of dead bodies in the basement. The corpses had once been other firefighters, their friends and coworkers, and several families that the station had let in after all hell had broken loose. But there hadn't been time to mourn.

It was a last-ditch effort to escape. Meg had observed the Variants from a distance for days. They never ate the dead, only the living.

After spending countless hours under the bodies, Meg had ordered Rex and Jed back upstairs. They had made it to the stairwell when they heard the ruckus of another one of the creatures searching for them upstairs and were forced to retreat to the gear closet. They'd been there ever since.

"Think it's safe yet?" Rex asked. He wiped the sweat off his forehead and squirmed.

"Shhh," Jed whispered.

Meg hadn't heard anything for a couple hours. The silence was starting to make her nervous. Was it possible the creatures were waiting upstairs?

That was a crazy thought, she realized. They would have come crashing down into the basement hours ago if they knew the firefighters were down there. Meg changed hands with the axe and pushed herself to her feet, using the blade as a crutch. The numbness in her right leg made her cringe as the blood began to flow again. She bit the inside of her lip and waited until it passed.

"Where ya goin'?" Rex asked.

Jed shushed the man again.

Straining her ears, Meg listened for movement. All was quiet. Eerily quiet. She was still getting used to the sound of nothing, especially in a city like New York. In the hours of monotony, she wondered if she had gone deaf. Or crazy. The truth was she'd entered a nightmare, a world where the only sounds were made by things that wanted to tear her apart.

Holding her breath in anticipation, Meg slowly opened the closet door. She glared back at Rex as if to say, *Keep your big-ass mouth shut.*

Stepping out of the closet, Meg raised her axe and held it close to her chest. *One step at a time*, she thought as she slowly crossed the basement. Rays of light bled into the room from the small windows.

Meg emerged from the shadows and made her way to the staircase, placing her back against the wall and peeking around the corner. She held in another breath, half expecting to see one of the monsters dangling from the ceiling or walking backward down the stairs like that girl in *The Exorcist*. But the stairwell was empty. She waved the others out of their hiding spot and started up the concrete steps.

Above, the garage had been completely ransacked. Suits, helmets, boots, and hoses that had been perfectly organized were now in disarray, pulled from their hooks and lockers and scattered across the floor.

Meg sighed. She doubted anyone would suit up ever again.

"Come on," she finally whispered, motioning for the others to follow. She crossed the garage carefully, side-stepping around gear and equipment, and then stopped in the open doorway to the stairs that led to the second floor.

Staring into the darkness was like looking into a portal. The thought of spending another minute up there made her pause. But the alternative was the basement, and she couldn't bear the idea of returning to the morgue.

Grabbing a railing, she climbed up the stairs. With every step, the sour scent grew. It was one of those smells she just couldn't exactly place. Maybe lemon. Or grapefruit. Meg wasn't sure. Whatever it was, it stank like an open garbage bin on a hot summer day.

Pulling her collar up around her nose, she continued toward the open door and the idle ceiling fans above. Meg paused again to listen.

Nothing.

She used the time to think. Although she'd come up with a plan in the closet, she wasn't sure she had the guts to implement it now. The idea was to leave the fire station and find other survivors, preferably the military. But the closer she got to their old hiding spot, the more she wanted to just hunker down. They had food and supplies. The only thing outside was death and hungry, crazed ex-humans.

Meg was a fighter. Always had been. She'd grown up

a tomboy and prided herself on the bruises she got from playing football with the boys. As an adult, she'd found there wasn't anything that got her blood flowing like kicking in doors and running into burning buildings. But her life had never been threatened as it was now. The danger was exciting back then. Now it was truly terrifying. She wasn't ready to die, especially at the hands of the monsters.

When she saw the empty room of beds and the boarded-up windows, she made her decision: They were staying put. She wasn't going to risk moving unless a damn chopper landed in the street outside.

Rex and Jed passed her and reclaimed their bunks. Rex pulled a plastic bag of food from under his bed and began rifling through the contents. How he could eat when the place reeked was beyond her. She laid her axe on the nearest bed, pulled her brown hair into a ponytail, and changed out of her wet clothes.

Meg had never been the bashful type. Working and living mostly with men had ensured that. And besides, at the end of the world, formalities like pissing in a toilet and changing in a bathroom had gone out the window. Pulling on a clean shirt, she sat down slowly, cautious not to make the bed squeak. For the first time in days, she felt the closest thing to safety.

The feeling vanished when the shriek of one of the creatures ripped through the night. Meg froze, her gaze falling on Rex's terrified features. Jed stood in place, his eyes locked on the window.

The screech was distant.

A second voice answered the call.

Meg waited anxiously for a third. Several minutes ticked by and she slowly relaxed again, her hand falling away from the axe.

Swinging her feet off the floor, she lay down and let her head sink into the pillow. What she needed was some good rest. She pulled her collar up over her nose again. The rot lingered, but she was tired enough not to care.

Closing her eyes, she crossed her arms and let her body and mind succumb to fatigue. She sank into the comfortable bed and had just started to drift off when a third sound came.

Meg jolted upright. This wasn't a screech, but the click-clack of joints.

"Shit," Jed said. He poked his eye against the gap in the boards. "Those things are..."

Rex dropped his bag of food and stood, his hands trembling.

Meg rushed to the window and nudged Jed to the side. She gasped when she saw the adjacent buildings. The creatures were perched on the rooftops, all of them staring at the fire station.

Stumbling away from the window, Meg looked to Jed for support. The marine didn't speak. None of them did. They were cornered, with no hope of escape.

The team was more than a mile into the tunnel systems when they came to the final hallway. Four orange drums and a wall of sandbags sat in front of two steel doors. Someone had gone to great lengths to seal the entrance.

"We're here," Chow said. "The hundred-gallon barrels are full of water. They've been down here a long time. Disaster supplies."

Horn threw the strap of his M249 over his shoulder and approached the blockade.

"Our makeshift shelter's on the other side," Chow continued. "Come on. Let's move these things."

Horn was already pressing his shoulder into the side of the closest drum to push it out of the way. After a few grunts he had created a gap wide enough for another body. Beckham squeezed through and helped him move the barrel against the wall. The plastic rumbled against the concrete as they moved. Chow and Jinx worked on the barrel to the right, and the team repeated the process for the second set. The four Rangers stepped through the narrow gap and began to remove the sandbags.

Sweat formed on Beckham's forehead. His uniform was wet by the time they finished clearing the doors, a mixture of perspiration and blood.

"Well?" Horn asked. "Is there a password or what?"

Chow pulled off his gas mask and rapped his fist against the metal three times. "It's Chow—open up."

The only response was a hollow echo.

Horn yanked on one of the handles. The locking mechanism clicked; it was locked from the other side. Chow pounded the door again. "Hey, Williams! You awake? It's Chow, and we have company." He pressed his ear against the steel and listened.

"Shit," he muttered, stepping away from the door.

"What do you mean, 'shit'?" Horn said. "You said you had this place guarded."

"It was," Jinx chimed in.

"It *is*," Chow corrected him. He tossed his M4 to Jinx and reached for a pocket in his vest, retrieving a small lockpick. "Williams is on security. He's probably patrolling the other hallways."

"He better be," Horn snarled.

"Keep it down," one of the Rangers said. The man's tag said RICH. He removed his gas mask and ran a hand through his hair. Then he took a drink and turned to scan the other end of the tunnel, his eyes roving back and forth anxiously.

"What the hell were you guys doing outside anyway?" Horn asked. "Why'd you leave the others?"

Chow glanced over his shoulder. "Supply run. We were trying to make it to an ammo depot when those things ambushed us. Lost two men."

Rich shook his head and walked over to the other three Rangers. Beckham's heart sank as the four men talked in hushed voices. He wondered how many other squads and teams had been torn apart like Team Ghost. So much death and loss, and all for what? For Colonel Gibson's fucking dream.

The lock clicked, and Chow pumped his fist in the air. "Got it," he said, smiling. He stepped back and reached for his rifle.

"Keep sharp," Beckham said. "You take point, Chow. You know this place the best."

The operator nodded and grabbed the door handle, eyeing each man in turn. After a beat he twisted it and pulled the door back to reveal an empty passage. There were piles upon piles of boxes stacked to the ceiling on the right-hand side.

Horn moved next, his weapon angled into the darkness. The damp hallway stank of stale water. Chow stopped at the first curve and propped his shoulder against the wall. Placing two fingers to his eyes, he flashed a hand signal to Beckham and Jinx. Beckham gripped his M9, tensed his body, and bolted around the corner. A beam of intense light hit him in the face, momentarily blinding him. He stared into it, his palm extended in an attempt to shield his eyes, his trigger finger dangerously close to squeezing off a shot.

"Friendly, friendly!" Jinx yelled.

Beckham blinked away the white spots in his vision and saw a Ranger standing in the middle of the corridor, a look of shock painted across his features. He couldn't have been more than twenty-one years old.

"Jesus, you scared the shit out of me," the man said.

Chow and Horn hustled into the hallway. "Well, Jinx just about shot you in the face, Williams," Chow said. "Didn't you hear the gunfire earlier?"

"I can't hear shit," the man said. "My ears have been fucked since the bombs dropped." He smacked the side of his helmet and scanned the new faces.

"Where are the others?" Horn asked.

"Who the hell are these guys?" Williams asked. "And where's Ricardo and Bonner?"

"These are Delta operators Horn and Beckham," Chow said. His gaze flicked to the floor in a moment of silence. Looking up, he said, "Ricardo and Bonner didn't make it."

"Fuck," Williams said softly. Anguish streaked across his face, and he gave his helmet another smack.

"Rich, Timbo, Steve, and Ryan—you guys secure that back door. Then report to Command," Chow said. He turned to Horn next and placed a hand on the man's shoulder. "You ready to see your daughters?" Chow asked.

Horn smiled. "Hell yes."

Kate stared at her food. She wasn't sure exactly what she was looking at. The man who had slopped the mush onto her plate called it meat, but maybe he was joking. It had the same consistency as mashed potatoes.

She'd learned to stop taking things for granted when she began her career in the field. Traveling to remote villages in India, Sudan, and Guinea had a way of changing people, making them realize how great Americans really had it. The majority of the world did not have access to clean drinking water, health care, or electricity, let alone porterhouse steaks.

Kate jammed a forkful into her mouth, chewed, and swallowed. It didn't taste that bad, actually. She told herself it was mashed potatoes and finished half the meal before checking on Ellis.

The doctor sat across the table, shoveling green peas in his mouth as he thumbed through pictures on his cell phone. With service gone, the devices were nothing more than picture albums or toys. Some of Kate's old apps still worked. Ironically, the plague game she used to play still functioned. Dismissing these trivial thoughts, Kate let her mind wander to the people she would never see again.

Her brother. Michael. Possibly her parents. And Reed...

Kate shook the thought away. Beckham was coming back. He would swim back to Plum Island if he had to.

"I miss CNN," Ellis muttered. He placed his phone on the table.

"I miss the Discovery Channel."

"We're living in a Discovery Channel documentary about the end of the world," Ellis said.

Kate wiped her mouth with a napkin. "I know. I just never thought I'd be one of the stars."

Ellis popped another scoop of peas into his mouth. "Do you think things will ever go back to normal?"

"Are you kidding?"

He shrugged. "I believe in miracles."

"Would take one hell of a miracle," Kate said.

"I still have hope. That's why I became a doctor in the first place."

He was right, and Kate knew it. She had a tendency to treat Ellis like a kid—like her little brother, Javier.

"I'm sorry," she said.

Ellis rolled his eyes and grabbed his cell again, swiping the screen with a greasy finger.

"Ellis," she insisted, "you're right. It's just..."

He looked back up at her.

"This documentary sucks," Kate finished.

Ellis laughed. "Yeah, yeah, it does. But, Kate, if it weren't for you, the hemorrhage virus would have infected an even larger percentage of the population."

The brief moment of humor faded away. Kate dropped her fork. "I know, but I can't stop thinking of Javier. VariantX9H9 killed him. I killed my brother." She cupped her head in her hands. "I killed my own brother," she whispered.

"Javier was probably already dead. Just like my family. You didn't want him to suffer, did you?"

Kate shook her head. "No."

"Do you know why I haven't completely lost my mind?"

She shook her head again.

"Because I direct my anger toward Colonel Gibson and Doctor Medford. Those bastards created the hemorrhage virus. And the way I look at it, we destroyed that virus." Ellis pushed his tray aside, focusing on Kate with a stern look. "We can defeat the Variants. We can take back the country. I believe that. I do."

Kate pulled her hands away from her face and sat up. Straight. Professional.

Ellis reached across the table with his right hand. "Kate."

The gesture took her by surprise. Ellis wasn't an emotional man, but the end of the world had a way of changing people. Things that didn't seem to matter before were important now. She gripped his hand in her own.

"You can't continue to blame yourself for the death of Michael or Javier or anyone else. You did your job," Ellis said.

"But I couldn't save them. Maybe with more data or more time I could have developed a cure..." she said. Her mind had run over the possibility countless times.

"But you *didn't* have those things. You tried your best."

"I know," Kate whispered.

He pulled out of her grasp and then patted her hand. "If you need anything, just let me know."

She smiled and brushed the threat of a tear away from her eye. "I will. Same goes for you."

"Shit," Ellis said. "Look who's coming."

Lieutenant Colonel Jensen was striding across the cafeteria.

"What now?" Kate said. Her stomach churned when she thought of Beckham. Did he have news?

"Doctor Lovato, Doctor Ellis," Jensen said. "I want to apologize for losing my temper with Colonel Gibson. That man… At any rate, I'm sorry."

"We understand," Kate said.

"Secondly, I need to share some intel with you," Jensen said. He threw a glance over his shoulder at a table of marines. "Perhaps it would be better if we discussed this in my office."

"Is it Beckham?"

Jensen looked uncharacteristically confused. "I don't know. We haven't heard from him yet." He checked the marines again and said, "Meet me in the CIC in fifteen minutes."

"We'll be there," Ellis said.

Kate stood, grabbed her tray, and hurried over to the trash bins. Jensen knew something—something he didn't want to share in front of the marines—and she was anxious to know what it was.

7

The weight pressing on Beckham's chest lifted the moment he spied the freckled faces of Horn's daughters. Relief flooded through him, the burden vanishing as the girls burst from a pack of civilians huddled together in the tunnel.

"Tasha, Jenny!" Horn shouted.

"Daddy!" the girls yelled. For a moment they stood there, as if they weren't sure what to do.

Horn held out his arms and dropped to both knees. His girls came running toward him then, and he scooped them up and kissed them each on the cheek in turn. He cried with joy as he pulled them closer.

Beckham gave them some space and walked over to Chow and Jinx.

"First happy ending I've seen in weeks," Chow said.

Jinx laughed. "Man, I could use a happy ending."

"Are you fucking kidding?" Chow said, slapping the back of his hand on Jinx's shoulder.

"Cut it out," Beckham said. "Do you know what Horn has been through, Jinx?"

"Look what you did now," Chow said to Jinx as Beckham snorted and walked away.

"Reed!" both of the girls screamed as he approached.

"Hey, Tasha! Hey, Jenny!" Beckham said, his smile widening further. Horn set his daughters down and they ran to Beckham, nearly tackling him. "Have you two grown?"

Tasha, who was eight, shook her head.

"I have!" Jenny said enthusiastically.

Beckham agreed. She looked older than five now. It had only been a few weeks since he'd seen them, but the gray soot covering their faces aged them both. "You're going to be as tall as your dad soon," Beckham said, taking a knee in front of them. He reached inside his vest pocket and pulled out a surprise he'd been holding on to since they left Plum Island. "Got you something."

Both girls grinned. They knew what was coming: He always gave them Hershey's Milk Chocolate bars. He pulled the candy from a bag and looked up at Horn for his approval. He nodded, and Beckham handed over the wrapped bar.

"Thanks!" the girls said.

Beckham stood and patted the girls on their heads. He found Horn's eyes. They were brittle. He hadn't had time to grieve at all for Sheila. The time for that would come soon, but first they had to get the girls back to Plum Island.

Focusing on the narrow hallway, Beckham realized it was going to be more difficult than he thought. There were at least fifty survivors. Some needed medical attention, and there were multiple children who would slow the group down. That meant three Black Hawks and a support crew. Jensen wasn't going to be happy, but Beckham knew exactly how to sell the mission. Jensen needed boots for Operation Liberty. Looking around him, Beckham saw something even better—two more Delta operators and a handful of well-equipped Army Rangers.

"Chow, get over here," Beckham said.

"Whatcha need?" the man asked. He placed his pack on the ground and stood as tall as he could manage. Strands of jet-black hair glistened on his forehead. The trim Chinese American operator was one of the most decorated men Beckham had ever worked with. Before he joined the military and was tapped for Delta Force, Chow had been training to be a mixed martial arts fighter. His experience and his skill in countless martial arts made Chow one of the best.

"You guys got a working radio? I can't get a signal down here," Beckham said.

Chow nodded. "Yeah, this way."

Beckham smiled at the girls and patted Horn on the back one more time. Then he followed Chow through the crowd of survivors. Men and women of all ages stared at him, their eyes pleading for reassurance and hope. He saw a young man with auburn hair lying on the ground. Two metal blades jutted out from under a filthy blanket in place of his lower legs. He was probably a veteran of the war in Iraq or Afghanistan. The sight made Beckham aware of his own legs and reminded him of Riley. He stopped and waited for the man to look up. When their eyes met, Beckham gave the man a nod of recognition.

A smile streaked across the soldier's dirt-stained face. He sat up and returned the gesture. "Good to have you here."

"Good to be here," Beckham replied. "Sit tight. We're going to move soon."

The man nodded and tossed the blanket aside. Putting his palms to the ground, he pushed himself to his feet as Beckham walked on. At the end of the hallway, another Ranger stood guard over a makeshift desk. Radio equipment and ammunition littered the surface. Chow nodded at the man and then pulled a chair up to the table.

Plucking a piece of paper from his vest pocket, Beckham handed it to Chow. "That's the encrypted channel for Plum Island."

"Hold up," Chow said. He fidgeted with the dial, white noise crackling from the speakers. "Think I got it." He handed the receiver to Beckham.

"Plum Island, this is Ghost One, do you copy? Over." Static surged through the narrow hallway, catching the attention of several children and a nurse handing them packets of food.

A female voice said, "Ghost One,—Corporal Hickman, at Plum Island. Good to hear your voice."

Beckham exhaled and brought the receiver back to his lips. "Good to hear yours, Corporal. We're requesting extraction at the following coordinates."

Chow handed him the GPS location that he'd scribbled on a piece of paper. "That's the location where we saved your asses," he said.

Beckham read the coordinates. "We need three Black Hawks and medical support. Evac zone could be hot. Extraction team should come prepared for hostiles."

"Copy that," Corporal Hickman replied. "Will relay info to Command. Stand by."

A few minutes later a stern voice came online. "Ghost One, Lieutenant Colonel Jensen. That's a hell of a lot of choppers."

Beckham glanced at Chow and then said, "Sir, we have located a team of Delta operators and Army Rangers. They would be a valuable addition to Operation Liberty. Horn's daughters are alive too."

Chow took the receiver and gave both Beckham and Jensen a brief rundown on the survivors—the number of wounded, the number of civilians, and the number of military personnel—before handing it back.

A moment of silence passed as Jensen considered the

request. The lieutenant colonel would be analyzing the situation, considering all of the variables, including the wounded. Three choppers were a lot to risk.

"Copy that, Ghost. Extraction at 0700 hours. You get those civilians out of there safely. You hear me?"

"Thank you, sir," Beckham said, breaking radio protocol again. He checked his wristwatch. That gave them ten hours to prepare the survivors and get to the evacuation location.

"Beckham," Jensen said. "There's something else. Doctor Lovato had a message for you about the Variants. She said they're evolving."

"Copy that, sir," Beckham replied.

The channel cut to white noise, and Beckham handed the receiver back to Chow.

"What the fuck does that mean? 'Evolving'?" Chow asked.

Beckham thought back to the female Variant in New York City. He could picture the blood on her face as well as if she was standing right in front of him. She'd pointed right at him and shown a type of intelligence the other creatures hadn't.

"You seen those things act differently at all in the past few days?" Beckham asked.

"Nah. They seem like basic predators to me—hunt in packs and attack like kamikazes."

Beckham scratched his chin. "Tell the rest of the men to be on alert. I don't want any surprises."

Chow flashed a thumbs-up and said, "Glad you made it, man."

"Me too, brother."

"I sure hope you have a good plan to get these people out of here."

"I do," Beckham said. He examined the other soldiers in the hallway. "I just hope we have enough firepower."

"You authorized what?" Smith shook his head in amazement. "With all due respect, you do this for them and every soldier on this post will request the same for their family."

"You don't think I know that?" Jensen exhaled and spoke calmly. "Beckham and Horn and anyone they can find with their level of training—those men are invaluable. We *need* them."

"I understand. But the other survivors are going to take up space and precious resources, like food and water. Not to mention medicine. And there's still the risk of infection."

Jensen considered the major's words. He was right. Everything he said made sense. The other soldiers on post would want the same treatment for their families. He'd already received two dozen requests for missions into the cities to look for survivors—requests he'd denied. Now he was bringing fifty men and women from Fort Bragg to the island. Even if he did it under the cover of darkness, he would need to find a place to house them.

"I need a plan," Jensen said.

Smith nodded. "Yes, sir, you do."

Clasping his hands behind his back, Jensen walked to the window in the CIC and stared out over the ocean. It was the only place he felt comfortable, the last place on earth he felt a sense of peace. The purple waves crashed against the shoreline. The view was soothing, an escape from the responsibility he felt to those under his command. Everyone stationed here had essentially won the lottery. It was one of the most secure locations left on the planet.

"That's it," he said suddenly.

The major raised his brows as he took a sip of steaming coffee. "What's it?"

"A lottery." Jensen hesitated for a moment to reflect; then he brightened at the idea and turned to his second. "What if we hold a lottery? Any person on this post can enter if they have family within the range of one of the birds. We'll select a random winner each week."

Smith stared at him as if he was crazy. "Where are we going to house these survivors? What if people don't volunteer to go? Are these going to be single-man missions?"

Jensen sighed. He wasn't thinking. *Fuck.* He wasn't thinking at all.

"I don't think you want to have riots on your hands," Smith added. "In time, we're going to have more problems to deal with. Supplies won't last forever. The military and what's left of the government may not be able to resupply us. We need to hunker down for the long haul."

"The most important resources aren't the supplies. They're people, Major." Jensen turned back to the window. "We can always find more supplies."

"I hate to bring this up, but what if soldiers ask to leave the post? When their enlistment is up?"

"This isn't a prison," Jensen replied quickly. "They are free to go when their service is complete."

Smith snorted his response. "I figured you would say that. But if we keep this post secure and safe, then we won't have to worry about riots, or soldiers asking to leave."

Jensen had considered this before, in the hours of the night when he couldn't sleep. Smith was right. The best way to keep the island safe was to keep those on it happy.

"Besides, even if we hold a lottery, most people on this

post lost their families weeks ago. There may not be anyone to rescue," Smith said.

The ugly truth was difficult for Jensen to stomach, but he had accepted the fact that his own family was likely dead. And most of the other men and women on the post would have done the same. Smith was right; a lottery would be a waste of resources.

A welcome knock on the door reminded Jensen that he'd requested Kate's and Ellis's presence. She would be pleased to know that Beckham was safe.

"Come in," Jensen said. He met the doctors and gestured for them to take seats at the messy metal table. "I have good news for you, Doctor Lovato. Master Sergeant Beckham has linked up with a group of approximately fifty survivors at Fort Bragg, and they've located Staff Sergeant Horn's daughters."

Kate covered her mouth with her hand.

"That's great!" Ellis said.

"When are they flying back?" Kate asked.

"Evac's at 0700 hours," Jensen replied.

Kate smiled. "Thank you."

Jensen nodded. "Least I can do for him." His tone hardened with his eyes as he took a seat next to Smith, who sat at the computer. "The reason I called you here is because I wanted your opinion on something. Major Smith, please bring up the data we have on New York."

The monitor filled with a map of the city. Kate and Ellis scooted closer as Jensen eyed the clusters of red. They looked as though they had grown, as if the Variants were continuing to gather.

"Zoom in on Manhattan," Jensen said.

Smith punched a few keys, and the map shrank. Several red blocks emerged within the confines of Manhattan.

"What are we looking at?" Ellis asked.

"That is the most recent data we have from Central Command on Variant populations. This specific cluster is in Manhattan, very close to Times Square. A squad of recon marines in the area put their numbers at around a thousand strong."

"That's it?" Kate asked, pulling her chair even closer to the table. "Can you show us a history of their movement?"

"Absolutely," Smith replied. His fingers dashed across the keyboard. "This was five days ago."

The map now showed small red dots all over Manhattan, much like the early maps of the hemorrhage virus. Smith punched a button, and the time lapse started. The specks slowly moved to a central location until they formed one group.

Kate brought a finger to her chin. "So the Variants have been on the move for days?"

"Yes, Doctor," Smith said.

"And you're wondering why they're gathering in one spot?"

"I have a theory," Jensen said. "I think they're grouping together to hunt. It's the typical hunter-gatherer behavior of our primitive ancestors."

"I think you've answered your own question. That's exactly what I was thinking," Kate said.

Ellis nodded enthusiastically. "I agree, but to clarify—the VX-99 chemicals turned on genes that harken back to long before any indigenous cultures were present in North America, though. Their behavior likely mirrors that of predatory animals like hyenas or lions. They hunt in groups and gather around natural resources."

Jensen ran a finger across his chin and looked toward the ceiling. "But that doesn't explain everything."

A moment of silence passed over the room, the tick of an unseen clock the only sound.

"As you can see, the clusters are showing up in multiple sections of the city. Command has put their numbers in the tens of thousands in these areas," Jensen said.

"Tens of thousands?" Kate stared intensely at the monitor. "I don't get it. Where are the rest of them?"

"That's why I brought you here—to ask you that exact question."

"There should be hundreds of thousands," Kate said before pausing. "No. There should be *millions*."

"These maps are accurate," Smith said. "Satellite imagery and recon marines don't lie."

Kate shook her head. "If approximately eighty-five percent of the population in New York State was infected with the hemorrhage virus, that means there were more than sixteen million cases before VariantX9H9 was launched. And if ten percent of those infected survived the virus and transformed into Variants, then that puts their numbers between one and two million. Even if this map focuses just on Manhattan, there's simply no way there could be that kind of discrepancy."

Smith chuckled nervously. "Maybe the Variants all ran away."

"More like vanished," Kate said, narrowing her eyes at the screen. "So the real question is what happened to all of them."

There was absolutely no rational explanation for the numbers being so far off, Jensen saw. Either the doctor was wrong or Central Command was planning an offensive with faulty intel.

"Corporals," Jensen said, looking toward the communications officers at the opposite end of the room. They both took a break from listening to the endless sea of radio chatter and waited for orders. "Get someone from Central on the horn ASAP."

Troop movements, armor, and air strikes were being

planned around maps that potentially showed only a fraction of the true Variant strength. They had to warn Command to delay Operation Liberty before it was too late.

Beckham couldn't stop thinking about Kate's message. "Evolving," he muttered a bit too loudly.

"What's evolving?" Horn asked, packing his gear bag while Tasha and Jenny sat a few feet away.

Beckham glanced over at the girls. They were oblivious to the conversation, playing with a doll Tasha had managed to bring with her.

"The Variants," Beckham whispered. "Kate said they're 'evolving' but didn't specify into what, or how."

"What's a Variant, Daddy?" Jenny asked. "Is that one of the monsters?"

Beckham sighed. He was going to let Horn explain this one.

"Is that what killed Mommy?" Tasha asked.

Horn's face turned crimson. Beckham's heart ached for him. He wanted to help his friend, but he didn't know what to say.

The man kneeled in front of his girls. Tears welled in his eyes. "Your mom was a very sick woman. She's with Grandma and Grandpa now."

"But I want her to be here with us," Tasha whimpered.

Jenny rested her head against Horn's flak jacket.

He reached for Tasha and pulled her close. "I know. I know; I do too. But we have to be strong so we can get to Plum Island with Reed."

Jenny looked up from her dad's vest. Beckham forced a smile, but the ache dug deeper when he saw the pain in her face. He thought of his own mother and traced a finger over his vest pocket; he knew exactly how the girl felt.

Beckham took two steps forward until he was within arm's distance of Horn and his girls. He'd suppressed memories of his mother his entire life, but seeing Tasha, Jenny, and Horn dealing with Sheila's loss brought them all surging back.

He put a hand on Horn's shoulder. The four of them remained in the damp hallway for several minutes, letting everything out. Tears found their way down Beckham's face. Three of the most important people in the world were right next to him. He would do anything to protect them.

"Gear check in fifteen," called a voice down the hallway. Five Army Rangers advanced through the crowd, checking the wounded and splitting the survivors into groups.

Beckham wiped his eyes as Chow and Jinx approached.

"Horn, I'm guessing you want to stay with your girls, right?" Jinx asked.

An incredulous look broke across Horn's face. Beckham had to chuckle.

"Copy that," Jinx said. He turned to Beckham. "We better get working on our formation. I just sent a scout out to check on the smoke. Good news there; it's changed course away from the evac zone."

Beckham considered the route they'd used to get to the tunnels and said, "The tunnel is filled with corpses. We have kids to think about."

Jinx scratched his nose. "With all due respect, the kids have already seen that shit and worse."

The words hit Beckham hard. He knew the horrors the kids had already seen, the same as he'd seen in New York and Niantic. These kids were going to grow up in a world where that was normal. If they were able to grow up at all.

"Other way is risky, man," Chow said, pulling out his map. "We've been using it for supply runs and recon, but we were ambushed there a few days ago. Worse than the tunnel."

"Four Delta operators and six Rangers to protect fifty people, against things that move like insects," Jinx muttered. "I don't like our odds."

"What's the distance of each route?" Beckham asked. He helped Chow spread the map against the concrete wall.

"Way we came in is about one and a half miles. Other way is three." Chow wiped a strand of hair out of his face and focused. Beckham could see it in the man's eyes—he wanted to take the way they'd come in. He didn't like the idea of exiting through a tunnel full of corpses, but maybe they didn't have any other option. Beckham looked to Horn for support.

"Probably the fastest way is the best way," Horn said, stroking Tasha's hair. "Especially if the smoke has cleared."

Beckham licked the roof of his mouth. Once again he was at the helm, but this time he had a shit-ton of civilians to look after. "All right. We'll exit the way we came in. Chow, you and I will take point. I want our best Ranger snipers on the rooftops along the route once we get out of the tunnel. Two'll have to go out ahead of us and stay ahead as we move, but they fall back to join the main group if they meet any threats. Horn, you and Jinx stay with the civilians. The other two Rangers will take rear guard. Buddy up every able adult with a child. Tell the kids to cover their eyes if they can. I don't want any of them seeing this shit if they don't have to."

Chow, Jinx, and Horn nodded simultaneously.

"You said those things won't follow us into the smoke, right?" Beckham asked and then remembered they'd already been followed into the tunnels.

"Correct," Chow said. "Except..." Clearly the man was thinking the same thing Beckham was.

"Maybe they came from a different location. Maybe they didn't follow us after all," Beckham said. "Do you guys have any smoke grenades? We can form a perimeter around the group when we get topside."

"Good idea," Jinx said. "I'll distribute a couple to each man."

Beckham paused to think. Was he missing anything? Was this the best way? His gut said it was. He swept his gaze over the tunnel, listening to the coughs and quiet whispers of the civilians. His eyes stopped on the veteran with the blades. He was standing behind Jinx—eavesdropping from the looks of it.

"What's your name, marine?" Beckham said, gesturing the man forward. He wore a pair of shorts and a black T-shirt with SEMPER FI emblazoned across the chest.

"Joe Fitzpatrick, but everyone calls me Fitz."

Beckham smiled. "You want to fight, Fitz?"

"Thought you'd never ask," the man said with a wide grin.

"Jinx, get this marine a weapon," Beckham said. "Whatever he wants."

"M4 or MK11, if you have it," Fitz requested.

Jinx grabbed an M4 and handed it to Fitz while Beckham looked at his watch. The birds would be en route now. It was time to start moving.

Kate opened the door to Riley's room quietly, just in case he was sleeping. An energetic voice greeted her.

"Hey, Doc! Hit the lights, will you?"

She smiled and flipped the switch. Riley was sitting up in bed, his arms folded and his hair sticking out in all directions.

"You're awake early," she said. "You've just been sitting here in the dark?"

"Couldn't sleep. Too worried about Beckham and Horn. I still can't believe they went to Bragg on their own." Riley pounded his sheets with a hand. His light blue eyes were focused, alert. He looked as though he'd been up for hours.

"I couldn't sleep either." Kate sighed. "Plus I'm waiting on more test results."

Riley flattened his wild hair with a pat of his hand. Kate chuckled when it puffed back out.

"Here, I brought you something," she said, tossing him a copy of *The Forever War* by Joe Haldeman.

He caught the paperback with a swipe and then stared at the cover with arched brows. "A book?"

"Not just any book." Kate took a seat in one of the chairs next to his bed. "I hear this is quite the story—aliens, soldiers, and *sex*. You should enjoy it."

Riley quickly thumbed through the pages. "Um, I don't see any pictures. What page is the sex on?"

Kate rolled her eyes but could not suppress a smile. "Start from page one."

He laughed and set the novel on his bed. "Thanks. Seriously, I appreciate it."

"No problem."

"So why are you really here? You got word about Beckham and Horn?"

Kate pulled her chair closer to his bed. "Three Black Hawks are en route to Bragg. Beckham found fifty survivors, including Horn's girls."

"What about Sheila?"

Kate shook her head. "I'm sorry."

"God," Riley said. He used his fingers to trace a cross on his chest and then bowed his head in a whispered prayer.

She put a hand on his bed. When he finally looked up, she said, "But two other Delta soldiers made it—Jinx and Chow. Do you know them?"

"Jinx and Chow!" He winced in pain as he repositioned his casts. "That's great news. Didn't think anyone could have survived."

"Me too," Kate said. "But I've got to ask—what kind of name is Jinx? Doesn't that mean bad luck or a curse?" Kate asked.

Riley chuckled. "Jinx is a nickname, and it's an inside joke. His real name is Drew Abbas, and trust me, Staff Sergeant Abbas is the opposite of bad luck. Him and Chow are the guys you want at your back when shit gets dark."

"That's good. I'm glad Beckham's got good men watching over him."

"I wish I was one of them," Riley said. He brushed something away from his eye and sat up straighter. "Thanks for coming to see me, Kate. And for the news. Sitting on the sidelines is the hardest thing I've ever had to do."

"I know," Kate said. "Seems unfair, doesn't it? Us being here, safe, while Beckham and Horn are fighting to save the helpless."

Riley nodded several times. "It's the ugly truth about war. Only a brave few fight while the rest of the world sits back and watches."

"It's been like that for centuries," Kate said.

"Yup." Riley picked up the book again. "Aliens, huh?"

"Beats zombies, doesn't it?"

Riley pursed his lips and changed the subject. "Listen, Doc, I know you and Beckham got this thing going on.

I kind of got a magical ability to read people like that. And I just want to say…" He paused as if he couldn't find the right words.

"Riley, it's not like that," Kate said, her cheeks growing warm. "We're just friends. I respect him."

"He's a good man. A good leader. Never been married, you know. Really hasn't had many girlfriends either. He cares about us more than himself. So I guess I'm just saying don't mess with his heart. He's probably got the biggest one out of any Delta Force operator to ever walk this planet."

Kate was completely taken aback. "I—"

"It's okay. I'm probably overstepping my boundaries here, but I see the way he looks at you. I can tell he cares about you. When this is all over, I just hope—"

"I care about him too, Riley," Kate said.

"Well, yeah," the soldier mumbled, stumbling over his words. "I know."

"You sound surprised. I thought you had this all figured out."

"I did, I did. You know, it's just good to hear it's reciprocal."

They shared a laugh and then fell into companionable silence. Kate imagined Beckham, Horn, and the survivors winging their way toward the island. She closed her eyes and said her own little prayer, pleading with God or whatever was out there to watch over them—to watch over them all.

8

Beckham slowly opened the door and swept the tactical light on his new M4 over the tunnel. A pungent, rotten smell hit him immediately. On reflex he pulled his scarf over his nose and nudged a Variant corpse away from the door.

Beckham took a guarded step inside, playing his beam over the way ahead.

Nothing moved.

He turned and motioned the others forward, his gaze falling on the boy to whom he'd given his gas mask. The child's chaperone grabbed his hand and told him to cover his eyes. Whimpers from the civilians followed as they inched forward. Beckham brought a finger to his mouth. Knots formed in his stomach as he took in a breath and proceeded. Beams from flashlights danced across the slaughterhouse scene, crisscrossing blood-splattered walls and mangled bodies.

Beckham thought of Horn and his daughters. No man should have to experience what he was going through, and no child should have to endure the horrors surrounding them. He hoped to God that Kate was right about the risk of infection being minimal.

A low croaking stopped Beckham in his tracks.

Balling his hand into a fist, he stopped the group and swept his tactical light over the concrete until he found the source of the noise. Just as he feared, one of the Variants was still alive. How, he wasn't sure; its legs were a twisted mess of exposed muscle and ligaments. Blood oozed from multiple bullet wounds, and one of its ears hung by a thin strand of cartilage.

Chow joined Beckham at his side. "Christ, man. How is that thing still alive?"

The Variant dragged its broken body toward the group, prompting several screams of alarm.

"Keep quiet," Beckham ordered. He stepped past Chow, leaving about twenty feet between him and the Variant.

"Tell the adults in the front to shield the kids from this," Beckham said.

Chow nodded and returned to the group.

Beckham waited a moment and drew his knife. The Variant clawed the air with one hand and crawled with the other. Kneeling, Beckham prepared to jam the blade into the monster's skull. Its eyes followed his motions, studying him, a hint of humanity still left inside. Without further hesitation, he brought the knife down into flesh and bone. There was a pop from the bulging sucker lips and then one last gasp of air as it fought for a final moment of life.

Beckham dislodged the knife and stood. The Variant collapsed on its stomach. He nudged the body to the wall with the tip of his boot and then motioned for the others to follow.

"On me," Beckham said, taking point. He trained his muzzle on the double doors at the end of the hallway. He stopped again when they were fifty feet away and waved Chow forward. Together they advanced to the doors. Heel to toe, heel to toe.

Chow inched the one on the right open and peeked through.

"Looks clear," he whispered.

Beckham put his hand on Chow's back. In tandem, the two men moved into the hallway. More carnage greeted them, bodies strewn on the floor just beyond the doors. The operators played their lights over every inch of concrete. This time nothing moved.

So far, so good, Beckham thought. He nodded at Chow and then began the walk up the sloped floor, checking his six every few steps. The adults kept the children in the middle of the group, doing their best to shield the young ones.

"Let's check that one," Beckham whispered to Chow, pointing at a small metal door with a glass window set into it. They ran ahead and took up positions on either side of the door. Propping his shoulder against the wall, Beckham nodded at Chow. The operator bent down out of sight of the window and crawled in front of the door. He slowly stood to peek through the glass. He instantly pulled back and raised his rifle as though he'd seen something.

"Contact?" Beckham asked. His muscles tensed as he waited for the high-pitched shriek.

Chow peeked through the glass again and shook his head. "Thought so at first, but must have just been the flicker from the emergency lights."

The observation wasn't reassuring, and Beckham dropped to his knees and then checked for himself. The light flashed, casting an eerie glow over the broken ceiling tiles.

"Clear," Beckham said. Behind them, the other survivors huddled together, some of them shivering. Beckham propped the doors open and, taking point with Chow, he motioned the group forward again.

Minutes later, Beckham was staring through ash-covered windows to the outside. A plastic bag sailed over the sidewalk. Bodies littered the lawn, cooking under a brilliant morning sun. The light cut through the smoke to the north, rays breaking through the plumes.

The knots in Beckham's stomach tightened. His senses told him something was off.

"Looks clear," Chow said.

Beckham held up a hand. "Got a bad feeling," he said. "It's too quiet."

Chow stared out the window. "I've had a bad feeling for weeks, man, but we have got to move. We've got a hike ahead of us, and those choppers are on the way."

A minute passed before Beckham finally pushed open the left door. Shouldering his rifle, he crossed the lawn to the street. He scoped the area a second time and caught a glimpse of the half-burned magnolia to the right of the building.

"Clear," Beckham said. "Let's move."

Chow led the civilians from the building in a tight line, the Rangers taking up positions alongside. Horn and his girls were near the back, both of them latched on tightly to their father. He smiled. Everything that had happened before this was in the past. Saving Horn's girls was a fresh start, a way to move forward. All that mattered now was extracting these people safely to Plum Island. Beckham was ready to rock and roll.

The two forward snipers moved out fast and began looking for hides along the route. Beckham and the others made sure the main body of the group proceeded at a sharp pace, probably too fast for some of the kids. Beckham checked the pack every hundred yards to ensure no one was falling behind.

He glanced down at his watch as they passed across the expressway on Zabitosky Road. The choppers would be close now. Beckham jogged a bit faster, his eyes sweeping the road, trees, buildings, and vehicles for contacts. The stretch of Zabitosky that ran through the forested area made him uneasy. They were surrounded on all sides by a canopy of thick trees—the perfect place for an ambush, and with no high ground for the snipers to provide good cover. Or advance alert to incoming threats.

The snap of a tree branch elevated Beckham's heart rate, taking him back to the first hour when they arrived at the post. He eyed the sea of green with a new sense of urgency. Beckham gripped his rifle tighter. They passed another intersection that crossed Honeycutt Road and continued around a mess of vehicles.

The civilians were silent. Everyone knew what was at risk, even the children. Beckham slowed to check the smoke from Womack Army Medical Center, which was finally starting to dissipate.

"Chow, take point," Beckham said, halting in the street.

The operator rushed past, with his weapon sweeping over the road. Beckham hung back to see how Horn was doing. He was running with Jenny on his back. Tasha held on to one of his hands. The two men nodded without uttering a word. It was all Beckham needed to know that his friend was okay. He continued on to the rear guard to check on the others. The two Rangers stood like statues, with their MK11s angled to the northwest. After a few beats, they lowered their weapons and jogged to catch up.

"See anything?" Beckham asked the man Chow had referred to as Timbo. He was a tall, bulky African American man, with a chin strap of facial hair. They ran side by side for a few moments.

"Negative," Timbo said in a gruff voice. "Pretty quiet so far."

"What about you, Steve?" Beckham asked.

The other Ranger shook his head.

"All right, I'm headed back up front. Keep sharp."

Beckham tucked his chin to his chest and broke into a run. The group was passing a tangle of wrecked vehicles when he heard a creaking in the distance. The noise was so soft it could have been the wind, but when he eased to a stop, his ears told him what his mind wanted to deny. There was something out there.

Not wanting to alarm the group, he jogged back to the snipers at the rear, waiting for the group to get ahead before saying anything. Both men had set their rifles up on the hoods of cars. Beckham watched their muzzles search the road to the north.

The sound came again, a scuffling like a rat scampering across the concrete. There were other noises too: low moans and the awful clicking of joints.

Beckham forced himself to look. The sound was coming from Honeycutt Road, about five hundred feet to the north. He readied his rifle.

Steve and Timbo trained their MK11s on the intersection. A solid wall of trees blocked the view to the east and west. Beckham threw a look over his shoulder. The civilians were a couple hundred feet to the south of the intersection now, making their way toward the Airborne Inn and a cluster of other civilian buildings. They were moving at a trot, slowing down. The kids and the injured were fatigued.

"Shit," Beckham said through clenched teeth. He knew the journey wasn't going to be easy. The sounds of the Variants erased any hope for a simple extraction.

"Twelve o'clock," Timbo growled, spitting onto the hood of the car as he repositioned his rifle.

Beckham glassed the concrete just as the first Variants burst onto the street. Tumbling bodies exploded across the intersection, somersaulting, crashing into cars and one another. From amidst the blur of bloodstained bodies, a Variant caught Beckham's attention, a man dressed in tattered camouflage shorts. The Variant leaped with ease onto the roof of a pickup truck. His muscles bulged, and blue veins webbed across his skin. He tilted his head, sniffed the air, puckered his sucker lips, and pointed a finger in Beckham's direction. The action shocked Beckham. He'd wondered if the woman in New York had been an anomaly, but the truth was perched on a car in the middle of Honeycutt Road.

Kate was right. They were evolving.

The ex-soldier released a raspy howl that would likely result in several of the kids in the group pissing their pants. The sound angered Beckham. He feared only one thing—not being able to protect the group. Beckham considered his options, but there was only one viable strategy.

"Change of plans," he said to the Rangers. "We'll hold them here. Screw the rooftops. We're not going to make it up there."

The response came in the form of sharp gunfire. Screams from the civilians followed. They had stopped in the middle of the road.

"Chow! Get them to the LZ!" Beckham yelled with his hands cupped around his mouth. "Jinx, you're with me."

Beckham searched for Horn, finding him quickly. They exchanged a nod, and then the Texan was gone, using his thick arms to corral the group forward. Beckham saw one man had remained behind. He cracked a half smile when he realized it was Fitz. The man jogged on his prosthetic blades holding the M4 Beckham had given him.

"Need some help?" Fitz said.

"Hell yeah," Beckham said. They took up position next to Steve, bracing their bodies against the car. Timbo and Jinx were busy thinning out the field from the car to the right. Empty shell casings rattled off the metal hood and onto the concrete. The chorus of war returned, and Beckham joined the fight.

He raised his weapon, brought the scope to his eye, and fired on the mass surging over the mangled frames of crashed vehicles clogging the intersection. Most of them moved on all fours, like a swarm of fire ants, their bodies painted with the blood of their victims.

They were met by a tide of gunfire, splattering the ground with gore.

Beckham squeezed off concentrated shots, aiming for vital regions. He hit a female in the face, taking off the top of her head. The high-caliber rounds did little to deter the wall of creatures. They charged forward, replacing those that fell.

"Changing!" Jinx yelled.

"Me too," Fitz said.

Beckham laid down supporting fire, a wide arc of bullets spraying over the road. Several of the Variants out front dropped, convulsing as their life force drained away. He hesitated when he saw the muscular male Variant still on top of the pickup truck. The creature crouched, its distorted hands waving madly through the air like the conductor of a symphony from hell. Beckham zoomed in for a better look.

"What the fuck?" he muttered as he watched the beast's face. His bulging lips moved, saliva dripping from the oval sucker. Beckham angled the scope down an inch to focus on the creature's clawed hands.

The Variant was giving orders.

Kate's warning finally made sense. They couldn't drive cars or fire weapons, but they were more than just crazed cannibals. They functioned at a very minimal level, a primal level. But they were learning how to hunt and kill more efficiently.

Beckham didn't hesitate any longer. With the cross hairs centered on the man's chest, he squeezed off a burst. The man's agonized screech rang above the gunfire as bullets caught him in the midsection. He fell off the back of the truck, disappearing from view.

Beckham had wasted ten seconds watching the man, but he'd confirmed what Kate already knew. The Variants were learning.

He finished his magazine as the horde of creatures fanned out across the road, inching closer and closer. There were too many of them, and even without their leader they would overwhelm his position in minutes. A scream in the distance pulled Beckham's gaze to the civilians. They were almost to the extraction zone, past the wooded area and moving toward the John F. Kennedy Special Warfare Museum.

"Fitz, get out of here," Beckham said. "I'll catch up with you."

"Nah, I'm good," he said between bursts.

Beckham's eyes were darting back and forth as he fired, trying to count the monsters, when he saw the smoke grenades hanging off Steve's gear bag. Snatching a pair, Beckham pulled the pins and tossed them over the cars. The grenades clanged onto the concrete and hissed as they poured out smoke, covering the roadway. Beckham then reached for a frag grenade and tossed it into the center of the smoke field.

"Fire in the hole!" he yelled. He grabbed Fitz by his flak jacket and pulled him away from the vehicles. Jinx, Timbo, and Steve sprinted after them.

The blast from the grenade shook the ground. Shrapnel whistled past Beckham's right ear. Steve let out a low moan as one of the pieces hit him. Beckham saw him cradle his right arm. Only a flesh wound—he would be fine.

The overwhelming reek of burned flesh mixed with the awful sour-fruit smell of the creatures. Beckham pulled his scarf back up, coughing into the material. When the ringing in his ears cleared, a different noise emerged. It was the beautiful sound of helicopter blades.

"Evac incoming!" Steve shouted.

Three black dots raced across the skyline. But any relief he felt was short-lived. Waves of Variants were already bursting through the smoke wall. Three of the creatures paused, their heads tilting, confused. They clawed at their noses, as if the smoke had knocked out their sense of smell. Another pair followed. Both were missing limbs, and the female on the right had a hole the size of an apple in her stomach. Blood gushed from the wound as she searched for food, her eyes roving, unblinking.

It was as though the Variants couldn't sense the team.

"Let's go," Beckham said, hoping the smoke would buy them time. His earpiece crackled to life as he turned to run.

"Ghost One, Echo One—en route, prepare for extraction."

"Copy!" Beckham yelled. "Will meet you at LZ. Do me a solid, Echo One," he said. "Thin out this horde chasing us."

The pilot replied calmly. "Copy that, Ghost One."

The whining scream of the chopper's guns came a moment later.

Then Beckham heard shouts and small-arms fire. He looked away from the birds. The civilians were stopped again. His heart pounded in his throat when he saw the flashes.

"No," he said aloud. They were trapped. The Variants

were piling in from south of Zabitosky Road. He couldn't bring himself to believe it was all coordinated, that the Variants had planned the ambush all along.

Rage boiled in the pit of his gut, warming his insides like a shot of whiskey. He scanned the area, desperate. Flicking his mini-mic to his lips, he yelled, "Echo One, Ghost One, get those guns on the group to the south. We'll hold the pack to the north."

"Copy that," the pilot said. "Good luck, Ghost One."

Beckham watched the choppers circle overhead. The door gunners opened fire with M240s, spraying 7.62-millimeter rounds that splattered the concrete with the blood of the Variants out in front. The gunners focused on thinning out the herd while the other chopper landed in the empty intersection to the south. Chow approached the troop hold and helped the children inside.

Beckham turned back to the north. The dazed creatures were starting to move again, and a dozen more stood in front of the dwindling smoke screen.

"Steve, Jinx, Timbo, Fitz," he yelled. "We hold them here. Not a single one of those things gets through. Got it?" Beckham examined Steve's injury. Blood dripped from his arm. "You good to shoot?"

Steve nodded. "Got two arms, don't I?"

"Fitz, you're with me," Beckham said. He reached for a fresh magazine and jammed it in with a click. Dropping to one knee, he searched for his first target. Fitz took up position next to him.

"We just need to buy them time," Beckham said, firing off a shot that took a leg off a lingering Variant.

Fitz replied by dropping three of the creatures.

Beckham nailed two targets of his own, blood and gore exploding out the back of their skulls. Screams of rage and pain combined with the gunfire as more of the Variants hit the pavement. This time Beckham and his team were holding the pack back. The smoke and the grenades had confused the creatures and culled their number. The tide had shifted, and the fight no longer felt like a battle. It was a slaughter.

The bark of the M240s stopped, and Beckham turned to see all three birds on the ground. The civilians piled in, Chow and Horn directing traffic.

Beckham patted Fitz on the back. "Time to move."

The marine finished off his magazine, and Beckham helped him up.

"Let's go!" Beckham shouted to the other three men. They stood and backpedaled, firing as they moved.

The half dozen remaining Variants suddenly changed directions, ducking behind the safety of vehicles and leaping behind trees on the side of the road. Beckham made a final dash for the choppers. Two of them lifted into the air and traversed the skyline. The third hovered a few feet above the intersection. Horn shoved the soldier on the M240 aside and took the reins.

Beckham put an arm under Fitz's shoulder. The man was struggling now, panting deeply. They lagged behind as Jinx, Steve, and Timbo climbed aboard the bird.

When they were fifteen feet from the chopper, Horn suddenly swiveled the machine gun and screamed, "Move!"

By the time Beckham turned around, it was too late. The muscular ex-soldier from Honeycutt Road was still alive and was charging him. The others had regrouped, following their injured leader.

A flash burst from the M240 as Horn trained the weapon on the pack of Variants. Beckham could hear their bones shattering as the rounds shredded their sick bodies. The gunfire ended as quickly as it started. Movement from his peripheral vision revealed the leader was still trailing him. They were in Horn's line of fire.

In one swift movement, Beckham pushed the marine toward the Black Hawk, swung his M4 toward the crazed face of the monster darting for him, and pulled the trigger. The bullets thunked into the man's barreled chest, the muscles jerking and seeming to absorb the rounds.

The magazine clicked dry, and he reached for his M9 as the Variant tackled him onto the concrete. Beckham's head hit the ground hard. Sharp pain jolted through his skull. He gripped the creature around its thick throat, trying desperately to hold back jagged teeth. Saliva flowed from the Variant's lips.

The taste of blood filled Beckham's mouth, his front lip gushing from where his teeth had torn it open. He squeezed the creature's neck harder, but it yanked free of his grasp. The Variant slammed its fists into Beckham's chest, driving the wind from the operator's lungs.

He fought back with a few haphazard punches of his own, but they only infuriated the creature more. It let out a deep growl, leaning back and tilting his head toward the sky. Then it butted Beckham in the chest with the top of its skull. He gasped for air as the creature clawed at his face. Fingernails dragged across Beckham's skin.

Beckham's vision faded in and out in time with the pulsating pain in his head.

He was going to die. It should have happened a dozen times before, but now he was finally going to die.

Beckham caught a glimpse of the chopper. "Go!" he yelled.

A fog clouded his vision.

He blinked and caught a glimpse of black, blood-stained boots. They were moving. Close now. Two steps away.

One step.

Beckham felt the weight of the creature fall off his

body. Or was he slipping into unconsciousness? He wasn't sure. He struggled to peel back an eyelid.

The Variant was gone. A new face was looking down at him.

"Get up," said a deep voice.

The freckled face of Horn came into focus. Fitz stood next to him, and together they reached down and grabbed Beckham under his arms. He went limp, his legs dragging across the concrete as they carried him back to the chopper. Rounds from the door guns zipped overhead.

Beckham's body was numb as he was lifted into the air and placed onto the floor of the chopper.

"Is everyone okay?" he muttered.

"Everyone's fine," Horn replied. "You did it, man. You saved everyone."

Beckham fought to keep his heavy eyelids open. He saw Tasha and Jenny staring at him behind Horn.

"It's okay now," Beckham choked, reaching for them. "You're going to a safe place."

9

Lieutenant Colonel Jensen had requested a call with Central Command, hoping to talk to someone with pull, someone who could get shit done. To say he was shocked when Hickman told him General Richard Kennor was on the line would have been an understatement. Kennor wasn't only the acting commander in chief; he was the mastermind behind Operation Liberty.

"Sir, video call in five minutes," Hickman said.

Jensen nodded, mentally preparing his thoughts. He had a real shot at saving countless American lives. All he had to do was convince the general that their intel was wrong.

After transferring the files, Jensen took a seat at the war table and typed in his credentials, wishing more than ever for a wad of juicy chewing tobacco. Instead he chewed on the inside of his lip and turned on the screen.

"Patch the call through, Lieutenant."

The wrinkled face of General Kennor appeared on screen. His lips and nose were angled in a way that made him look as if he had a bad taste in his mouth. With his saggy skin, the general reminded Jensen of a bulldog—which wasn't far from the truth. The man's career was defined by his aggressive war strategy. If the US military had an attack dog, Kennor was it. He'd overseen countless missions in the War on Terror and was responsible for killing or bringing to justice close to one hundred terrorists.

"Jensen," General Kennor said, "I hear you have some important intel."

The lieutenant colonel cleared his throat and said, "Yes, sir, very important. It's about the Variant populations in New York City."

Kennor raised a bushy gray brow. "I'm listening."

"Sir, Central Command sent us projections of the population in Manhattan, specifically the clusters in Times Square, around Rockefeller Center, and near the New York Public Library. The data shows only about two thousand Variants in the area."

The general studied a piece of paper in front of him and then shrugged. "Good. Should make it that much easier for your strike teams and First Platoon to clear the area and set up a forward operating base."

"Yes, sir, it would, but I believe the intel isn't accurate. Doctor Lovato, the CDC doctor who designed the—"

"I know who she is," Kennor replied, looking up to meet Jensen's eyes. "Relay my gratitude when you get a chance."

Jensen nodded and continued. "I will, sir, but as I was saying, she believes there are hundreds of thousands more Variants in the area that aren't being picked up by satellite imagery or the recon scouts."

"Nonsense."

"Sir, I understand how this sounds, but please check the encrypted file I sent a few minutes ago. I apologize for the delay, but I had to check with Doctor Lovato to ensure the numbers were correct."

Kennor slid a laptop across his desk and flipped the top open. "Give me a second."

"Yes, sir." Jensen pulled open the file and reviewed the numbers himself.

"For the sake of time, why don't you explain this to me?" Kennor said.

Nodding again, Jensen said, "Doctor Lovato believes approximately eighty-five percent of the population in New York was infected with the hemorrhage virus. About sixteen million people. After VariantX9H9 was launched, the infected population was reduced to ten percent. The Variants should then number between one and two million in New York City. The map should be crawling with them, sir. The numbers just don't add up."

"This map focuses *just* on Manhattan," Kennor replied gruffly.

"Yes, sir, but if you add up every other cluster in the metro area, you'll see there are only fifty thousand of the creatures accounted for. So where the hell did the other million-plus go?"

Kennor closed the lid to his laptop, folded his hands, and cleared his throat. "I'm going to be blunt here. Doctor Lovato was clearly off in her calculations. I appreciate her work, but let's be honest, Jensen: That many people don't simply vanish. And we've been running recon missions for weeks. Between flyovers, scouts, and satellite imagery, we have a pretty good idea of what we're up against."

Jensen picked at a hangnail under the table, out of view. He could feel a bead of sweat forming on his forehead.

"Sir, I understand how this sounds, but we could be walking into a trap in New York. Why not insert several Special Ops teams into the city? The Variants could be underground, in the subways or storm tunnels. I'd request that you delay Operation Liberty until we know—"

Kennor shook his head. He knit his eyebrows together, forming a hundred more wrinkles. "Absolutely *not*," he growled. "Do you realize how much coordination and planning has gone into this operation? New York is only one of a hundred other cities. The marine company in New York and the teams you will supply are only a small piece of the overall puzzle here. We need you in this fight. *I* need you in this fight. And I need you to keep your goddamn cool. This is just the sort of claim that could cause panic or desertion."

The general scratched a day's worth of gray stubble on his chin. "Quite frankly, we're running out of time to take back our country. Every minute we wait, more survivors are brutally murdered and eaten by those *things*."

Jensen bit back a response.

"Besides, you're forgetting one key piece of information here," continued Kennor.

"Sir?" Jensen asked.

"We are part of the United States military. And we have the most advanced weapons in the world at our disposal. The Variants are the equivalent of our distant Neanderthal ancestors. They don't drive cars or fly jets. They can't even fire a handgun. So I don't care if there are one thousand or one million. Operation Liberty will crush them. The battle will be a slaughter."

Yeah, thought Jensen, *that's what General Custer said right before the "savage" Indians killed every single one of his men.*

"General Kennor, if you won't delay the mission, at least provide me the opportunity to insert a team of my own. I have some Delta Force operators here at Plum Island who have proven to be great assets."

Kennor seemed to consider the request for a moment but then shook his head. "We have recon marines in the city, no need to waste more time on a useless mission."

He looked down at his watch. "Operation Liberty will launch as scheduled."

Jensen fought the urge to speak his mind. General Kennor was panicking. He was anxious as hell to get this all over with, no matter what it took. And there was nothing Jensen could say that would change the man's mind.

"Anything else?" Kennor asked.

"No, sir."

"Good luck," Kennor replied, reaching to shut off the feed.

The screen went dark, and Jensen pounded the desk with his right fist. "The man is delusional!"

"Maybe so," Major Smith said from the observation window. "But he's right about the firepower. What can Variants do against missiles and tanks?"

"You don't get it, do you?" Jensen said. "Those things are evolving. Our teams could be heading into a trap. We can't afford to underestimate the enemy. One mistake could send the human race spiraling toward extinction."

Hickman grabbed her headset and slipped it back on. "Sir, I'm receiving a transmission from Echo One."

Jensen rushed over to the communications equipment, forgetting the conversation with Kennor.

"Echo One, Two, and Three are en route to Plum Island. They have fifty-two survivors in total," Hickman said. "Echo Three requests medical support for—" Her eyes shot up to his face with concern. "For Master Sergeant Beckham."

"How bad?" Jensen asked.

"Not sure, sir."

Jensen cursed. With Operation Liberty still moving forward, he would need to find someone else to lead a team. Beckham's fate affected many on the island, including Kate Lovato. He would need to tell her before the Black Hawks returned.

"Your briefing is in thirty minutes," Smith reminded him.

Jensen nodded. Every man and woman on the island was waiting for his report. He'd made them a promise that he would keep them informed, a promise he fully intended to keep. But first he needed to meet with Kate.

The moment Riley had closed his eyes, he had fallen asleep. The pain medicines were powerful, and even the Delta operator couldn't resist them for long. Kate watched his chest move up and down for a few minutes, just to make sure he was out. Then she checked his biomonitor one last time and walked out of the medical ward, pausing in front of the doors to the ICU to see if she could catch a glimpse of Colonel Gibson's room. The dimly lit corridor revealed two marines standing guard.

The sight meant he was still alive. *Good,* she thought. Maybe after Operation Liberty was complete, Central Command would have the time and assets to try the man for international war crimes. If things ever did return to seminormal, the trial would draw the same sort of press that Nuremberg had after World War II.

She left the building in a hurry and ran past the two Medical Corps guards posted at the entrance without uttering a word. Kate was anxious to get back to the lab. Ellis had assured her that they would finally have blood samples of Variants from around the country.

The midmorning sun cast a beautiful trail of light across the concrete drive that connected the campus of domed buildings. A cool breeze rustled through her hair as she jogged to Building 1. Overhead, a seagull dotted the blue sky. The bird spread its wings and then swooped toward the ocean, vanishing into the sunlight.

Kate shielded her eyes and stopped to check her watch. The choppers would have extracted Beckham and the other survivors by now. They would be back in hours. She suppressed a prickle of anxiety and ran up the steps to Building 1.

Inside, she suited up and concentrated on the tasks ahead. Compartmentalizing her schedule took the edge off, gave her something to focus on. Gibson hadn't given her anything she could work with. Nothing new, at least. Only tests would determine how the Variants were truly changing and hopefully reveal a way to stop them before it was too late. It was up to her team now, and to whatever teams were left across the country.

She zipped up the back of her suit and slipped on her helmet. Cindy Hoy, the young scientist and engineer assigned to Kate's team, was already busy working on the other side of the lab's glass wall. Ellis sat at the adjacent station, staring at his computer screen. Behind them, the other compartments were all bustling with activity.

Kate held her key card over the security panel. A chirp followed as the doors hissed open.

"Good morning," Ellis said, keeping his focus on his monitor.

"Morning," she replied. "Did we receive the samples?"

"Sure did. They came in during the night." Cindy typed a few keystrokes and brought up a myriad of data streams. "I've already started the tests you requested."

"And?" Kate moved to the right so Ellis could point at the screen. His finger stopped on the middle row of data.

"They're changing, Kate," Ellis said, his voice low but clear over the comm system.

Kate gestured for Cindy to scoot over. Grabbing another stool, Kate pulled it up to the display.

"Check the confidential file that Command sent us," Cindy said, pointing at the folder.

"This came from a team somewhere in DC," Ellis added.

Kate didn't hesitate, quickly clicking on the small folder. A message formed on the screen.

CLASSIFIED—TOP SECRET

EYES ONLY—CDC—PLUM ISLAND

Examination by unauthorized persons is a criminal offense punishable by fines up to $100,000 and imprisonment up to fifteen years.

If you are Cindy Hoy (USAMRIID) or Dr. Kate Lovato or Dr. Michael Allen or Dr. Pat Ellis (CDC), please proceed and enter your electronic signature.

Seeing Michael's name hit Kate in the gut.

"Kate," Ellis said, putting a hand on her arm, "you good?"

She nodded and entered her electronic signature. The message disappeared and a PDF filled the screen.

The following are field observations and test reports on the Variant population as of May 6, 2015.

Tests on Specimen 45Y yielded the following results:

Subject was provided both living and nonliving animals.

Subject showed a strong prejudice toward living flesh.

When isolated for long periods of time, the subject engaged in self-mutilation and self-cannibalization.

Kate scrolled down to the picture of Specimen 45Y. The Variant was curled up on the floor of a brightly lit holding cell. He'd bitten a large chunk out of his own arm.

The next page revealed a female subject. The blurred picture showed a snapshot of the Variant moving vertically along the concrete side of her holding pen. A second image provided an enhanced look at the subject's palms.

"See that!" Ellis said. He pointed at the microscopic bristles on the skin. He zoomed in and, each time he did, the bristles split into smaller and smaller hairs. "If you look closely, the Variants have those all over their hands, legs, and arms. These are setae, microscopic hairs or bristles—the same thing that allow geckos and spiders to walk up walls. They take advantage of the attractive interactions between individual molecules. Normally, those attractive forces are pretty weak, but if you have millions of these setae, like the Variants, over a surface area even as small as a quarter, you can support a human's body weight."

Kate nodded slowly as she read the results.

Tests on Specimen 49Y yielded the following results:

Subject is able to climb on both vertical and horizontal surfaces utilizing microscopic hairs and by altering articulation of joints. Furthermore, Specimen 49Y has developed nails that aid in movement.

She continued to the next picture. A magnified image of the nail on the specimen's index finger filled the screen. A tape measure showed the yellowed blade was four inches long. The sharp tip curled at the end, more like a talon than a nail. Specimen 49Y confirmed the creatures' physiological traits were continuing to develop, resulting in a more efficient killing machine.

"We already know this stuff. Give me something I can work with," Kate said, scrolling farther through the document. She stopped on a section entitled "Physical Senses."

"Here we go," she whispered.

The next image was taken during the autopsy of Specimen 49Y. The subject's nasal cavity was exposed, and the olfactory nerve severed. Another picture revealed the dissected eye of the same subject. The vertical pupil was enlarged and the dual membrane peeled back. Kate had never seen anything quite like it. Unsettled but deeply curious at the same time, she continued reading.

Specimen 49Y has increased olfactory receptors. Sense of smell continues to evolve. Subject has a significantly higher rod and cone count, allowing for pupil dilation far past the limits of the normal human eye. This in turn aids the patient's ability to see in the dark. Furthermore, subject is able to focus on near and far objects by stretching her lenses.

In addition, specimen was found to have increased auditory sensitivity due to a regeneration of cochlear hair cells. This results in hearing loss reversal and improvement.

"This explains their enhanced ability to hunt," Cindy said.

"Their senses are heightened. So what?" Ellis said.

"We still haven't found a smoking gun that explains exactly how the epigenetic changes take effect. Without that we won't have any way to treat them."

Ellis spoke as though developing a treatment was possible. Kate wasn't as optimistic. There might be a way to stop further changes if they could discover how they worked, but looking at these pictures proved the creatures were beyond saving.

Kate ignored her colleagues and continued scrolling through the report. The next image was of a middle-aged, dark-skinned Variant labeled Specimen 14Y. Patches of skin and muscle hung loosely off the bone. A second picture, dated two days later, revealed soaked bandages covering his legs. Two days after that, the bandages had been removed. The final shot showed thick, wrinkled skin over the subject's legs.

"This can't be right," Kate muttered. No one could heal that quickly. She moved on to the conclusion, reading it aloud to the others.

"Specimen 14Y shows remarkable healing ability. Tests show concentrations of fibrocytes circulating in the bloodstream, allowing rapid healing of dermal layers. Further tests reveal the subject displays improved vascular regeneration, allowing expedited growth of blood vessels to injured regions. This in turn restores physiologic nutrient and oxygen delivery as well as cell-waste removal."

"A true supersoldier," Kate said.

"Yup. I can't wait to see this all in person," Cindy replied.

Kate looked at the younger scientist. "What did you say?"

Cindy raised a glove. "I know how you're going to respond, but the request has already been approved by Lieutenant Colonel Jensen. I just heard it this morning.

Central Command has authorized all medical facilities to perform live testing on Variants."

Kate lowered her head in dismay. She'd known this was coming, and this time she wasn't going to fight it. The Variants weren't contagious anymore, and they needed a live specimen. But if they got out again...

A buzzing from the PA system interrupted her flashback to Patient 12, the Variant that had attacked her a week before. Jensen stood behind the observation glass, his finger jammed against the comm button. "Doctor Lovato, may I see you for a moment?"

"Sure—one moment," Kate said. She glanced over at Ellis and Cindy. "I want a full synopsis of this document ASAP."

"No problem," Ellis said, taking her place at the monitor.

Kate went over the facts in her mind as she crossed the lab. The Variants had developed microscopic hairs and talons to help them move faster and more efficiently. They had heightened physical senses. And they had the ability to heal more rapidly. Combine that with the overwhelming desire to find and devour fresh meat, and Colonel Gibson had created the perfect weapon: a creature with no regard for human life and little, if any, regard for its own.

Sighing, she strode to the glass where Jensen waited. She paused when she saw his face, his lips pressed into a tight line below his mustache.

"Beckham?" she choked.

Jensen nodded and pressed the comm button. "I only know that he was injured in the evacuation of Fort Bragg."

Kate suddenly felt trapped behind the glass wall. She breathed deeply, her suit tightening around her chest. "When?" She sucked in a gasp of air. "When will they be back?"

"Two hours, max," Jensen replied. "I just wanted you to know. I'm sorry, Doctor, but my briefing starts in a few minutes."

Kate reached toward the glass. "Wait!"

"My apologies, but I really need to go." Jensen nodded stiffly and stepped away from the glass.

Kate drifted back to her lab station, unable to decide if she should sit or stand or fall to the floor in tears. She leaned up against the lab table, bracing her gloved hands on the metal.

"You okay?" Ellis asked.

Kate slumped into her chair, staring at the lab notes on her monitor. The screen blurred, the text replaced by a mental image of Beckham's broken body. She let out a sharp sob. No amount of work could save her from her thoughts this time.

Lieutenant Colonel Jensen walked into the mess hall, wondering if he was doing the right thing. The room was overflowing. Soldiers and support staff sat at metal tables, speaking in low voices. Others huddled in small groups, waiting patiently. He didn't see a single open seat.

He faltered briefly, uncertainty amplifying in his chest. Smith was right; Plum Island was already operating at a maximum capacity. Bringing in more survivors would put a burden on their resources.

But seeing the faces of those who had taken a pledge to their country gave him a great sense of pride. He wanted to lead them in a fair and just way. That meant providing the same opportunities to *everyone* on the island.

The crowd quieted as Jensen and Smith marched to the center of the room, but not as quickly as they had silenced themselves for Colonel Gibson weeks before. That meant one of two things: Either they had feared his predecessor, or Jensen had some work to do to gain their trust. *Maybe both*, he thought, clearing his throat and checking the mic with a double tap of his finger.

"Good morning, everyone." Jensen worked the group with a quick sweep of his eyes. He'd seen other men master the gaze; they usually ended up as generals. He still needed some practice. "As many of you already know, General Kennor and Central Command have been organizing a mission designed to take back our cities from the Variants: Operation Liberty."

Jensen ran a finger over his mustache and continued. "Command has asked us to provide multiple strike teams to support a mechanized platoon of marines in Manhattan. This is part of a bigger mission to take back New York. There are four other platoons that will operate in the other boroughs. Each will set up a forward operating base as the first phase of Operation Liberty in New York. All will be mechanized, and all will have air support."

"Only one company in New York?" a slender marine asked from the front row. Jensen glanced over at him. He wasn't taking questions—this was a briefing, not a Q&A—but the man's eyes begged for reassurance.

"Truth is, we're still trying to clean up the mess that was Operation Reaper. We lost a lot of men and equipment in the first few days of the outbreak. Most of what's left comes from our navy fleet, which beelined it back from hot spots around the world. Every city west of the Mississippi is getting far less support than we are. Trust me—a company is a goddamn *army* in terms of the assets we have left."

The marine nodded.

"Your COs will meet with those of you selected for

the mission after this briefing. But before they do so, I want to inform you of another development."

Jensen sucked in a short breath, unsure of how the subsequent information would be received. He reminded himself that leadership required guts.

"Thirty hours ago, I authorized a mission to Fort Bragg. Two Delta Force operators were inserted to look for survivors there. They found approximately fifty, including a small team of other Delta Force operators and Army Rangers. As expected, the post had been overrun by Variants. I'm proud to report that we were able to evacuate all of the survivors, and they are currently en route to Plum Island via three Black Hawks."

There were a few immediate protests. Support staff, from the looks of it—nonmilitary. Jensen raised a hand. "Please!" he shouted. "Let me finish."

Major Smith took a step toward the crowd.

Lowering his hand, Jensen said, "The moment I took command of this post, I promised to keep you all informed of the situation outside. I lifted the communications cloak so you could attempt to reach your families. But the hard truth is most of our families are gone. The man or woman next to you is your family now. We are all in this together and must remain vigilant. With that said, I hope you will all welcome the survivors from Fort Bragg with open arms. They will become a valuable part of our extended family."

He waited for the crowd to transform into a mob like the one he'd seen days earlier. To his surprise, the room remained still. A beat passed and then another before an unfamiliar noise finally broke the silence. In the back of the room a marine stood and began to clap. Jensen nodded at the man with gratitude. The man clapped louder and the entire table of marines stood and joined in. Before Jensen could respond, the mess hall erupted with applause.

Jensen scanned each face, one by one, from the line cook with a filthy apron to the navy pilots in uniform. The men and women of Plum Island had finally pulled together, something he hadn't been sure he would ever see after the truth about Colonel Gibson had emerged.

He glanced over at Smith, who smiled and joined in the applause.

Maybe I'm getting closer to mastering that gaze after all, Jensen thought.

10

Echo 3 tilted slightly to the east and swooped low over the teal ocean waves. Beckham rested on his side next to the open chopper door. A female nurse whose name he didn't know was hovering over him and treating his injuries.

He looked down at the shadow of the chopper flickering on the water. The thump of the blades drowned out the nurse's voice. When he didn't respond, she leaned down next to his ear and said, "This is going to burn."

He winced as she pressed an antiseptic pad against the cut over his left eye. The pain told him it was deep. Maybe even stitches deep.

"Thanks," he muttered.

With a nod, she crouch-walked to another patient. Beckham scooted closer to the open door. Echo 3 was filled to the brim with passengers.

They were safe now—a miracle by anyone's standards. But surviving was both a blessing and a curse. He caught the gaze of a child sitting in a soldier's lap, the same boy he'd given his gas mask to. He looked six, maybe seven years old. Yet where Beckham saw an innocent child, the Variants saw food.

The monsters were the most ruthless enemy he'd ever

faced. Children, women, the old, and the injured—they were all the same in the eyes of the creatures.

Beckham rested his helmet on the floor. The long flight back to Plum Island would give him plenty of time to replay the mission. He'd safely evacuated everyone from Fort Bragg, but what he'd seen during the escape had changed his opinion of the war. The Variant that had broken his face wasn't some barbarian but the general of a demon army.

Rolling onto his back, Beckham glanced up at the refugees. Faces blurred together as the morphine took hold.

"Almost there," a man said.

The sunlight shifted into his eyes. Beckham blinked and saw the dirt-stained face of Fitz staring down at him.

"Nice shooting back there," Beckham said.

Fitz smiled and then looked down. "I was the best in my unit when I was a marine, before an IED took my legs. But I still got it!"

Beckham chuckled and said, "You're still a marine."

"Yeah," Fitz said. "Hang in there, man; we're heading home."

The bird pulled to the right and the light faded, darkness filling Beckham's field of vision. He closed his eyes and held his hand over his shirt pocket, thinking of his mother as the chopper descended. He was glad she was in a better place. At least she had been spared the horrors of this new world.

The rumble from a low-flying jet faded away, and with it went the clicking of the monsters as they retreated into the sewers.

Rex was hunched over, his face pressed against the

boards. "Are they gone?" he asked, tilting his head. "Looks like they're gone."

Meg watched the final creature disappear into a manhole and then returned to her bed, collapsing onto the sheets. The roller coaster of near-death experiences had taken a toll on her. God, she just wanted to sleep. She'd been up for—how long now? She'd lost track, the hours blending together.

"Think they live down there?" Rex asked.

"Obviously," Jed said. "They don't just go down there for shits and giggles."

Rex backed away from the window and glared at the marine. Then, without a word, he walked back to his bunk and grabbed a bag of chips.

Hours slipped by as Meg dozed in and out of sleep. Her dreams took her back to the world she missed so desperately, to dinner parties with her husband and friends. But every time she awoke, reality would slowly sink in, filling her with a sickening dread. She'd wrap her fingers around her axe handle, but the sight of the cold steel blade prompted flashbacks of its own—to the moment she had taken her best friend's life.

Anxiety forced her eyes open, and she stared at the ceiling fan over her bed. The walls around her seemed to narrow, squeezing. She felt like a caged animal, and she wanted out.

Meg swung her feet over the side of the bed onto the cold floor. The overcast sky had cooled the room, and the wind outside wouldn't let up. Jed had replaced Rex at the boarded-up windows, keeping a watchful eye over the streets.

Crossing the floor as quietly as she could, Meg joined him. "I've been thinking," she said. "Maybe we should move."

Rex responded from his bunk exactly the way Meg

thought he would. The man's freckled nose flared, and his eyebrows came together to form a single red line. "Are you crazy?"

Meg looked to Jed for support. The marine's chiseled jaw remained stiff, his features stone cold. He put an eye back to the gap in the window and scouted the rooftops.

"We haven't seen any survivors for days. Haven't even heard a shot fired," Meg said, keeping her voice just above a whisper. "Our supplies won't last forever, and those things *will* be back."

"I'm not leaving, Meg," Rex said.

Before Meg could respond, Jed crossed the room, grabbed Rex by the arm, and commanded his gaze. "You need to get your shit together. Be a fucking man."

A floorboard creaked above, and their eyes all gravitated to the ceiling. Meg's imagination raced. Three weeks ago, she would have ignored that sound, but now it terrified her. Every familiar noise was a possible threat. She and the two men stared at the ceiling for what felt like eternity. Another gust of wind shook the building, making the old windows rattle again. Meg let out a breath she hadn't realized she was holding.

"You're right," Jed finally said. "We need to get out of here. At the very least we need to find some weapons." He scanned Rex from boots to receding hairline. "If you don't want to come, then you can stay here."

Rex shook his head, pleading with hands outstretched. "You can't leave me."

"We can. And we will," Jed replied. "If we stay, we die."

Meg caught a drift of rotting fruit in the stagnant air. Every muscle in her body tensed. But the stench quickly passed. Was she finally losing it?

"They're least active in the afternoon, when it's hot. I say we pack our shit and start planning," Jed said.

"Where will we go?" Rex asked.

"My squad was ambushed ten blocks from here. I say we start there, load up on guns, and find a vehicle."

"We're just going to drive on out of the city? Have you not seen the streets out there? They're gridlocked." Rex snorted.

"Better than sitting here and waiting to die," Meg said. She turned to Jed. "I'm with you."

The marine nodded, and Meg hurried back to her bunk and put her boots on. The longer they stood around and talked, the more time she would have to change her mind. Rays of light shot through the holes in the boarded-up windows as Meg laced up her boots. The trio turned to watch the sunlight.

"There isn't a cloud in the sky," Jed said.

"Now's our chance," Meg said. "Let's go."

Beckham woke up in a hospital bed. He turned on his side to see he was alone. The movement sent a shock wave of pain through his entire body. Everything hurt.

He wondered how long he'd slept. He vaguely recalled the chopper ride, but he had no recollection of landing or how he had made it to the medical facility.

Using his hands, he scooted back toward the headboard. Sharp pain attacked his rib cage, as if someone was holding a hot knife there. He felt the injury, checking for cracked bones, wincing. The bones were bruised, but not broken. That was good news. He could still fight.

A rap on the door pulled his attention away from his injuries.

"Sir," came a gentle voice. The door creaked opened and a nurse stepped into the room. His shoulders sagged in disappointment that it wasn't Kate.

"I'm Tina. Doctor Holder will be in shortly." She stopped at his bedside, checking his vitals. "How do you feel?"

"Like I got my ass kicked."

The nurse smiled but kept her focus on the biomonitor. "I'm told you're a lucky man."

He nodded and glanced around her at the open doorway. "What time is it?"

"Just after two p.m. You've slept all day."

Beckham fought to remember how he'd gotten here. He wondered where Horn and Kate were. And Riley. Where was the kid?

The nurse handed him a cup of water and a pill. "Take this. It will help with the pain."

"Where's Riley?"

"Down the hall," the nurse replied. "You can see him soon. But you need to rest."

"I'm fine," he said, throwing back his head and swallowing the small dose. When he opened his eyes, he saw a thin shape standing in the doorway behind Tina.

"Reed?" The voice was soft, sweet. His heart kicked when he saw it was Kate.

"Hey," he said, struggling to sit up.

"Sir, I'm serious. Don't push it," Tina said, placing a hand on his shoulder.

Beckham looked her in the eye. "I'll be fine."

"Yes, but you need to rest," Tina said sternly. She stepped aside to make way for Kate. With a firm glare, Tina said, "Please try to make this short."

Beckham motioned Kate closer to his bed as the nurse left the room. He caught the woman's eye through the slightly ajar door. *So much for privacy*, he thought.

"Oh my God," Kate said. She bent over his bed and wrapped her arms around him. "I'm so glad you're okay."

"Watch the ribs," Beckham choked.

"Sorry, sorry!" She covered her mouth with a hand. "I'm so sorry."

Beckham chuckled and ignored the pain. "It's okay."

"When I heard you were injured, I thought—"

He reached for her but stopped just short of taking her hand. "It's going to take a lot to put me out of business."

Kate whimpered and laughed at the same time. "So now that you're back, you're going to stick around for a while, right?"

Beckham looked down at his body, unsure if he would be able to fulfill his promise to Jensen. Operation Liberty was happening with or without him, and he couldn't bear the thought of Horn and the other men fighting on their own.

"I heal quickly," he said.

"Have you seen yourself?"

Beckham fidgeted, winced, and then relaxed. "I'm guessing I look like shit."

"Uh, yeah."

"Trust me, I've looked worse than this—"

"There's something I need to tell you, Reed," Kate said suddenly.

Beckham scooted over to make room for her and patted the bed. After throwing a glance over her shoulder, Kate carefully sat next to him.

"I have intel for you too," Beckham said. "Something I saw at Bragg."

Kate shied away. "You go first."

"You were right, Kate. The Variants are evolving. We encountered a group right before we reached the LZ. One of them seemed to be in command—like he was giving orders." Beckham knew his words sounded insane, but they didn't seem to disturb Kate.

Her voice was brittle when she replied. "This is just the beginning. The epigenetic changes are irreversible, but they're not stable. The Variants *are* evolving at a rapid rate, and I don't think they're going to stop."

Beckham reached for his right leg, a charley horse attacking his calf. "Shit," he mumbled. His ribs burned from the sudden movement.

"What's wrong?"

Gritting his teeth, he said, "Cramp. Ribs."

She was searching him, concern radiating from her blue eyes. "And you think you can fight like this?"

Beckham nodded. "I told you, I've been worse." He glanced up, struggling to keep his swollen left eye open. "What did you want to tell me?"

Kate looked away. "It was nothing. Just glad you're back, is all."

Meg felt the nagging tug of regret. They weren't even two blocks from the fire station, and she had already started questioning her decision to leave the safe house.

She ran behind Jed and Rex, keeping low and close to the storefronts. The only motion she saw was swirling trash and their reflections in the glass windows that hadn't shattered.

To say she felt alone was an understatement. The despair ate at her with every step. New York City, the place where she'd grown up and lived her entire life, had transformed into a ghost town. Every street corner, every sidewalk was littered with corpses. The blood that hadn't washed down the storm drains had dried on the street. Bodies baked under the bright afternoon sun, their decomposing flesh filling the city with an invisible cloud of rot. As a firefighter, she was used to seeing her fair share of blood and chaos. It had never bothered her, until now.

Taking a knee behind a yellow cab, she studied the scene. Dark red pools had coagulated around fallen bodies, like spilled paint. A few feet away, a middle-aged man lay facedown in a puddle of dried crimson. The breeze chipped away at the edges of the stain.

The victims had all bled out shortly after the jets swooped over the city. Jed had said the military created a weapon to destroy the hemorrhage virus, that it was their last hope. The result was thousands, millions of bodies, some piled on top of each other where they'd succumbed to whatever biological weapon the air force had dropped.

If it weren't for the CBRN suits they'd taken from a FEMA shelter weeks before, they would have had to endure the putrid smell of decay. Now all she could smell was rubber.

They advanced in single file down the sidewalk, with Jed taking point. All three of them carried axes from the fire station. The sharp edge did little to relieve the spike of anxiety growing inside of Meg.

Whispering breezes and the rap of their boots followed them through the streets. Every few steps Jed would stop and listen for the creatures. He glanced up at the buildings towering above, scanning the rooftops.

Meg stopped in front of Mickey's, an Irish pub, where the fire crew had spent many nights pounding shots of whiskey and bottle after bottle of beer. A woman in a space suit glared back at her in the window, a woman she hardly recognized. She closed her eyes and pictured the night she'd polished off a bottle of Hennessy with her husband and Eric and his wife. It was hard to believe the four of them would never share another drink.

"Come on," Jed said.

Meg pressed a hand to the glass, bowed her head, and then trekked after the others. Walking in the open, exposed to the buildings around them, was terrifying.

She had to gain control of herself. The only way out of the city was forward. She had to let go of the ghosts in her past and leave them behind.

Ahead, Jed stopped next to a police car. He climbed inside the vehicle and searched for weapons but came back empty-handed. Using two fingers, he motioned Meg and Rex to continue. They rounded the next street just as the sun vanished behind the clouds. Shadows swallowed them before they could react. They darted behind a FEMA truck and waited for the sun to reemerge.

The sound started off as a faint creaking. Then came the popping of joints and dragging of nails, like the gruesome combination of a crab and a spider skittering across concrete. All three of them heard it. And not even the cloud cover could hide the look of pure terror behind Rex's visor.

Slowly, Meg peeked around the side of the truck and examined the rooftops. A blur of motion shot across the top of a four-story building at the end of the street.

"What do you see?" Rex whispered.

Meg looked past the man and found Jed's worried gaze. "How much farther to those Humvees?"

"Two blocks," he said, then paused. "I think."

Risking another glance, Meg scanned the roofs. This time she saw one of the creatures. The half-naked male Variant perched on a ledge, sniffing the air. Even from this distance, she could see the blue veins crisscrossing its pale flesh. Another three shapes climbed onto the smooth concrete ledge.

Meg ducked behind the truck. She sat there paralyzed by fear, listening to the snuffling monsters. "We have to make a run for it," she said.

Jed nodded, but Rex reached out and grabbed Meg's arm. "No. We can't. We have to stay here."

For the first time in the years she'd worked with Rex, Meg felt an overwhelming anger toward him boiling inside of her. She wondered if she should have left him back in the fire station.

"Please," Rex begged.

The only way out of the city was past the monsters in one of the Humvees. Meg didn't want to hide anymore. The walk through the death-infested streets had taken another bite out of her soul; if they stayed much longer, there wouldn't be anything left. She was sick of waiting to die and was prepared to take her chances.

The cloud cover broke and sunlight flooded the streets.

"When those things move, we move," Meg said firmly.

Rex slowly nodded, and Jed flashed a thumbs-up. Meg craned her neck to see around the side of the truck. The rooftop was empty now. She caught a glimpse of one of the creatures as it ran for cover from the bright sunlight.

"Okay. Now's our chance," Meg said. Keeping low, she led the men around the side of the truck, and they took off running through the maze of abandoned cars. Rex panted behind her, but Meg didn't slow down. She ran like a woman possessed, rounding the corner to the next street on the tips of her toes.

The skyline revealed another cluster of clouds moving over the city. She slowed to a trot and watched the armada of dense gray crossing over the buildings. The shadows filled the streets like a flash flood.

"Run," Meg said. "Run!"

Raw fear took over as she pushed on. She wedged past abandoned vehicles, ricocheting off open doors and bumpers. She ran harder still when the shadows washed over her. Ahead, two cars blocked the route. Instead of going around them, she jumped on a hood and then leaped for the concrete below.

But when she should have landed, she continued to fall.

Meg tried to scream, but all that came out was a choked whisper.

She dropped her axe and reached for something to hold on to. Her gloved hands dragged down the concrete walls of the manhole she had fallen into, slowing her only slightly as she descended into darkness.

The drop took only seconds, but by the time she landed in a stream of sewage water, she was certain she'd fallen off the edge of the earth. The impact sucked the air right out of her lungs, causing her to bite her tongue.

Meg coughed uncontrollably. She thrashed through the muck, reaching for something, anything to hold on to. Her fingers finally found a ledge. She held on and glanced up through the manhole where she'd dropped. If it hadn't been for the water, the fall would have broken both her legs. Gasping, she pulled herself onto the concrete, wiggling her chest up onto solid ground and stretching her arms out. Meg lay there, half of her body over the ledge, the other half still submerged in the sewage. Stunned, she rested her helmeted head on the floor and tried to catch her breath.

A moment passed. There was no sign of Jed or Rex. No sounds. No shouts.

Nothing.

Had they seen her fall? Would they leave her down here?

She knew Rex wouldn't think twice about it if it meant saving his own skin, but she trusted Jed.

When Meg looked up again, the manhole filled with light. The cloud cover broke, and she could see the buildings above. But where were Jed and Rex?

She considered calling out for help but shoved the idea away when she saw the dark tunnel behind her. The sight provoked a surge of fear, and she quickly pushed herself farther onto the ledge, sliding her stomach across the concrete. The pain from the sudden movement made her wonder if she'd broken something after all.

"Shit," she muttered. "Just what I needed." The words were lost in the sound of splashing water. Meg's head shot up. She scanned the tunnel to the right and then to the left. There was no sign of movement in the inky darkness.

"Guys!" she finally yelled. "I'm down here. I'm hurt! I need help!"

No answer. She saw a skeletal ladder extending up the narrow passageway to the street. The bottom steps hung four feet above the water, just near the ledge. With no small amount of effort, she repositioned her body so she was facing the channel on her stomach, but she couldn't stand; her legs were too weak, in too much pain. Using the rays of sunlight to guide her, she swatted at the closest rung, but her fingers slipped and she fell back to the platform, nearly stumbling over the edge.

The faintest of scuffling sounds came from the right. She wiped her visor clear of grime and squinted into the darkness.

There was another splash. Closer.

Meg didn't dare move.

A shape emerged.

No.

An apparition wading through the sludge.

Were her eyes playing tricks on her?

Petrified, she stayed in a crouched position and watched. A moment later, a second and then a third shape appeared in the tunnel, both of them trailing the leader.

Meg made another grab for the ladder. Her fingers brushed the metal and missed again.

The slurp of splashing water pulled her gaze back to the darkness. The shapes were approaching the barrier that separated the light from the darkness. Out of reflex, Meg swept her hands across the ground for a weapon—a rock, her axe, anything that would protect her.

Meg looked back at the approaching creatures. The closest monster came into clear view, white and glistening with the wet sewage. Illuminated by a single ray of light, it lifted its head and sniffed the air, the joints in its neck cracking as it searched. The creature blinked, vertical slits locking onto her, smoldering with hunger. A swollen tongue shot out between its bulging lips and flicked back and forth.

Out of desperation, Meg flailed for the ladder again. This time her fingers found the bottom rung, and she used every ounce of her strength to pull herself to her feet, leaning against the ladder. Tears from the burning pain welled up in her eyes as she started climbing. Years of working and training as a firefighter had given her the strength to pull herself up the ladder using mostly her upper body, but it was slow going. Too slow.

A deep howl reverberated through the tunnel. Meg let out a cry of her own and threw a glance down the ladder over her shoulder. Waves rippled across the water.

Another shriek answered the first as more of the monsters climbed onto the platforms that lined both sides of the canal. They scuffled and skittered across the surface, fighting to be first in line for their feast.

Meg reached for the next rung. Then she saw the original creature point in her direction. In the blink of an eye, the monsters charged.

"Help!" Meg screamed.

She was moving faster now, forcing herself to climb through the pain. She was halfway up the ladder when something caught her foot. The grip was powerful, dragging her down so hard that she almost lost her hold, the pain so intense her vision was fading in and out.

"Help!" she screamed again.

Tilting her visor toward the sky, she saw two helmets staring down at her. Another hand gripped her other leg. Claws sank into her flesh.

"Rex! Jed! Please, help—" Meg's fingers slipped, and then she was falling. She landed in the water with a splash. The sharp claws quickly found her, tearing from all directions. Thrashing, she burst through the surface. Framed in the circle of light high above, she saw Rex and Jed staring down at her.

Instead of coming to her rescue, they drew away. Their white helmets vanished, leaving behind a view of the perfect, cloudless sky.

"I'm sorry!" came a voice.

"*No!*" Meg cried in horror. "Don't leave me down here!"

The last thing she saw was the manhole cover sliding back into place, sealing her into a watery tomb as the monsters dragged her under.

11

Heavy footfalls, unlike those of the padded shoes the nurses wore, woke Beckham the next morning. Someone in uniform was coming to visit him.

He sat up and brushed the hair from his eyes. It was getting long now, long enough that he would have caught shit if his CO was still around to yell at him.

Kate slept curled up in a chair next to his bed. She had said she was only going to stay a few minutes, that she had work to do, but she'd slept through the night. He reached over to rouse her as the footfalls stopped outside the door.

Kate stirred and her eyes flickered open. "Crap. What time is it?" She looked for a clock and yawned, stretching. Then she slumped back in her chair. "Great. Wasted hours I won't get back." She rubbed her eyes and gave him a quick look. "How do you feel?"

"I'm good," Beckham lied. His ribs were still tender, but the swelling was down. His injuries were mostly superficial, nothing serious. If it weren't for the doctor's orders of bed rest, he would have already been back in the barracks.

Someone knocked on the door. He heard muffled voices on the other side, familiar but hard to place.

"It's open," Beckham said. He shifted in his bed, sitting up as best he could.

Lieutenant Colonel Jensen and Major Smith strolled into the room. They removed their berets and tucked them under their arms.

"Doctor Lovato," Jensen said, offering a smile.

"Good morning," she replied.

Jensen examined Beckham. "Looks like you had one hell of a trip."

"Oh, this." Beckham ran a hand over his body. "I've been beat up way worse."

Jensen didn't laugh. "I wish I was here with good news, but I'm not."

Beckham sat up farther when he saw the stern look on the lieutenant colonel's face.

"As you know, the countdown to Operation Liberty continues. We're twenty-eight hours out. I'm still hoping you're able to lead a team—"

"Are you crazy?" Kate said. She stood and positioned herself directly in front of the bed.

"Kate, please, sit down. I'm fine," Beckham assured her.

She stood her ground.

"Really, Kate. It's *okay*," Beckham said.

Kate glanced back at Beckham for a moment and then uncrossed her arms.

Jensen waited for her to sit and then continued. "Before we discuss your condition, I need to know if there's anything you can tell me about the Variants."

The pain of Beckham's injuries flared as flashbacks to the creature that had put him in the hospital tore through his thoughts. Shaking his head, he turned to the window to watch the play of sunlight on the distant waves. The crimson rays seemed divine, captivating in a way. It was still hard to believe that the world was gone.

"I'm not sure how to explain it, sir," Beckham said.

He turned to the lieutenant colonel. "The Variants are unpredictable. When we got to Bragg, they were suicidal. But as we were leaving, we encountered some sort of a leader, a Variant that seemed to be in control of the pack. I saw something similar in New York, but this was different. This was a coordinated attack. They flanked us."

Major Smith swore under his breath.

Jensen scratched his mustache. "What else did you see?"

"Smoke seems to screw with their senses. Besides that, not much. You already know it's hard to take them down. Head shots seem to do the trick, but I saw one of 'em that had about a dozen holes in it and still kept coming."

"Holy shit," Smith said.

"Anything else?" Jensen asked.

"No, sir," Beckham replied.

"All right," Jensen said. "The doctors said you're good to go. I'm going to hold a briefing with the other team leads in two hours at the CIC."

"I'll be there," Beckham said. He refrained from looking at Kate, but he heard her scoff in annoyance.

"You aren't seriously considering—"

An enthusiastic voice in the doorway cut her off. "Guys!"

Beckham couldn't help but smile as Riley guided his wheelchair through the door.

"Hey, boss. You look like shit too!" He laughed and then grunted as the chair caught against the doorjamb. "Damn it, I hate this thing," he said, fighting with the wheels to make it into the room. Kate walked over to help him.

"The stupid nurse said I couldn't see you earlier," Riley said. He wheeled himself to Beckham's bed.

"Since when did you start listening to anyone who told you not to do something?" Beckham asked.

"She's cute, and I was trying to be on my best behavior,"

Riley said. "Not many girls to pick from at the end of the world, you know."

Beckham shook his head and changed the subject. "How are you feeling?"

Riley shrugged. "Doctor said I won't be back on my feet for a while." He chuckled. "But at least I don't look like you."

"You should have seen the guy that did this to me. He was bigger than Horn."

The room grew silent at the mention of their friend. Kate put a hand on Beckham's shoulder. Riley bowed his head.

"I heard about Horn's wife. But you guys were able to rescue his girls—that's a miracle in itself. Tell you the truth, I figured everyone would be dead at Bragg," Riley said.

"There weren't many left."

Riley glanced up. "Jinx and Chow made it, though, right?"

"They saved our asses."

"Small victories, I guess," Riley said. "So what's next?"

"Operation Liberty," Beckham said.

Kate backpedaled from the bed. Her jaw tightened, her lips a thin line of disapproval as she retreated to the door. She was giving him the distance he needed, but it was clear she wasn't happy about it.

"Wish I could go with you," Riley said.

"Me too, Kid. Me too."

A dense fog crawled across Plum Island. Beckham stood outside the medical facility with Kate by his side, watching the haze slowly consume the base. The horizon threatened yet another storm.

Beckham acknowledged the two guards outside with a nod. Grabbing the handrails, he made his way cautiously down the steps and into the knee-deep mist. He squinted at three soldiers approaching in the distance. They walked at a brisk yet graceful pace, side by side, the muzzles of their rifles bobbing up and down over their shoulders. As they got closer, he saw the thin outlines of their body armor and the sculpted muscles that reflected constant training.

"Who are they?" Kate asked.

Beckham smiled. "My men."

Even in the fog, he knew the slender, defined frame of the man on the left belonged to Chow, and that the beefy man in the middle was Horn. The man on the right had to be Jinx.

The three emerged from the gray and formed a line, shoulder to shoulder. Horn stepped out and saluted. "Sir."

Beckham wasn't sure how to respond. The gesture was completely unexpected from Horn, not to mention unnecessary. Beckham recalled Riley's laughter from earlier and figured a little humor might do them all some good. Snapping his heels together, he returned the salute, then dropped his hand quickly.

"All right, knock it off now," Beckham said.

Horn laughed and held out a fist. "Good to see you standing."

"Luck," Beckham said, bumping his knuckles against Horn's. "I think mine's got to run out soon."

"Horn saved your sorry ass," Jinx said.

Beckham looked at the men in turn, remembering all of their fallen brothers; then he reached forward and wrapped his arms around Horn, patting his back before pulling away. "Thanks again, bro." He leaned forward and put his forehead against his friend's.

"I always got your back," Horn said gruffly.

Chow snapped his fingers. "We better get moving. Briefing in a few."

The operators walked in silence through the fog. The CIC was packed by the time they arrived. Officers and enlisted men and women huddled around the war table, staring at crinkled maps. Lieutenant Colonel Jensen stepped away from the observation window and made his way through the swollen crowd.

"Let's get started," he said and paused, scanning the assembled men and women. He addressed a tall and slender marine with the build of a marathoner. "Sergeant Peters, you've got Team Alpha." The man nodded and made eye contact with his nearby team.

The next marine Jensen called looked more like a linebacker, with broad shoulders. "Sergeant Rodriguez, you've got Bravo." He scrutinized the stern faces around him as if looking for someone in particular. "Where's Chipper?" Jensen asked.

"Here, sir," a short Army Ranger said. He pushed his way forward from the edge of the group.

"You've got Team Charlie."

The man nodded and swept a hand over his bald head.

Then Jensen's eyes found Beckham. "Master Sergeant, you have Team Delta."

He turned to his second and said, "All right, everyone. Major Smith will provide a sitrep."

Smith bent over the table and flattened several maps. Grabbing a remote, he clicked on an overhead projector. A map appeared on the room's west wall. "This is New York City, all five boroughs." Smith used a laser pen to identify the five main sections. "Recon teams and satellite imagery show these locations are where the Variants seem to be gathering."

"I'm going to be straight up with you," interrupted Jensen. "We don't believe these numbers are accurate. According to intel from Command, the Variants are grouped in the areas in red," said Jensen.

Smith nodded and pointed to one of the marked areas. "Reports estimate one to two thousand at each of these hot spots, and your mission is to help set up a forward operating base and then assist First Platoon in clearing the streets."

Jensen waited for the info to sink in. "I believe Command is wrong, and Doctor Lovato is going to tell you why."

Without hesitation, she walked up to the table. "Gentleman, as Lieutenant Colonel Jensen and Major Smith have already stated, these red blotches represent the known Variant populations. General Kennor believes those are the only Variants left. If that's the case, then you won't have much of a problem taking back New York. But I'm here to tell you that I think General Kennor is wrong." Kate's eyes scanned the soldiers, her gaze catching Beckham's for a moment before she continued.

He nodded, admiring the way she handled herself in a roomful of military personnel.

"And not by just a little," Kate said. "I believe he's wrong by a whole hell of a lot."

Kate pulled up a chair to the table's monitor and plugged in a thumb drive. Keying in a few commands, she transferred the information to the projector and pointed to the wall. "As you can see, the clusters ballooned in these areas.

"My projections show the Variant populations should number somewhere between one and two million, not one and two thousand," Kate continued. "That's a far cry from Command's calculations."

Nervous chatter broke out all around them. Beckham

tensed his muscles. How could Command be so far off? If Kate was right, then New York was lost. There was simply no way a company of marines and strike teams could take back the city.

Jensen raised a hand. "Everyone keep quiet. Let the doctor finish."

"Thank you," she replied. "I'm not sure exactly where the Variants have vanished to, but I do know that the creatures are changing, evolving. They are growing more intelligent. Some of them even seem to be leading packs. They're faster, stronger, and can heal quicker than anyone in this room—even you, Master Sergeant Beckham," Kate said with a half smile.

The subsequent chuckles were short-lived. The grim reality of Kate's projections lingered on everyone's mind. If true, the numbers were daunting: They were facing a battle that the military had no way of winning. Beckham discreetly sized up the men in front of him. Some of them had seen action, fighting insurgents in the War on Terror, but most of them had never gone up against a Variant. And this time they wouldn't face just a couple hundred. There were millions. The idea was madness—even if the enemy was armed with only teeth and claws.

"Thank you, Doctor Lovato," Jensen said. "I've asked Command to delay this mission until we know where the Variants are hiding. They denied that request. In just over twenty-four hours, we are expected to provide four teams to help set up a forward operating base and remove any Variant threat from the area. Refusing to do so would amount to desertion, but frankly a court-martial is the least of your worries. I've decided that I will take full responsibility for Plum Island's actions. For that reason I'm making this a volunteer mission. I hope the leads will stay, but I can't force you."

There were a few whispers, but Jensen spoke right over them, his voice swelling until it filled the whole room. "The fate of our species hangs in the balance. And there's no doubt in my mind each and every one of us will play an important role in the fight to save our comrades, our country, and our world."

Goose bumps rippled across Beckham's skin. The speech reminded him of the ones Lieutenant Colonel Clinton had given before ordering Team Ghost into the pits of hell on the other side of the world. He hadn't trusted Jensen up until this point. Now he was ready to follow the man into war.

Beckham wedged in next to Kate. "Sir, may I say a few words?"

"Absolutely," Jensen replied.

"Horn and I have fought these things in Atlanta, Niantic, New York, and Fort Bragg. I've seen what they are capable of. They move like animals and are only interested in killing. I've watched them turn on each other, and I've watched them organize. They are unpredictable and extremely dangerous." Beckham raised a battered brow as he scanned the skeptical sea of faces. "These are not sick human beings. They are not zombies. These are deadly predators. And they will kill you without a single thought."

"I hope you all heard Master Sergeant Beckham," Jensen cut in. "He's the only one of us who has led a team against the Variant threat. You can see he's come back alive, if a bit worse for wear."

Beckham saw the look in Kate's eyes and knew that she wanted to protest, but he had a job to do. He knew that she understood that too.

"I'm on board, sir," Beckham said to Jensen.

"Me too," Horn said, patting Beckham on the back.

"I'm in," Jinx said.

"Wouldn't miss it," Chow added.

One by one, confident voices called out, each warrior stepping up to support Operation Liberty. But deep down Beckham knew they were volunteering for a mission that they had little hope of accomplishing.

That night, while the rest of the base was prepping for war, Beckham snuck through the personnel-quarters wing of Building 1. Getting past the guards had been the easy part; they didn't ask questions when they saw his rank. His business was none of their concern, and the men let him pass without notice.

He moved from door to door, searching for Kate's room. Halfway down the hall, a woman stepped out of the restroom in a towel, her hair wrapped up in a glistening black bun. They nearly collided.

"I'm sorry," Beckham said. She shied away, clearly terrified. He'd been so focused on finding Kate that he'd forgotten his injuries. He probably looked like Rocky Balboa after fifteen rounds against Apollo Creed.

"Um, excuse me—what exactly are you doing here? This area is for science officers and support staff," the woman said.

Beckham felt his cheeks flare. "I'm looking for Kate. Doctor Lovato."

The woman pointed down the hallway. "She's in Room Fifteen." She caught a glimpse of the color rising in his cheeks and smiled. Giving him a once-over, she chuckled and continued down the opposite corridor.

Embarrassed, Beckham let out a sigh. He wasn't sure if he was doing the right thing. Sneaking in to see Kate had seemed like a good idea at the time, but now he wasn't so sure. The chemistry he shared with her was undeniable. But maybe this was all wrong; maybe they should stay friends.

Go with your gut, he thought, eyeing the numbers on the doors. His gut said, *Talk to her.*

He found her door and raised a battered hand. He wasn't even sure if she would be there, considering she pretty much lived in the lab, but a few seconds later the door creaked open and Kate peeked out.

"Reed? What are you doing here?"

Beckham couldn't see her face in the darkness. But there was something about her tone—a trace of nervousness. Apprehension.

Fuck, he thought. Maybe he shouldn't have shown up this way. He looked terrible.

"Reed?" Kate asked again. She stepped into the hallway in a pair of exercise shorts and a small white tee.

Beckham took a sidelong glance to ensure the woman in the towel wasn't eavesdropping. He considered making up an excuse, some pretense of official business, but came up with nothing. "Thought I would... um..."

Kate's mouth turned up in a half smile. The banks of fluorescent lights in the panels above spread a soft glow on her olive skin. Without thinking he reached forward and pulled her chin toward his, kissing her softly. A small moan escaped her lips when he pulled away.

She dragged him into the room, slamming the door shut behind them.

They kissed on their way to her bed, tossing clothes on the floor before crashing onto the small twin mattress. Beckham ignored the pain shooting through his ribs. He didn't care. All that mattered now was Kate.

She ran her finger in a circular motion around a bruise on his chest, kissing the tender skin. Her muscular legs confirmed she didn't spend all of her time in the lab. She had told him she was a runner, but he never imagined that her lab coat covered such a gorgeous body. She was slender and fit, but also had natural curves. His eyes slid along those curves, savoring every inch of her.

"You're beautiful," Beckham whispered. "No—you're gorgeous."

Kate didn't shy away from his gaze. Confidence radiated from her blue eyes—eyes that roved his body with the same intensity he felt.

"I don't know what the future holds, Kate, but I want you to know that—"

She put a finger on his lips. "You don't need to say anything."

Staring down at her, he realized how long he'd gone without the touch of a woman. Team Ghost had spent the better part of the last year in Afghanistan. Yet he wasn't nervous. He burned with desire, but he also felt calm, at peace, as if he'd found a quiet place at the center of a raging storm. His lips found her collarbone and then her breasts, sending Kate's body arching in pleasure. Maneuvering on the narrow mattress was hell, but he managed to blaze a trail of kisses along her taut stomach. He paused, looking up into her eyes, questioning one last time.

"I want you," she said. There was no hesitation, no uncertainty. Wrapping her arms around his muscular triceps, she pulled him to her. For hours, they lost themselves in each other, their sweaty bodies moving under the radiant moonlight. Thoughts of broken promises and the postapocalyptic world that surrounded Plum Island were forgotten. His pulse raced as adrenaline flooded his system. He made love the way he fought, with an all-consuming passion.

His movements became more powerful, faster, and intense. Kate wrapped her legs around him, pulling him deeper. Her moans grew louder. Beckham buried his face in her hair and kissed her neck. Their bodies shook, and Beckham locked eyes with Kate. He had never had time for love in the past. Women had come and gone, but his promise to protect his men and his country had always been his top priority. It was funny how the end of the world changed a person. Looking down at Kate, he made another promise.

"When this is all over, I will come back for you."

She looked toward the window, gasping for breath. "You don't have to go."

Beckham slid his body off hers and rolled onto his side, propping his head up with a hand. "I do, Kate. You know I have to."

"I know," Kate said. "But I'm going to hold you to that promise. And if you break it, I'm coming after you."

Beckham smiled. "Good," he said. "I wouldn't expect anything less from Doctor Kate Lovato."

12

A small crowd of military and civilian personnel gathered at the edge of the tarmac. Beckham nudged his way through the group, stopping when he heard someone calling his name. Throwing the strap of his pack higher over his right shoulder, he turned to see Fitz.

"Hey, Fitz, how are you holding up?" Beckham said with a smile.

"I'm good. But I'd be even better if you did me a favor."

Beckham halted. "What do you have in mind?"

"I'd like to join your team." Fitz stood a bit taller on his prosthetic legs. "I want to help."

The weight of Beckham's bag suddenly felt much heavier. He wasn't prepared for the request, but when he saw Kate and Riley standing on the sidelines, he knew exactly how to respond.

"We need you here. With so many of us going to New York, the base is going to be vulnerable. Lieutenant Colonel Jensen could use a sharpshooter on one of those towers," he said, pointing.

Fitz frowned but then nodded and flung a glance over his shoulder. He eyed one of the towers and then extended a hand. "Good luck, Beckham."

"Keep everyone here safe."

"Will do," Fitz said with confidence.

Crew chiefs and engineers crowded around the four Black Hawks, making last-minute adjustments and checks. A crewman loaded one of the door guns on Echo 3. It was the same bird that had extracted Beckham from Fort Bragg. He knew the threat in New York was greater than any these men had ever faced before.

Horn, Jinx, and Chow were camped out past the chopper. Two of the Rangers from Bragg stood a few feet away. Beckham had finally had a chance to learn their real names and ranks. Gerard Ryan and Brad "Timbo" Timmins, both corporals, were performing their final gear and ammo checks.

The new Team Ghost was ready.

"'Sup," Horn said as Beckham approached.

"Sorry I'm late."

Horn finished looking through the scope of his M249 and then gave Beckham a full once-over. "What the hell, bro? Were you up all night or something?"

Jinx grinned from ear to ear. "Bet the good doctor was giving him a last-minute physical."

"Watch it," Horn snorted.

Chow stood glaring a few feet away, slowly shaking his head at Jinx. "Maybe we should have given you a different nickname."

" 'Shithead' was my first choice," Horn said.

"What does Jinx mean anyway?" Timbo asked, curiously. "I thought that was bad luck. If so, then am I missing something?"

"Oxymoron," Chow said. "Staff Sergeant Abbas is the last thing from bad luck. The only time Jinx is bad luck is when he's your wingman at a bar."

"Hey, man, that's not cool," Jinx said. "Not cool at all."

"Cut the crap," Beckham said. He was fine with a bit

of joking around—it calmed pre-mission jitters—but the last thing he wanted was a rift in his team before they went back out there.

Horn rolled up a sleeve, revealing several of his tribal tattoos. That was Hornspeak for *shut the hell up*. After silencing the men, Horn pivoted toward Beckham and whispered in a voice only he could hear.

"You good, boss?"

"Yeah, I'm good."

Horn reached down to pull the skull bandanna up around his neck and tightened the knot. Then he put a hand on Beckham's shoulder.

Beckham nodded and looked him in the eye. "I'm fine, really. I'm more worried about you, Big Horn."

He exhaled a long breath. "This has to be done," Horn said. "We need to take back New York."

A final nod passed between them, and the two men returned to their preparations.

"Grab all the ammunition you can," Chow said. "I don't know if Doctor Lovato is right or not, but if she is, then we're going to need every round we can carry."

Beckham had picked up an extra M9 and strapped it to his leg. "Listen up," he said. "You guys already know the drill, but I have a few more details."

Beckham crouched and pulled a map from a pocket in his vest. Spreading it out on the concrete, he pointed toward a solid red blotch covering several blocks in Manhattan, just east of Times Square. "This is where we rendezvous with the mission commander, Lieutenant Gates, and First Platoon. The others are being deployed to the other four boroughs."

"So once we hit the LZ, we're pretty much on our own?" Horn asked.

"Afraid so. We're meeting the marines here, at Pier 86," Beckham said, pointing at the map. "That's where the armor is being dropped." He ran his finger away from the dock. "We follow First Platoon to the main target area, here."

"Rockefeller Center?" Chow asked.

"Looks like there's several subway stations in that area," Horn said.

"The Variants could be using the abandoned tunnels," Chow said. "Just like we did at Fort Bragg. That one bunch followed us in, remember?"

Timbo leaned over the map, his massive shadow covering the pages. In a gruff voice, he said, "So we're clearing each city block and wiping out the main cluster of Variants and then setting up an FOB?"

"That's the plan," Beckham replied.

"What about infected? Is it possible we'll encounter anyone with the hemorrhage virus?" Ryan asked.

"Command has assured us that the virus has burned out in New York. They dropped VariantX9H9 in the area without mercy. Not a single infected has been spotted since then."

"What's Doctor Lovato say?" Horn asked.

Beckham stood and crossed his arms. "She said that infection is highly unlikely. The biggest threat, obviously, is the missing Variant population." He paused to feel his left eyelid. The swelling was finally down, but it had left an ugly shiner. It was a wonder Kate had even wanted to touch him. He pushed any thoughts of Kate aside, knowing there was no room to relive the memory of last night during this mission. He had to remain vigilant, focused on Operation Liberty and on keeping his men alive.

"Look," Beckham said. "I don't like this any more than you guys do. Those things could be hiding anywhere. Or, if we're all really lucky, like win-the-fucking-lottery lucky, maybe Doctor Lovato is wrong. Either way, we have a job to do. The air force is going to soften the area before we move in to clean up the mess. They'll be on standby if we run into any problems. I've been told the flyboys still have plenty of bombs."

"That's reassuring," Horn grunted. He rolled his neck, cracking it audibly.

"Any other questions?" Beckham asked. He looked at his team in turn. Everyone in the group had seen action. They all knew what came next.

"All right. Once you finish your gear prep, say your good-byes." Beckham folded the map and put it back into his vest pocket. He dug inside and pulled out a copy of the picture of his mother. The original picture had been snapped thirty years before, in Rocky Mountain National Park, long before the cancer had reduced her to a skeleton. She stood on a peak overlooking a lush valley, with her arms wrapped around Beckham. Her curly black hair blew slightly in the wind, and she wore a smile of pure joy.

"She looks so happy," Horn said. Beckham was so engrossed in the image he hadn't felt the man's presence.

"Yup, and look at me. I look annoyed."

"You were a kid. No one likes having their picture taken with their parents at that age."

"How are the girls doing?" Beckham asked.

Horn shrugged. "They miss their mother and they don't want me to go."

"Maybe you should—" Beckham had begun to say when Horn punched him softly in the shoulder.

"We just went through this, boss. I'm with you."

Beckham knew better than to argue with his friend. The man was here, and that was enough for him. "I told Kate and Riley to look after the girls. Fitz is going to keep an extra set of eyes on them too."

"Thanks," Horn said.

Beckham scanned the crowd. Riley sat in his wheelchair, his hands in his lap. The kid wasn't used to sitting on the sidelines, but this time he had no choice. Kate stood behind him, with Jenny and Tasha at her side. The girls waved when they saw him looking.

Beckham turned to focus on the men who were new to his team. Ryan was an entire head shorter than Timbo, with dark olive skin, a large nose, and a thick Queens accent. The man jammed a magazine into his MK11 and scoped the skyline. Timbo checked his secondary weapon, an M4 that he kept slung over his flak jacket. Unlike the armor the operators wore, the Rangers had ceramic armor. It wasn't as advanced as the high-density polymer and plastic beneath Beckham's vest, but it had saved countless lives.

Lastly, Beckham examined both Rangers for signs of anxiety. Not that he would blame them if they were nervous, but he needed to make sure they were good to go. He had been part of joint missions before and typically knew the men under his command. Both Rangers had performed well at Bragg, but New York was going to be very different.

"Fifteen minutes!" shouted a voice across the tarmac. Major Smith and Lieutenant Colonel Jensen walked around the teams, overlooking the last preparations.

"Better say good-bye," Horn muttered. He nodded toward the crowd, and Beckham followed him away from the birds. Riley, Kate, and the girls watched from behind one of the concrete barriers. Both men hopped over the block and Horn took a knee in front of Tasha and Jenny. Horn yanked his skull bandanna down and then pulled both girls against his armor, wrapping his arms around them.

"I'll be back in a few days," he assured them.

"Promise?" Tasha asked, pulling her head away from his chest.

Horn nodded.

Tasha looked at Beckham and said, "You promise to take care of my dad?"

Beckham put a hand on Horn's shoulder. "I promise. I owe him one."

Tasha smiled. "He saved your butt."

Riley chuckled. "Not the first time!"

Leaving Horn to tend to his children, Beckham walked over to Kate. She smiled but didn't speak; they'd already said their good-byes earlier in the morning. She wrapped her arms around him as best as she could, hindered by the armor and ammunition. "I'll be okay, Kate," he said.

"You'd better."

With Kate pressed up against his chest, he looked over at Riley. "You take care of these ladies. You hear me?"

"No problem, boss," Riley replied.

"Good luck," Kate whispered. She pulled away and searched his eyes.

"We'll be back before you know it," Beckham said, forcing a smile. He waved and then tilted his chin toward the choppers. Horn said his final good-byes, and then they climbed into Echo 3, leaving their loved ones behind.

The thump of helicopter blades had faded by the time Kate looked away. She'd secretly hoped Beckham would stay behind, that his injuries would excuse him from Operation Liberty, but she knew the man well enough now to know that staying behind had never been an option. The dread in Riley's face as he watched his brothers fly away without him reminded her these men were warriors. They had a job to do. A duty. Asking him to step away from a mission was just like asking her to stay away from the lab.

The blue and gray horizon stretched as far as she could see, infinite and empty. Somewhere on the other side of the Atlantic Ocean, Kate's parents might be looking up at the same sky. She felt a tug on her sleeve and looked down into Tasha's wide, curious eyes.

"Where's our dad going?" the girl asked.

Kate crouched next to the girls.

"He's going to help people in New York City. Have you ever seen New York City?"

Jenny buried her head into Kate's side and cried.

"He'll be back soon," Riley said, repositioning his wheelchair so he could face them. "Your daddy and Beckham will take good care of each other."

Jenny wriggled her head away from Kate to get a better view of the injured man. Riley grinned and said, "Will you girls push me back to my room?" He cupped the back of his head and let out a long sigh. "I'm too tired to do it myself." He faked a yawn and winked at Kate.

Tasha and Jenny slowly pulled away from her side, examining Riley curiously.

"How old are you guys again?" Riley asked. "I want to make sure you're old enough for a wheelchair license."

Kate let out an uncontrolled laugh. Jenny fidgeted nervously, her lips pursed and ready to speak. She held out five fingers instead.

Riley nodded. "Five. Let me consult my mental rule book." He counted with his right fingers.

The younger girl hunched over, gripping her stomach and giggling. "Come on!"

"You're good to go," Riley finally said.

Tasha grabbed the right-side handle to his chair and said, "I'm eight, so guess I'm good too."

Together, the two girls pushed Riley slowly across the

path back to the post. Kate trailed close behind, ensuring the girls didn't topple his chair. They turned the job of pushing him into a game. Kate smiled, but the sight of the white dome of Building 1 reminded her that their situation was no game. It loomed above as they walked farther through the base. Kate studied the architecture as they walked. From the outside it looked clean and pure. But the weapon she'd designed inside made the building nothing more than an ammunition factory. VariantX9H9 had killed more people than any other weapon in the history of the world.

She felt nauseated.

"Wait up," a man called out.

Kate turned to see a soldier running on two metal blades attached just below his knees. "Doctor Lovato, Staff Sergeant Riley," he said. "Girls."

"What happened to your legs?" Jenny asked.

Tasha glared at her little sister. "That's not polite."

"Sorry," the younger girl said.

A streak of red crossed the man's freckled face. He was young, probably in his early twenties, Kate thought.

"I lost them fighting bad guys," he finally replied.

"Oh," Jenny said. "They're really cool."

The man smiled at that; then his eyes gravitated to Riley and he said, "Beckham and I fought those things together back at Fort Bragg."

"That's what I heard. He said you could nail a fly from a quarter mile away."

"I don't know about that, but I was the top marksman in my unit, back before..." His voice faded as a gust of wind passed over the group. A few seconds of awkward silence followed.

The man probably experienced that silence a lot, Kate thought. Her heart hurt for him.

Clearing his throat, he extended a hand. "I'm Joe

Fitzpatrick, but you can call me Fitz. Beckham asked me to look after you guys while he's on the mission. I'll be on one of the guard towers, but thought I'd introduce myself to y'all."

Riley reached out and shook the man's hand. "Damn good to have you here, Fitz. I'm Riley. And this here is the savior of the world, the woman behind the weapon that destroyed the hemorrhage virus."

"Nice to meet you," Fitz said. He turned to Kate with an outstretched hand. "Pleasure, ma'am." He had a Southern accent—a gentleman, Kate thought, by anyone's standards.

"Not everyone thinks I'm a hero," Kate said.

Fitz held her gaze. "Not everyone is intelligent."

Riley laughed. "I like this guy already!"

Wind rustled Kate's hair. Rain clouds were moving in rapidly from the west. They were heavy and dark, a collage of purple and black.

"Looks like another storm," she said.

"We better get inside," Riley said. He craned his neck. "Girls, if you would, please."

Kate laughed as Tasha and Jenny pushed him forward. They stopped in front of the barracks.

"This is me," he said.

Fitz stepped forward. "Me too. I'll take him from here."

Kate wasn't surprised to see Riley sink a bit farther in his chair. It was obvious the man wasn't used to people taking care of him, and that he'd only asked the girls for their help to get their minds off their dad. The barracks hadn't been built for wheelchair access. There were no ramps or ADA fittings. *A state-of-the-art facility that doesn't even adhere to federal access laws? That's strange*, Kate thought.

"I'll take the girls to dinner around six o'clock tonight, if you'd like to join us," she said.

Fitz made a slight bow, as if he was tipping a hat. "Would be my pleasure."

"Count me in," Riley said, repositioning his chair so his back was to the steps. With narrowed eyes he found Fitz. "Take it easy on these, man."

The two guards at the top of the ledge stepped down, eager to help. "We got you."

Riley sank even farther into his chair, his eyes locking with Kate's. There was despair there he couldn't hide. She offered a reassuring nod. "See you in a bit."

13

Echo 3 and the other Black Hawks raced toward the storm. Judging by their speed and the trajectory of the clouds, Beckham guessed they would meet in New York City. Balling his right hand into a fist, he flexed his forearm and felt the first wave of adrenaline pumping into his system. He reached for his vest pocket and pulled out the picture of his mother. More adrenaline rushed through him as he kissed it. Mentally, he was ready to go.

Snapping his NVGs into position, he checked one last time to ensure they were working properly. Then he counted his ammo. Eight magazines protruded from his vest, two more than he normally carried. The extra weight was welcome if it saved him from the teeth of the Variants.

Next he checked his headset. "Testing."

The word drew laughter from Horn. The man stared down at a clogged highway below. "Testing? What is this, high school?"

Beckham frowned. "New equipment means problems and—" The bird hit a patch of turbulence before he could finish his thought.

The shadows in the compartment shifted to reveal the stern faces of Ryan and Timbo. The two Army Rangers stood toward the back of the chopper, the muzzles of their MK11s aimed at the open doors. Timbo offered a nod when he saw Beckham's gaze had fallen on him. The Ranger adjusted his headset and said, "Works."

Grabbing a handhold, Beckham waited for the rough patch to pass. "Listen up," he said in a voice just shy of a shout. "We'll be on the ground in twenty. Do one final check of your gear and weapons. I don't want any surprises."

"LZ in fifteen," the lead pilot said over the comm.

Beckham hunched to steal a glance out the windshield in the cockpit. A flash of lightning streaked across the horizon as the bird continued toward the New York skyline. They were close enough to see the extent of the destruction. Pockmarks peppered the skyscrapers where missiles had hit weeks before. Some of the structures had collapsed entirely, covering roads and crushing the smaller adjacent buildings. Most of the fires had fizzled out, the result of above-average rainfall since the military firebombed parts of the city in the early days of the hemorrhage virus.

"Fucking A, man," Ryan said, pulling himself closer to the doorway. "This is insane. We did this?"

"Yup," Horn replied.

"When I signed up for this mission, I thought I would be coming back home. But this..." Ryan shook his head. "The city is gone. There's nothing worth saving down there."

"There could be survivors," Beckham replied. "And once the Variants are gone, we'll rebuild. Just like we rebuilt the Twin Towers."

Ryan kept his eyes on the destruction.

"Where you from?" Beckham asked. He had to keep the man engaged and focused before they landed. Losing him now would make him a liability.

"Queens," said Ryan flatly.

"Hey, we found my daughters and rescued them. You can't give up hope. You hear me?" Horn said. "Ryan," he repeated when the man didn't reply.

The Ranger turned slightly. "Yeah, man, I hear you. Don't worry. You can count on me." Ryan patted his helmet with his palm. "Good to go, good to go."

The storm hit as soon as the Black Hawk crossed over Times Square. It started as a drizzle, hitting the bird from the side, but rapidly grew into a downpour. The rain pelted the metal sides of the craft as the pilots descended toward the LZ.

Pier 86 was already bustling with military activity. Several navy boats raced away from the dock, a powerful wake trailing them. The chopper banked to the left and hovered for several seconds as the pilots made contact with 1st Platoon, and then angled toward the dock, setting them down next to Echo 2.

Without hesitation Beckham jumped out, his boots splashing in a puddle. Ducking the blades of the chopper, he ran for the marines gathering around a makeshift camouflage tent set up next to a trio of Humvees, all mounted with M240s. Two Bradleys dwarfed the trucks. The sandy-brown armored vehicles were a sight for sore eyes. The armor, the mounted TOW missile launchers, and the 25-millimeter cannons prompted a moment of hope that made the situation seem less dire, even if they were grossly outnumbered. The display of firepower gave him the fuel he needed to kick this mission into gear.

Beckham spun to watch Echo 1 and Echo 4 land. The other teams from Plum Island piled out. Their arrival sealed the deal: There was no turning back. Operation Liberty was under way.

Beckham scratched the wound above his eye and approached the main tent. Two marines stood outside.

"Master Sergeant Reed Beckham, reporting from Plum Island."

One of the men checked a sheet of paper in a waterproof case. "Says here you're a Delta Force operator," the man on the right said. He seemed older, maybe fifty-five or sixty, and Beckham was surprised to see that he was a lance corporal.

"That's right," Beckham replied, worried by the realization that the military was more than desperate for boots on the ground.

"Glad to have you here, Master Sergeant," the man said. "Please proceed."

Beckham offered a short nod and then ducked into the tent. Crates of equipment greeted him. Support staff worked quickly to unload the gear. He spied an officer hunched over a metal table. The man was drawing circles on a map with a red pen. Two other officers flanked him. They eyed Beckham as he walked toward them.

"Lieutenant Gates, sir?" Beckham asked.

The man glanced up from the table, removing a pair of glasses and positioning them high on his bald head.

"Yes, and you are?"

"Master Sergeant Reed Beckham, reporting from Plum Island," he repeated, standing at attention.

Gates slipped his pen into a vest pocket. He walked around the table and extended a hand. "Welcome to New York."

Beckham shook the man's hand. "Happy to assist in the fight to take back the city."

"How many of you are there?"

"There are four of us, sir, and two Army Rangers."

Gates arched a brow. "Four? That's it? Central assured me there would be more."

"There are three other teams from Plum Island, but we're all that's left of Delta Force Team Ghost and Team

Titanium, besides an injured man who was forced to remain behind."

Gates shook his head. "I'm sorry to hear that, truly I am. This war has already taken so many lives. Most of First Platoon and the others in this company were pieced together from surviving units on the East Coast. And the casualties continue to mount. That's what makes Operation Liberty so important."

"Lieutenant," said a deep voice from behind Beckham. He stepped to the side to watch the muscular frame of Lieutenant Colonel Jensen walk into the room. Combat gear covered him from head to toe. He adjusted the strap of an M4 and ducked under one of the tent's support beams on his way to the table.

"Master Sergeant," he said.

"Lieutenant Colonel," Beckham replied.

Gates stiffened and threw up a salute. "Sir, are you taking command of First Platoon? I hadn't heard from General Kennor."

Jensen shook his head. "No, and General Kennor won't be hearing from you that I'm here either. You're in command, Lieutenant, but I reserve the right to pull rank." He paused and looked to Beckham. "I'm here to fight alongside my men."

Gates hesitated and glanced over at his team.

Beckham felt a grin breaking across his face. He remembered something he'd learned in training. Years ago, a master sergeant had told him that in order for a commander to earn respect from those under him, he had to be their equal and their leader. By showing up to the fight, Jensen had done just that. Beckham felt a growing respect for the man.

"Is that a problem?" Jensen asked.

"No, sir," Gates finally replied. "Happy to have you here, sir."

Jensen nodded and pointed at Beckham. "I see you've met our best. He looks pretty beat up, but trust me, the man can fight."

Gates nodded. "Truthfully, I was hoping Command would send more."

"I'm afraid there weren't more to send."

He followed Gates to the other side of the table, and they huddled around the map. Two other drenched marines walked into the tent a beat later. Beckham recognized them as the other team leads, Rodriguez and Peters.

"I'll be leading a strike team, as will Beckham, Rodriguez, and Peters," Jensen said, introducing the marines.

"Welcome," Gates said to the men. He pointed at a marine with a nasty scar on his chin. "This is Sergeant Vince Valdez."

Valdez grunted a response Beckham couldn't hear.

Gates looked back at Jensen. "Sir, when Central Command told me they were sending support, I figured it would be more than four teams. And I certainly wasn't expecting the commander."

"I couldn't let my men do this alone," Jensen said. Reaching into his pocket, he removed a bag of chewing tobacco. "Besides, I've been itching for some chew for weeks." He jammed a wad into his bottom lip.

After the introductions, Gates uncapped his pen and leaned over the map. "All right. After the air force hits their targets, we're rolling in with the armor. Take a left onto the West Side Highway, then a right onto West Fiftieth. Satellite imagery shows this is the clearest route. Most of the other streets are covered in rubble from Operation Reaper. We've fitted the Bradleys with cowcatchers to help clear the roads. It's going to take us a while to get through some of these areas, but this is the best direct path to our target and the area where we will set up an FOB. That brings us to the bombing zones."

Gates circled Rockefeller Center. "This is the primary target. Intel puts the largest number of Variants at this location. Our flyboys are going to level every building in the area. Then they're going to firebomb from here to here," he said, drawing a red line down several streets surrounding the buildings. "Any Variant that isn't killed in the first attack will be cooked in the second."

"Hell yeah," Sergeant Valdez grunted.

"The wind is blowing to the northwest, which should keep smoke to a minimum," Gates added. He glanced up and said, "We probably won't be able to get much farther than Avenue of the Americas. This is where I expect the most resistance. We'll clear any surviving hostiles and then move south to the intersection at West Forty-Second Street."

Gates circled the New York Public Library. "We've seen a lot of Variant activity around this entire area. This is where we'll set up our FOB. I want all strike teams to secure the Bank of America Tower and take up position there. It has the best vantage of the area. Command does not want the public library destroyed if at all possible. Something about some historic bullshit, but I guess when the world ends, you want to save whatever you can."

"So we won't have air support?" Beckham asked.

Gates looked up from the map and said, "Only if absolutely necessary. I'm putting my men before books, so don't worry too much about that."

Several chuckles followed the lieutenant's words, but Beckham didn't miss the man's eyes flicking to meet Jensen's, as if asking for his approval. The commander's face remained set, his jaw chomping on the wad of tobacco. Beckham didn't so much as crack a smile either. If he was in charge, he would level the library and every other location where the Variants were spotted. He was happy to see Jensen seemed to be thinking the same thing.

"What kind of numbers are we expecting?" Jensen asked. He rolled up his sleeves and crossed his arms.

"Command put the numbers at around a couple thousand but told us that there might be more," Gates said, again studying Jensen for a reaction.

He didn't reply. Instead he bent over the table, pretending to be deep in thought. "That's odd," he said. "Our projections put them much higher."

Gates removed his glasses again and placed them on the map. "Sir?"

Jensen stepped away from the table and cleared his throat. "Doctor Lovato, the scientist who designed VariantX9H9—heard of her?"

Gates nodded. "Of course, sir."

"Well, she claims there should be up to two million Variants throughout the five boroughs and beyond."

"Impossible," Gates said, shaking his head.

Jensen shrugged. "Maybe. But everyone thought the spread of the hemorrhage virus was impossible too."

Beckham hung back as Jensen worked his magic. He knew exactly what the man was doing.

"If that's true, then Central Command is sending us to our graves," Gates stated, his eyes hardening.

"*If* it's true, of course," Jensen replied. "How many men did you say First Platoon has?"

"Thirty-two. Plus your men, which puts us just shy of sixty."

"I can see why you're glad to have us here, then," Jensen said. "If Doctor Lovato is right—and she has been about most everything so far—then you're going to need every single one of us."

Gates's shoulders sagged, and he reached up to massage his temples. It was a look Beckham had seen before, the look of a commander who had shoddy intel but had to proceed with a mission regardless.

Outside, the diesel engine of one of the Bradleys snorted, telling Beckham it was time to start moving.

Gates checked his watch as a rumble shook the tent. "Right on time," he said, moving away from the table. "Follow me. I think you'll want to see this."

Beckham and the others filed out of the tent just in time to watch a squadron of F-18 Super Hornets screaming over the city. His blood tingled at the growl of the fighters. It was the most reassuring noise he'd heard all morning. He counted six of the black dots as they roared through the storm clouds and vanished. A second later the jets reappeared. Every man and woman on Pier 86 stopped what they were doing and followed the planes as they swooped through the city and released their payloads.

The ground vibrated as the bombs and missiles found their targets, deafening explosions drowning out the cheers and shouts from the marines standing on the dock. Beckham's ears popped. The vacuum from the blasts sucked away the air. Rain beat down on his helmet, and he squinted to see the explosions.

"Incoming!" yelled a marine on top of one of the Bradleys.

Everyone dropped to the ground and covered their eyes to prepare for the shock wave. The gust of smoke and heat broke across the pier. The heat from the explosions burned Beckham's exposed skin, the wind so powerful it swept up the tent and sent it sailing.

Even blocks away, the aftershock was enough to disorient the most experienced soldiers, including Beckham. Shaking his head, he rose to his feet. Flames licked the sky, creating crimson skyscrapers. He pulled his scarf over his mouth and nose in preparation for the incoming smells of burning rubber, charred metal, and the awful stench of burned corpses, mixed in with the sour scent of the Variants.

"We start moving in fifteen," Gates yelled. He walked back to the now exposed command post, barking orders at staff scrambling to collect equipment toppled by the shock wave.

Beckham checked the deck for Horn and the others. His team waited near a crate of ammunition.

"Need some grenades?" Horn asked. He reached in and grabbed several, clipping them to the only real estate left on his vest.

Another detonation in the distance rocked the concrete.

Beckham reached into the box and pulled out two grenades. "Chow, you're going to be on point. Jinx, you got rear guard. Timbo, Ryan, you make sure nothing sneaks up on us from above and to the left. Horn, you're with me on the right."

The rain let up, now just a drizzle. Beckham clipped both grenades to his vest and considered a few words to get the team riled up for action, but the stone-cold looks they all wore told him they were ready. Gripping his M4, he eyed the swirling smoke one more time and wondered exactly what the hell they were about to walk into. He didn't trust Command's long-term strategy, but there wasn't anything he could do about it now.

Eyeing his team, he said, "You all heard the man. We move in fifteen."

14

Hours had passed since Beckham and the other men left for New York City. Kate stood on the concrete steps of Building 1 with Ellis, her chaotic thoughts threatening to take over. She'd left Jenny and Tasha with a technician named Leila, who'd offered to look after the girls while Kate spent a few hours working.

The whipping of helicopter blades pulled Kate's attention to the skyline. A Chinook raced toward the island and then hovered over the tarmac as the pilot waited for permission to land.

Two Medical Corps guards shouldered their rifles at the bottom of the steps. One of them glanced up at Kate and Ellis.

"Doctors, you better go inside," he said.

Kate crossed her arms. She needed to see this—to remember what they were dealing with.

A few minutes later, the bird touched down. The doors opened, and six soldiers in what looked like riot gear emerged. Working together, they pulled three stretchers from the belly of the chopper, split into two-man teams, and then hurried across the runway.

Kate couldn't see much, but she could glimpse the Variants. They were held down by blue restraints that covered their arms, chests, and legs. She watched with fascination as the teams moved closer. A Medical Corps guard met them at the edge of the tarmac and pointed toward Building 4.

"Well, look at that," a voice said from the doorway. Kate hadn't heard Major Smith open the doors. He stepped outside and joined Kate and Ellis on the stoop. He chuckled and said, "I hope their passengers are sleeping."

"I'm sure they used tranquilizers on them," Kate replied. She took a step back as the men approached Building 1. She stared at the stretchers, studying each one. The creatures' mouths were covered with a metal contraption that looked a lot like the grille of a football helmet.

The soldier helping carry the first stretcher looked up at her, his eyes hidden behind a mirrored visor. Before he could react, the Variant he was helping carry shook in its restraints, jerking from side to side.

"Shit! Put it down!" one of the men screamed.

The stretcher toppled over, and the Variant fell face first onto the ground. The other soldiers put down their loads and retreated from the squirming creature. They formed a perimeter and then aimed their weapons.

For a moment, the men just stood there, waiting, as though none of them knew what to do. The Variant fought against its bands, twisting and shaking. It let out a muffled shriek that made Kate's heart leap.

She covered her ears and backed toward the door of Building 1. As her back hit the metal, a gunshot rang out. One of the Medical Corps guards on the bottom step loped forward, emptying his magazine into the creature. Blood pooled around the Variant as its body was riddled with bullets.

"Let's go," Smith ordered, suddenly very stern. "You don't need to see this." He opened the door and gestured for Kate and Ellis to go inside. When they were clear, he shut the door. Kate watched the major through the glass windows as he pulled a pistol and ran down the steps.

"Shit," Ellis said. "That's one less specimen to study." He turned away from the window and walked toward the hallway.

"One less specimen?" Kate replied, her arms trembling. She focused on her breathing and her pounding heart. Ellis had seen a lot over the past month—they both had—but his lack of emotion bothered her.

Ellis stopped, and then walked back to her when he finally realized what she was thinking. "Sorry, Kate. I know that must have been hard for you to see after what happened."

She held up a hand. "I'm fine."

He nodded and twisted his lips to the side, as though he wanted to say something else. Then he continued down the corridor.

Thirty minutes later, Kate was holding out her arms, waiting for Ellis to zip up the back of her suit. Her racing heart had finally calmed to a normal pace.

"There you go," he said. "You sure you're ready for this?"

Kate shrugged and then helped secure Ellis's suit. "We have no choice. It's the only way we're going to learn more about them. I just hope to God they don't get out again."

She thought of what Gibson had said about Lieutenant Brett as she finished assisting Ellis. *He was an animal. Rabid, deadly, and forever changed. We couldn't control him.*

The words were disturbing, but there was no turning back. She zipped up Ellis, patted his shoulder, and then checked her own suit one last time. When they were ready, she held her key card over the security panel.

The doors whispered open to the lab where she'd spent so many hours over the past couple weeks. White light from the overhead fluorescent lights blinded her for a brief moment. When her vision cleared, she saw her pale reflection in the glass wall across the room. She looked past it and watched the scientists and technicians in CBRN suits moving back and forth in their individual chambers.

The dead Variant outside, the motion, the bright lights, the chill of the oxygen filling her suit—it was all too much. Kate could hear Ellis's breathing behind her. Then there was a hand on her shoulder.

"You okay, Kate?" he asked.

She didn't reply. Her mind was a scrambled mess. She was overwhelmed with flashbacks of the horror she'd seen since the outbreak began, all of them as vivid as if she were watching a video of her past. There was Dr. Allen holding his injured arm, back in Atlanta. She heard his final words before he jumped from the chopper: *In order to kill a monster, you'll have to create one.*

She pictured the twisted face of her brother, Javier, with bloody saliva webbed across his mouth. Although she hadn't seen him succumb to the virus, she had heard his agony on the phone just before she lost him forever. Kate shivered. She wanted the thoughts to stop—for everything to just stop.

"Kate," Ellis said.

Closing her eyes, she took a deep breath and let the anxiety in her slowly diminish.

"Sorry," she said. "I'm okay. Just needed a minute." She crossed the lab and paused behind Cindy's station. "Do we have a live feed?"

"Yup," Cindy replied, swiveling the right-hand monitor in their direction. "Both specimens are in their cells and are coming to. Check this out."

The display showed a video of Holding Cell 14. A female Variant huddled in a corner of the room, away from the bulk of the bright light. She clawed the wall sluggishly. The tranquilizer still hadn't worn off completely.

"Never seen one of them do that before," Cindy said. "Interesting." She keyed in several strokes, and the video camera zoomed in on the creature.

"Check out her arms," Ellis said. "Are we seeing more of the epigenetic changes?"

Blue veins bulged from exposed skin—not the thin blue ones she'd seen before; these were thicker and more wormlike. Kate had never seen a Variant with such pronounced veins.

"Can you get someone on the comm?" Ellis asked. "See if they can redirect the lights."

Cindy typed in the request and brought up a feed to the lead guard at the isolation facility. The face of a young soldier filled the left screen.

"Station Two," he said.

"Yeah, this is Doctor Pat Ellis. We're watching the feed to Cell Fourteen and are having a hard time seeing anything."

"Our instructions are to keep the lights dimmed," the man said.

"I'm overriding that," Kate said. "You can tell your CO."

The man shrugged. "She ain't going to like it..."

A few seconds later, the right-hand monitor brightened as the fluorescent lights intensified inside the cell. The creature let out a pained shriek, clawing at the light. Hunching down into a ball, the female covered her eyes with an arm, her body trembling.

"That good?" the guard asked.

"Yeah," Kate mumbled, captivated by what she was seeing.

"Anything else I can do for you, Doctors?"

"Nope, that's it," Cindy replied.

"They must be forming a sensitivity to light," Ellis said.

The creature peered up through a gap between her arms, focusing on the camera. Kate gasped as the subject's vertical slits widened, focusing, as if she could see through the camera into their lab.

Kate looked away and tapped Ellis on his arm. "Did you see anything in the report we received from Central Command about a response to UV radiation or bright lights?"

Ellis shook his helmet without taking his eyes off the monitor. "Could be another change we haven't seen before."

With a nod, Kate said, "Cindy, bring up the feed of the other specimen."

With a few clicks, the woman's gloved fingers moved from the mouse to the keyboard and then back to the table, tapping nervously. "This is Cell Fifteen."

The monitor showed another female patient on the floor. Agonized shrieks filled the audio as she contorted her body. She fell to her stomach, squirmed, and then clambered onto all fours. Her arms and legs cracked and popped as she scuffled forward and launched herself onto the wall with a screech that hurt Kate's ears.

"God, turn the volume down," Kate said, cupping her hands over her helmet.

"Sure, sorry about that," Cindy replied.

The audio feed cut out, and Kate could hear only her own breathing. The Variant clawed at the lights and then dropped to the ground and darted to a corner, shielding its eyes with a naked arm.

"This is amazing," Ellis said. "The sensitivity to light is remarkable. I think we finally found a weakness!"

"What's causing it?" Cindy asked. "Do you think it was from the Ebola infection? The virus could have damaged their optical nerves."

"No," Kate said firmly. "These Variants have all recovered from the virus. What we are witnessing is a result of the epigenetic changes from the nanostructures found in VX-99."

In the blink of an eye, the creature hunched, coiled, and sprang toward the ceiling. She grabbed at the bank of lights and tore them out of the ceiling. She hung there, swinging back and forth by an electrical cord before it snapped and both creature and lights crashed to the floor. Glass shattered into hundreds of tiny fragments.

The Variant darted into a dark corner and Kate lost sight of her. Her heart leaped. She tried to convince herself the creatures couldn't get out again, that they were locked away in cells that would hold them this time. But deep down, she wasn't convinced. The longer she watched, the more she realized how insane holding them on the island was. They'd gotten out before. What would prevent them from doing so again?

A flash of motion on the monitor caught her attention. The female Variant crawled out of the shadows and crouched at the border between light and darkness. Tilting her head, she sniffed the air and puckered her lips. Her pupils dilated, refocusing in the darkness.

"What's it doing?" Ellis asked.

"Hunting," Kate whispered. She brought a hand to her helmeted head, an epiphany hitting her so hard she could hardly breathe. "My God—I was right."

Cindy rose from her stool. "About what, Kate? I'm not following."

Kate hurried toward the comm panel to call Major Smith, talking as she moved. "The Variants have acquired a sensitivity to UV rays, and they've developed night vision to compensate." She turned and searched her colleagues' eyes. They still didn't understand.

"The Variants *have* gone underground," she said. "Beckham and his team are heading into a trap!"

Fifteen minutes turned into four hours. Lieutenant Gates ordered 1st Platoon to stand by and wait for the smoke to clear. Command had picked a really shitty day to launch Operation Liberty; the wind had shifted almost immediately after the bombing, carpeting 1st Platoon's path with smoke. Beckham was surprised Command hadn't delayed the mission further, but General Kennor had a hard-on for killing the Variants. He wanted his streets back and he wanted them back yesterday.

The wait provided every man on the pier the chance to soak in the rain and the apocalyptic view of Manhattan. Black plumes blew across the skyline, rising from a smoking crater of rubble where the buildings of Rockefeller Center had towered just hours before.

When the armored vehicles finally choked to life, the morning had turned to afternoon. "Move out," Gates yelled. He climbed inside one of the Humvees marked with a medical cross and slammed the armored door.

Horn huffed as they followed the convoy off the pier. "Man, I told my girls monsters weren't real." He shook his head and then regarded Beckham with a wolfish grin. "Doesn't matter. We're going to kill all of 'em."

"Don't be overconfident. That's killed plenty of men before," Beckham said sternly. "And wipe that grin off your face."

Horn pulled his skull bandanna over his nose. "Just gearing up for the mission, boss."

"This isn't Fallujah or Sudan," Beckham said. His

knife hand shook, his fingers trembling. He didn't want to be back out here again; he didn't want to be leading these men to open graves. And now was *not* the time to fuck around. Horn should know better.

"Hold up," Beckham said. He waited for Jinx, Chow, Timbo, and Ryan. They formed a circle at the edge of the pier, a phantom border separating them from the decay and death of Manhattan. Beckham caught a glimpse of Jensen leading his team across the street. His posture reflected that of a combat vet, but Beckham didn't remember the man ever mentioning having seen action.

Turning back to his men, Beckham said, "You all know that we could very well be walking into a trap. Those things could be anywhere, and those Bradleys," he said, pointing, "they only have so much ammo."

He studied each face, stopping on Horn's. The man's eyes were focused above his bandanna. That was the Horn he knew; that was the man he needed right now.

The sound of metal crunching and grinding announced Operation Liberty was officially under way. Marines rushed past Team Ghost, their helmets bobbing up and down as they followed the armored vehicles into the street.

"Let's move," Beckham said. "Straight line. Combat intervals."

The cough of diesel engines, pounding of boots, and rustle of gear would have made Beckham's skin crawl on other missions. Any enemy within a square mile would hear them coming. But Operation Liberty wasn't about stealth. It was about firepower. General Kennor had made sure of that.

The Bradleys groaned and snorted as they smashed abandoned vehicles out of their path. Beckham pulled his scarf up over his nose and braved the street. The moment he stepped off the pier, the overwhelming smell of decomposing bodies and waste penetrated the cotton. He stifled a gag and secured the scarf with a tight knot.

Everywhere around him marines removed gas masks from their rucksacks. Beckham ordered his team to do the same. Across the street to his left, Timbo and Ryan were one step ahead of him and had their masks in hand already.

The convoy inched forward, passing hundreds of bloated corpses lining the street. They had all bled out from Kate's bioweapon, and crusted blood clung to the sidewalk like red moss. Most of the marines didn't seem to notice, but a few of them slowed for a better look. One man bent over, pulling his gas mask away from his mouth to puke.

A green recruit, Beckham thought. He checked the other marines, one by one, wondering exactly how many of them had even made it through training before the outbreak hit. Judging by their posture and movements, he decided the most action they'd probably seen was at the shooting range.

First Platoon was a ragtag group after all, cobbled together from what was left of the Marine Corps. He'd heard the casualty reports from Operation Reaper and should have known. He just hoped these men knew to stay out of his line of fire when shit hit the fan.

Beckham tightened his grip on his weapon, his biceps flexing as he kept the muzzle at a 45-degree angle. The gas mask provided two narrow oval views of the post-apocalyptic world they were venturing into. He told himself not to think of this as New York City—it was like any other enemy territory, no different than Baghdad or Fallujah despite what he'd told Horn. The iconic buildings of one of the world's favorite cities were dark, a grim reminder that New York was really gone. And it was probably never coming back.

"Pretty quiet," Horn said.

"For now," Beckham replied.

The convoy moved slowly, plowing through the graveyard of empty cars one at a time. The vehicle commanders stood inside the hatches of the Bradleys, scoping the road with binoculars behind the TOW launchers.

The Hudson River snaked along on their left, the calm waters devoid of boats. There were no tourists walking along the road, staring out over the polluted harbor or the seagulls perched on piers. Billboards jutted off the roofs of buildings on the right side of the street, displaying ads featuring Armani models and rap stars.

Two blocks in, the wind shifted again. A cloud of black smoke crossed the path of the convoy. The Bradleys groaned to a stop, and the Humvees parked a few feet behind them. Marines fell into line behind the armored vehicle. They waited for several minutes before Beckham's earpiece crackled to life.

"Command has ordered us to continue the mission through the smoke." It was Lieutenant Gates, and he sounded irritated.

The transmission ended. Beckham glanced over his shoulder and signaled Team Ghost forward. The vehicles disappeared into the black wall, swallowed as if they had entered a portal to another dimension.

"I don't like this," Horn said.

Beckham watched the swirling cloud. "Me neither, but the smoke messes with the Variants' senses."

"Messes with ours too," Horn said. "And remember what Kate said? Their senses are evolving or something." Horn adjusted his gas mask with his free hand.

"Just stay focused," Beckham replied. Holding his breath as if he was about to jump into cold water, he followed the rest of 1st Platoon into the smoke. The crunch of the Bradleys' tracks guided him.

When they reached the intersection at West Fiftieth, the smoke began to dissipate. Beckham searched for the rest of his team. Timbo and Ryan had their eyes and muzzles trained on the buildings nearby. Jinx and Chow eyed the skyline. An eerie gray haze lingered over Manhattan. Somewhere out there, the Variants were hiding.

Waiting.

The Bradleys tore onto West Fiftieth Street, taking turns pushing cars to the side of the road. Beckham watched the wreckage for signs of anything unusual. A bloated corpse slumped partially out of the window of a cab. The Bradley on the left reversed and then smashed into the tail of the car, sending the dead driver flying. The body skidded across the concrete and then hit the brick wall of a building covered in graffiti and murals. Its skin burst open, peppering the artwork with gore. Beckham cringed. He jumped onto the sidewalk and hugged the brick wall lining the right side of the street.

"Where the fuck *are* those things?" Chow asked over his shoulder. He'd moved to the middle of the street a few yards ahead of Beckham and Horn's position.

Horn pointed to the skyline. "Maybe the bombers got all of 'em."

"I wouldn't count on it," Beckham said.

Three blocks in there was still no sign of the Variants or survivors. A steady rain drenched the convoy as it charged forward. The final layer of crusted red blood on the streets streamed into storm drains. It would only take a few months for Mother Nature to cleanse the city. The corpses would decay, and the rats would finish what the hemorrhage virus and Kate's bioweapon had started. New York City had a shortage of many things, but rats weren't on the list. He suspected that wouldn't change anytime soon.

Beckham kept to the sidewalk on the right side of

the road, careful not to cross in front of any windows or doors that weren't boarded up. He had his urban combat senses on now. Every nook and cranny held a potential threat. Horn followed close behind him. Jinx and Chow held their places in the middle of the street, with Jinx rotating as he walked to regularly check their six. Timbo and Ryan kept up across the street, watching high and low for contacts.

At the end of the block they reached the first high-rises, a pair of modest brick apartment buildings. The Bradley on the left smashed a Honda Civic into the front of one building, blocking the entrance—one less door the Variants could use to ambush the convoy. Beckham sidestepped the crushed Honda and continued on.

Timbo stopped down the street to stare up at the building. Beckham glanced up to see what had caught the man's attention. What he saw stopped him midstride.

A body in a CBRN suit hung halfway out a window some five floors above, its head hanging down unmoving. Dead.

Suddenly there was a blur of motion in the window behind the body. Beckham took a step back and saw a Variant latched onto the back of the man's suit, feeding.

"Contact!" he yelled. "Fifth floor, eight o'clock." It had to be a recent kill if the Variant was feeding, which meant there were others in the area.

Leaping into the street, he took up position next to Horn. The Bradleys skidded to a stop. The commander manning the TOW launcher in the turret on the left dropped back into the vehicle and secured the hatch. The M242 25-millimeter chain gun squealed as it maneuvered toward the building. Marines fanned out across the road, shouldering rifles and taking up position behind the armor of the convoy.

"Shoot it!" someone yelled.

The marine Beckham had seen puking earlier screamed, "There's another one!"

He was right. More of the creatures shot their heads out of the building's open windows to check on the fresh meat gathering outside. Dozens of Variants emerged, their lips puckering and popping.

Before Lieutenant Gates could bark a single order over the comm, half of the platoon was firing their M16s. Beckham and the rest of Team Ghost ran for cover across the street, kneeling behind a car one of the Bradleys had flipped.

The crack of automatic gunfire echoed through the city as marines emptied their magazines. Bullet casings pinged off the concrete, and wounded Variants fell to their deaths, smashing into the street with loud cracks. Back in Iraq, Beckham had learned exactly what sound a body made after falling from a tall building. These were no different. Each crunch was as loud as a shotgun going off.

The sky was raining monsters.

"Hold your fucking fire!" came a voice over the net. "Conserve your ammo!"

It was Gates, and he was too late. Most of the platoon was already feeding the building with rounds from their second magazine. Beckham checked on his own team. The men all had their weapons aimed at the high-rise, but none of them had taken a shot.

A minute later, every window in the apartment building was shattered. Bullet holes pockmarked the brick exterior. A half dozen mangled creatures lay in puddles of blood on the sidewalk and street.

When the smoke cleared, the marines gathered around the first casualty of Operation Liberty. Beckham shook his head when he saw the body. The kid who had puked earlier and then prematurely started the Fourth of July celebration was lying facedown on the sidewalk. A panel of broken glass had sliced him nearly in two.

Sergeant Valdez went to work a few feet away, smacking helmets. He swooped down to check the man's lifeless body. He then pointed at the corpse and said, "This is what happens when you aren't careful! From here on out, no one fires unless I give the fucking order!"

Valdez checked the dead marine one more time before storming off toward the Bradleys. The sound of the engines reclaimed the afternoon, and the panic of the first battle faded. Marines fell back into position, some of them looking sheepishly at the ground, knowing they'd just participated in Operation Overkill.

The Bradleys advanced into the next intersection, and Beckham motioned his men forward. He passed the body of the dead marine, pausing briefly to say a short prayer. Two PFCs were standing over the kid. They watched Beckham pass and then glanced back down at their friend.

"He never even finished his training," Beckham heard one of them say.

"Neither did I," the other marine said.

15

Kate trembled with anger.

"What do you mean you can't get a message through?" she asked.

"Doctor, I assure you, Command is fully aware of the Variant threat in Manhattan. First Platoon is well equipped to deal with it too," Major Smith said from behind the glass.

"Bullshit," Kate replied. "The Variants have gone underground. There are hundreds of thousands, if not more of them, beneath the city!"

Ellis put a hand on Kate's shoulder, but she pulled away.

"Major, all you have to do is get on the phone and inform Central Command. Tell them I told you. Tell them the Variants are sensitive to UV rays. They've developed night vision, or something close to it, and I can guarantee you that they've gone underground. New York is riddled with sewers, storm drains, and utility tunnels, not to mention the subways. It's a *trap*."

"You are one hundred percent certain of this?" Smith asked.

"Yes!" Kate said, her voice just shy of a shout.

Smith nodded. "I'll see what I can do, but I can already tell you General Kennor is plowing full steam ahead."

Kate sucked in a breath and said, "There are a lot of lives at stake. You don't want that on your conscience, do you?"

The major paused at that, but then continued walking.

Kate felt a hand on her shoulder again.

"I'm sorry, Kate," Ellis said.

She exhaled and strode over to Cindy's station. "Talk to me," she said, filing away the conversation with Smith and her concerns about Beckham and the others.

Cindy avoided eye contact, her hand tapping nervously on the desk. "We just received new test results from Central Command. They sent us a video from a lab in Colorado."

"Did they find the same thing as us?" Kate asked.

Cindy nodded. "The creatures are evolving at an incredible rate. But so far the other teams haven't found any weakness besides the sensitivity to light."

Kate gritted her teeth. When the video feed came up on the screen, she saw Cindy was right. The creatures had transformed even further. These new specimens hardly looked human.

The video feed showed a female subject that barely resembled her former self. Wisps of thin blond hair hung off her pale scalp. Veins bulged from her nearly translucent flesh. And her face had gone through a grotesque alteration, her lips fully developed into what could only be called a sucker. If it weren't for the specimen's breasts, Kate wouldn't have known the patient was female.

Ellis broke the silence as the team stared at the monitors. "Technicians here are reporting the same thing with our two subjects."

Kate sucked in a cold breath of filtered air.

"All of the specimens are expressing traits of species that make them excellent predators," Cindy added.

"The flexible limbs and joints, the microscopic setae on the skin, the nails, the increased cones and rods in the eyes, and the regeneration of cochlear hair cells in the ear," said Ellis enthusiastically. "Think about how far back those genes could go. We're talking primordial ooze here. I remember reading about an extinct mammal that—"

"I know, you've already told us this," Kate said. "But unless you can tell me exactly which genes of the twenty thousand-plus that make up our genetic code cause this, then I'm not interested."

Ellis's cheeks flared red behind his visor and he turned back to his monitor. "Well, I may not be able to tell you exactly which genes, but looks like the first toxicology results finally came through for the blood samples we sent them yesterday. Give me a second to read these."

Kate raised a brow and joined him at his station. She was freezing and she desperately wished she could rub her eyes, but her chilly space suit made that impossible.

"Interesting," Ellis said after a few minutes. "Toxicology found several vital pieces of information. First off, the nanostructures of VX-99 are virtually gone in our new batch of Variants. Seems like Doctor Medford may have created his untraceable bioweapon after all."

Kate didn't want to think about Medford, or Gibson. "Keep going."

With a nod, Ellis continued. "Second—and this is fascinating—histology reports show the Variants seem to have lost the taste receptors for sweetness. They are no longer expressing the amino acids responsible. But like cats, they seem to have developed taste receptors for adenosine triphosphate, a molecule responsible for energy found in all living cells."

"So that explains their desire for flesh," Cindy said. "They've been reprogrammed as carnivores."

"Yup," Ellis replied. "Plus endocrine cell signaling is causing an increase in the stem cell population within dermal and bone marrow tissues."

Kate squinted. "So we can explain their healing ability and their affinity for the protein in meat."

"Correct," Ellis replied.

"So what?" Kate asked, irritated.

"Think about it, Kate," Ellis said. There was a note of almost manic enthusiasm in his voice. He pulled up a stool next to her. "These changes are occurring at a cellular level and are happening very quickly. The Variants aren't just evolving; they're adapting. All of the epigenetic changes we've seen are just part of the overall picture."

Kate nodded, once, then twice, then more rapidly. Ellis was right. The changes they were seeing were the result of something they couldn't see with their naked eye.

"Can't we find a way to turn those genes off?" Cindy asked. "I mean, wouldn't—"

Ellis cut in. "I've thought of that. Which is one reason I'm so interested in which genes the VX-99 nanostructures activated," he said, glancing at Kate. "Epigenetic changes have been reversed before, but we're talking about single cell cultures and turning off one easily identified gene. Changes at this scale and magnitude?" Ellis shook his head. "I'm not even sure if that's possible. It's simply beyond the realm of modern medicine. It would be like trying to devolve a human back into an ape."

"I've said it before: There's *no* bringing these things back," said Kate. "The Variants have evolved into an entirely new species. We have to focus on killing them, not treating them."

"Contact!"

Beckham waited for gunfire that never came. The convoy rolled to a stop in front of the wall of haze.

A large man in a CBRN suit emerged from the swirling gray. He walked past the armored vehicles and then stopped in front of the Humvees. Marines surrounded him with shouldered rifles.

Beckham balled his hand into a fist, and his men halted.

The man stumbled away from the vehicles with Sergeant Valdez shadowing him. "Stop where you are!"

Whoever he was, he kept walking aimlessly down the street as though he hadn't even heard the sergeant.

"What the fuck is wrong with this guy?" Horn asked.

"I have no idea," Beckham replied. He raised his M4. "Stop or we open fire!"

Beckham's earpiece flared to life. "Strike teams, don't let this guy escape. Proceed with caution."

With his muzzle angled at the concrete, Beckham approached the man. They were only about twenty yards apart now. "Sir, we aren't going to hurt you. Please, stop and put your hands above your head."

The man continued walking, unfazed by the small army surrounding him.

"We're here to help you," Beckham said, letting his M4 hang from his chest. He raised a hand. "Please, sir, we're here to help."

The man suddenly froze. He tilted his filthy, bloodstained visor and stared at Beckham. Then he wiped a sleeve across the pane of his helmet, revealing a freckled face. He stared back, unblinking.

"What's your name?" Beckham asked.

The man flinched and said, "You can't help me." He turned and scanned the marines surrounding him. "None of you can help me!"

That was good, Beckham thought. At least he had the guy talking now. "Calm down, man," Beckham said. "What's your name?"

His hands trembling, he looked at Beckham and said, "Rex."

"You a doctor?"

The man looked down at his suit as if he hadn't realized he was wearing it. "No, I was a firefighter before..." He paused, his gaze shifting to the skyline.

"Are you by yourself? Where is everyone else?"

The man let out a nervous chuckle. "Meg thought we could get out of the city. So did Jed. They thought we could run..."

"Rex, tell me where they are," Beckham said. "The other survivors."

"Jed's dead," Rex said. Then he pointed straight down at the pavement. "And Meg's down there with everyone else that tried to escape."

Seven hours into Operation Liberty, 1st Platoon was finally closing in on their first objective. The convoy crawled at a turtle's pace; the silhouettes of marines followed the armored beasts like ghosts. Dust and ash rained down from the sky, mixing with a light drizzle. Everything was covered with a layer of gray.

Rushing wind hit Beckham when he stepped into the intersection of Broadway and West Fiftieth. He stood there in the slush of ash and dirt, taking in the view. No matter how many times he told himself this was no longer New York City, his surroundings still awed him.

A billboard for a play that would never be seen again hung at an angle from the building next to an Applebee's restaurant. Up ahead, Fiftieth Street was choked with charred vehicles and burned, mangled corpses. The contents of food vendors' carts littered the concrete. Every window in sight was shattered. The air force had used firebombs designed to scorch everything in their path. He tried to picture what it must have been like hours earlier when the jets swooped in. The incendiary bombs would have detonated at street level before spreading to the surrounding buildings, blowing out every window and burning every square inch. The military had used the same strategy during Operation Reaper in an attempt to stop the spread of the infection.

It hadn't worked then, and Beckham was starting to wonder if it had worked now. The lone survivor they'd picked up could tell them more—if he was talking. The man was in the troop hold of one of the Bradleys, a medic tending to him. He hadn't said a word since they put him inside. Maybe the man was crazy, or maybe there were survivors underground. Either way, 1st Platoon's main objective was to clear the area of Variants and set up a base, not to explore the subways and sewers.

Beckham flinched as a strong hand patted him on the shoulder. Horn walked past, his M249 angled at the dark entrance to an underground parking ramp a few feet away.

"You good, boss?"

"Yeah, Big Horn. I'm good."

They walked side by side toward the target zone. Beckham kept his team on the rear guard, hugging the walls of nearby buildings and keeping an eye on the broken windows above. Jensen's strike team and the other teams from Plum Island had the same idea. They kept to the sidewalk rather than walking through the middle of the street like most of 1st Platoon. There wasn't any danger of being caught out in the open, but Beckham still liked the comfort of a solid wall at his back.

The convoy slowed a block away from Avenue of the Americas. Beckham scoped the skyline with his M4. A hole in the darkening sky spilled rays of light over the city. He still wasn't sure why, but the Variants seemed to avoid the sunlight. Maybe it was their pale skin, or some of those epigenetic changes that Kate hadn't explained. He didn't really give a shit either way. As long as they weren't setting up an ambush, they could hide all they wanted.

The vehicles rolled to a stop in the middle of the intersection at Seventh Avenue. Lieutenant Gates jumped out of his Humvee and joined Sergeant Valdez on the back of a Bradley. The lieutenant used a pair of binoculars to scope the street as he spoke with the vehicle commander in the hatch.

Horn stopped next to Beckham. "What's going on?"

"Not sure. I'll check it out," Beckham replied. The illustrations on the side of the Bradleys caught Beckham's eye as he jogged ahead. The armor on the left had the name BLACK REAPER painted in red on the vehicle's sandy-brown hull. The Bradley on the right bore an image of a snorting buffalo, and above that the words STEAM BEAST. These marines had some impressive artistic skills.

Several of the men watched him curiously as he passed, their eyes gravitating to his weapon. Their nods told him they were happy to have Team Ghost along on this operation.

Gates was already climbing off the track when Beckham arrived.

"Problem, Lieutenant?" Beckham asked.

Before he could answer, Sergeant Valdez jumped onto the concrete. "Yeah, there's a fucking problem." He raised a muscular arm and pointed over Steam Beast at the intersection with Seventh Avenue. "We got a clogged artery ahead that would make a heart surgeon shit a brick."

"Lots of dead soldiers up there," Gates said. "Looks like some of the vehicles from Operation Reaper."

Beckham stood on his toes and caught a glimpse of a fuel tanker turned on its side. By some miracle, it hadn't exploded. The entire street had been spared from the firebombs.

"Any way around?" Beckham asked.

Gates shook his head. "We could go back the way we came, but satellite imagery showed the other streets were worse."

"Someone at Command really fucked this up good," Valdez snapped. "How they miss an overturned tanker must be above my pay grade."

Beckham ignored the sergeant and climbed onto the back of the track. Valdez was right; the road ahead was a clusterfuck of abandoned military vehicles and a ton of bodies. Marines were sprawled out across the sidewalks, draped over the hoods of Humvees. Some were hanging from turrets. All had been torn to shreds by the Variants.

The track commander regarded Beckham from the hatch. "Never seen nothin' like this," he said.

Beckham swung his M4 to eye level and scoped the road. The tanker lay at a 45-degree angle across the street and sidewalk. There was a short gap on the right side. It would be a tight fit, but maybe they could get around. He swept the gun downward and checked for any sign of oil. He saw something dark on the ground, but it wasn't gasoline—it was blood from the fallen marines.

"Lieutenant," Beckham said. "Can you come up here for a second, sir?"

The officer climbed onto the rear of the track and joined Beckham near the hatch. "Take a look, sir. One o'clock." He let his weapon fall against his chest and pointed toward the curb.

Gates nodded and turned to the vehicle commander. "Think you can push those Humvees to the side and then sneak around the tanker?"

The commander shook his head and then let out a long sigh. "I don't know, sir. We'd have to go in single file. And if we clip the truck..." He used both hands to mimic an explosion.

Gates shifted his gaze from Beckham to Valdez as though he was looking for reassurance. *Well, I'll be damned*, Beckham thought. The puking marine who had died a few blocks back wasn't the only greenhorn in the platoon. Gates's inability to make this simple decision told Beckham that this was his first mission at the helm.

"Get the platoon into a line. Have every marine buddy up. We start with Steam Beast," Beckham said, patting the track with a glove.

He searched the vehicle commander's eyes. There was terror there. Despair. The man fidgeted with his helmet and gas mask before nodding.

"What's your name?" Beckham asked, pretending he hadn't already glanced at the man's tag.

"Matthews," the commander replied. Even with the breathing apparatus, he sounded terribly young. He couldn't have been more than twenty-two.

"Matthews," Beckham said, "a lot of marines are counting on you today, and I know you're scared. Shit, I'm scared too, and this is my fourth time in the field since the outbreak. But I've seen your maneuvers. I've been watching. You were born to command this track."

Matthews cracked a half smile and nodded twice. They were confident nods. Beckham's work was done.

"You got this," he said, patting the man on the shoulder. He turned and followed Gates. Valdez was waiting on the concrete, his right hand massaging the scar on his cheek.

"Get the men in line," Gates said. "Have them buddy up. Matthews is going to clear us a path. Then we send the rest of the convoy around the tanker in single file."

Valdez dipped his head toward Beckham and winked. The gesture took him off guard, but it told him that the sergeant's behavior toward Gates earlier wasn't just an act. The man was probably the most experienced marine out here. And that experience was *exactly* what 1st Platoon needed.

Beckham cracked a half smile when he saw Team Ghost waiting for him at the end of the street. They reminded him that maybe 1st Platoon had a chance after all. Glancing up, he saw his theory was about to be tested. An armada of storm clouds was rolling into the city, and in minutes they would carpet Manhattan with shadows.

Kate's brain felt as if it had melted inside her head. The only neurons firing were the ones that pulled her back to the night she'd spent with Beckham. She tried to remember what they'd learned about the Variants, replaying her conversations with Cindy and Ellis. The Variants were evolving. Check. The Variants were a new species. Check.

The list of their strengths was extensive, but they seemed to have only a few weaknesses. Their sensitivity to light wasn't even really a weakness. The sun didn't kill the creatures; they just really didn't like it. They weren't vampires. After wrapping a four-hour session in the lab, Kate was relieved to spend some time away from science. She picked up Tasha and Jenny from Leila and swung by the medical ward to pick up Riley. He was waiting in the hallway, doing wheelies in his chair.

"Hey, we're going to be late," he said when he saw Kate. "I think we told Fitz 1800."

"Yeah, it's only..." Kate glanced at her watch. It was already after six. "Crap."

They hurried to the mess hall and found Fitz waiting with his back against a wall. He smiled when he saw them.

"Sorry we're late," Kate said. "Lost track of time."

Fitz shrugged. "Not like I have any place to be—not yet anyway. Still no orders."

Kate felt a tug on her sleeve. Jenny was looking up at her, her eyes dull and sad. "Is my daddy coming back soon?"

When Kate didn't reply, Riley jumped in. "He's going to be back soon, honey. Reed and him are just out on a mission to help people."

"Okay," Jenny whispered.

"I'm hungry," Tasha chimed in.

"Well, let's get some food," Kate said, leading the girls toward the end of the line. The survivors from Fort Bragg had added significantly to the island's growing population. The sight of other children was reassuring: To Kate it meant that humanity still had hope, a fighting chance. But she missed her own family. Grabbing two trays, Kate moved up to the counter with Tasha and Jenny.

"What do you girls want to eat? Anything you want," Kate said.

A middle-aged cook wearing a backward New York Yankees hat flashed her an incredulous look. "Sorry, Doc, but tonight we're only serving soup."

Kate examined the empty buffet. She was so lost in her own thoughts she'd failed to see the single-serving bowl of soup the man was handing each person. No wonder the line was moving faster than normal.

"Soup it is," she said, forcing a smile. She carefully passed bowls to Tasha and Jenny. Kate refused the third bowl. "I'm not hungry. Better save it for the others."

"Suit yourself," the man replied, handing the bowl to Fitz.

"You should eat, Kate," Riley said. He cradled a bowl of soup on his lap as he wheeled forward.

"I'll be fine," she replied.

They found an empty table, and Riley maneuvered his wheelchair under the opening at the end. Tasha and Jenny sat next to Kate, grabbing their spoons and attacking their soup as though they hadn't eaten in days.

Most of the soldiers and support staff around them ate in silence. Small talk seemed unimportant. With supplies dwindling, conversations had shifted from lost loved ones to concerns about food and resources. Kate found herself staring at Tasha and Jenny as they lapped up the broth in front of them. Their mother's death and the horrors they had witnessed at Fort Bragg would be with them the rest of their lives.

Sighing, Kate broke the silence. "You said you didn't get assigned a post. Is that right, Fitz?"

He nodded. "Not yet. Apparently things are backed up at the administration building with all of the new refugees."

Riley glanced up from his bowl. "Did you tell them you're a bull's-eye waiting to happen?"

Fitz grinned. "Yeah, I mentioned it."

"I bet you could outshoot most of the turds on this island."

"Not my daddy," Tasha said in a very matter-of-fact tone.

"He'd give me a run for my money," Fitz said.

"What's that mean?" Jenny asked.

Both men chuckled, prompting several looks from the adjacent tables. Laughter was rare these days.

16

"Clear a fucking path!" Valdez yelled as Steam Beast jolted forward. "And maintain a straight line. Keep your intervals. Five meters apart!"

The marines who had clustered fanned out.

"Master Sergeant, what the hell did you say back there?" Jensen asked. He held his gas mask in a hand and spat brown juice on the ground.

Beckham shrugged. "Just gave the track commander a kick in the ass."

Jensen snorted a laugh and then slipped his mask back over his face. "I'm just waiting for a gigantic fireball when that tanker goes up in flames."

"And I'm just waiting for the Variants to show up," Beckham replied, watching swollen gray clouds roll into the city.

The lingering smoke pressed in on 1st Platoon. Helmets gravitated toward the sky as a giant shadow covered Manhattan. Within seconds, visibility was limited to a few hundred yards, and it was diminishing with every beat.

Jensen shouted, "Hold your positions. Stay sharp!"

The scraping of metal continued. Steam Beast worked on the first Humvee, pushing the truck toward the sidewalk. A bloated corpse in the turret slid over the windshield and disappeared from sight. Bones crunched.

A few agonizing minutes later, the Bradley successfully cleared the abandoned vehicles to the side of the road. That left the gap between the tanker and the building on the right. Beckham scoped the pass again. The street seemed smaller now, just a sliver of road and sidewalk. Every eye in 1st Platoon watched as the track snorted full steam ahead, gears grinding and diesel engine groaning.

Beckham checked on Timbo and Ryan, but could see only their fuzzy shapes in the smoke. They were set up at a curb, their sniper rifles sweeping the terrain for hostiles. Satisfied, Beckham watched Steam Beast. The machine flattened a light pole with a screech and then lurched forward. The cowcatcher didn't look as though it was going to clear the back of the tanker.

Thunder boomed in the distance. Rain poured from the pregnant sky. The wall of smoke thickened, squeezing the convoy.

"Hold position," Gates said over the comm.

Beckham shot his team a flash of hand signals and yelled, "Regroup!"

They met on the sidewalk, facing the smoke together. Other voices joined in, confused marines shouting orders and questions that Beckham couldn't quite make out. He searched for Jensen through the smoke but saw only the outlines of a few scattered men.

A shriek broke out.

At first Beckham thought Steam Beast was moving again. But the scream was guttural. Deep. It wasn't a noise human engineering could create.

Horn grunted. "It's a fucking trap."

"Jesus," Beckham said. "They weren't hiding from the sun; they were waiting for the smoke to shift again." He could hardly believe it.

The rifle crack of automatic gunfire sounded from down the street.

"You got eyes?" Chow shouted.

"Negative," Jinx replied.

"Stay focused and conserve your ammo," Beckham added.

"I can't see nothin'," Ryan said.

Beckham strained to see through the smoke. The engines of the convoy were drowned out now by the high-pitched screams of the Variants. The noise was coming from everywhere and nowhere, all around them. The snapping of joints and grinding of claws came from above, then below.

Beckham spun around just as one of the pale monsters came crashing out of a storefront window.

Kate sat staring at her laptop screen in the conference room of Building 1. Ellis had compiled a list of species that resembled the Variants. A variety of creatures filled his notes, some she'd never seen before.

She skimmed through them more out of curiosity than for research. Ellis hadn't left a single rock unturned. He'd connected the Variants to a host of multicellular organisms: mammals, amphibians, reptiles, insects, and invertebrates. Each image had a note underneath, explaining what trait the species shared with the Variants.

There were leeches and other segmented worms, some with one sucker and others with two. Next were half a dozen spiders. An odd-looking crustacean that was an ancestor of the hermit crab filled the next screen. A chameleon the size of a human finger followed.

The list wasn't surprising, considering Ellis's fascination with Charles Darwin and evolution. Over the past few days, he had become obsessed with linking the Variants to other species. He was convinced the chemicals in VX-99 had turned on genes he could identify. And with the proper equipment and time, he would find out which genes those were.

But so what if he could link the Variants to the leech or some hairy spider? It didn't matter. She'd said it for days now—there was no bringing these people back. Ellis was finally starting to believe her. There was simply no precedent for that type of gene therapy. It was too far in the future. Even if they could find a way to reverse or stop the changes, what would be left to save? The Ebola virus had likely caused brain damage in most of the Variants. There would simply be no quality of life for the creatures.

A voice from the past boomed in her head. It was her brother, Javier, his dying words replaying like a broken record. She couldn't help but wonder what she would do if he was still alive—if he had turned into a Variant. Would she try everything to save him, even if he never returned fully to the brother she remembered?

She realized the answer was more painful than the memory: The answer was no. She wouldn't want him to live like that, because she wouldn't want to live like that.

Kate let her grief pass with a deep sigh, rousing the curiosity of Tasha and Jenny. Both girls fidgeted impatiently in the chairs next to her.

Jenny tapped Kate on the arm. "What are those things?" she chirped.

Kate flipped the lid of the laptop down. "Just some pictures."

"Can we see?" Tasha asked. "I'm bored."

Kate stood, stretched, and faked a smile. "I have a better idea."

Both girls glanced up, their eyes curious.

"How about we play a game?"

Jenny clapped her hands together. "Like hide-and-seek?"

"Yeah," Tasha replied. "Can we play hide-and-seek?"

Kate shook her head. "I don't think this would be the best place to play that game."

Tasha's shoulders sagged. She twisted a lock of red hair with her fingers and said, "When's Daddy coming home?"

"Soon, honey. He and Beckham will be back before you know it." She held out her arms and said, "Come here."

Tasha and Jenny stepped into Kate's embrace. She held them tight, feeling warm tears on her neck.

"I'm scared," Jenny said.

"Everything's going to be okay," Kate said. "You're safe here."

"Promise?"

"I promise."

But she knew it was a lie. She couldn't promise anything in this new world.

Beckham whirled and blasted a Variant in the face. It skidded to a stop a few feet away from the shop entrance.

"Hold the line!" he shouted. As soon as the words left his mouth, he saw how fucked they were. He was staring into a blackout zone. Fiftieth Street was shrouded by smoke. The thick curtain of haze seemed to cling to the concrete. But it was too late to retreat now. The only way out of this mess was to fight.

Gunshots cracked from every direction. Beckham saw marines rushing for cover—or were they Variants? He couldn't make out a damn thing.

More gunfire. Screams from wounded men and dying monsters.

It was chaos.

A round whizzed past Beckham's helmet. He ducked for cover. Two more bullets hit the concrete ahead of him, chunks of rock hitting his exposed skin.

He scrambled to his feet and grabbed the man next to him. Was it Horn? No, too skinny. Had to be Chow.

Beckham shouted again. "Fall back!"

A blast from the other end of the street shook the ground. The shock wave from the explosion hit Beckham's position, covering him in dust.

"Why the fuck are they using antitank missiles?"

A second explosion came from above. The missile hit one of the buildings. Dust and fragments of metal rained down on the street. Beckham was on the sidewalk now, Team Ghost surrounding him. The Variant that had crashed out of the shop lay in a puddle of blood a few feet away. Their only protection was an overturned food vendor's cart. Blackened hot dogs and scorched pretzels littered the concrete.

There was more gunfire, and a third shot from one of the Bradleys.

The sidewalk trembled.

Then the chain guns flared to life. The 25-millimeter rounds pounded the building, impacting with the force of mini-missiles. Beckham scanned the smoke screen for his own target. There, barreling toward their position, was a Variant on all fours. Raising his weapon, he fired and sent the creature tumbling head over feet back into the smoke.

Another came from the side. Then another. He fired again, and again, the sound of gunfire drowning out the clicking of joints.

Drops of rain hit his visor. Or was it blood? Beckham wiped away the liquid and searched for the next target.

A fourth blast from a Bradley's TOW launcher rang out. The concussion sent a shock wave of compressed air through the street. The sound of screaming marines found its way past the ringing in Beckham's ears. Adrenaline flowed through him, and his internal processor clicked on. He fired on instinct. A bullet clipped his rucksack and sent him spinning. He dropped to the concrete and then pushed himself back up on a knee, just in time to see another Variant rushing across the street.

He squeezed the trigger without restraint, screaming into his mask.

The creature's chest absorbed the rounds, jerking on impact. A high-caliber round from one of the Rangers finished the job, taking off its head.

Another Variant took its place. Then a second. And a third. The trio waited in the periphery between smoke and light, hunched, searching. The smoke swirled around their deformed bodies.

Beckham fired relentlessly, aiming for their heads. The bullets took off the first creature's limbs. It flopped on the concrete like a fish struggling for air. His next shots were more precise, splattering chunks of skull and soft tissue on the car behind the Variants.

"Smoke's clearing!" Horn shouted.

Beckham finished off his magazine, killing three more of the creatures that were making a run for his position. Their bodies slumped to the concrete, twitching. Blood oozed from multiple gunshot wounds.

"Hold your position," Beckham yelled. Reaching for a new magazine, he added, "Changing!"

The ringing in his ears waned. Snapping the fresh mag into his weapon, he froze and listened. A few shots rang out in the distance. When the echo ended, an eerie quiet passed over the convoy. He couldn't hear a thing. As the haze lifted, Beckham raised his muzzle and swept it over the battlefield, expecting to see marines sprawled over the terrain. Instead he only saw a couple mangled Variant corpses. There wasn't a single dead marine in sight. And there were no moans or screams from any wounded men either.

Beckham turned to his left and counted five helmets. Team Ghost was accounted for. Across the street, Jensen emerged from behind a crushed cab with Team Charlie. Alpha and Bravo stood behind a squad car a hundred yards to the left.

There were only a handful of marines stumbling away from the protection of the Humvees. He counted twelve, including Sergeant Valdez.

"Where the hell are all of the bodies?" Horn said, changing a magazine.

Beckham examined the street again. Where there should have been corpses, there were only streaks of blood.

"Sitrep! Give me a fucking sitrep!" Valdez screamed. "Where's Rodney and Libby? Where the fuck is everyone?"

The adrenaline that had fueled Beckham earlier broke down in his system. Dread replaced it when he realized where the closest blood trail led. He followed the red streak across the concrete, moving slowly, the muzzle of his weapon leading the way. He stopped at the edge of an open manhole. Dropping to a knee, he bent and peered inside.

He didn't need a flashlight to see the crimson water below. The Variants had dragged away half of the platoon into their lairs. He finally understood why the satellite imagery and recon teams had accounted for only a couple thousand of the creatures.

"We better get moving, boss," Horn said. "It'll be dark soon."

"Someone better get Command on the line," Beckham said. "Tell them we found their missing Variants."

A hand on his shoulder pulled his gaze upward. Jensen stared down at him. He stripped the mask away from his mouth. "Goddamn," he muttered. "What are the odds of General Kennor ordering in an air strike with thermobaric missiles? We could pound the shit out of those sewers and subways!"

"I doubt that's going to happen," said a voice. Gates strolled over to the hole with Valdez on his flank. "I just got off the line with Command. We've been ordered to continue to the target zone and set up the FOB."

"With all due respect, sir, we aren't going to make it to the FOB if we're attacked again," Beckham said.

"Those are General Kennor's orders," Gates said.

"Does he know what we're dealing with?" Jensen spat on the concrete and wiped a sleeve across his lips.

"We did receive a warning from Command. Apparently they received a message from Plum Island," Gates said. "A doctor there claims the Variants can see in the dark and have moved underground."

Beckham spoke without thinking. "Kate."

Gates regarded him with a quick glance. "Yeah, Doctor Lovata."

"Lovato," Beckham corrected. He peered back into the dark manhole. The concrete under his feet suddenly seemed paper thin. He stood and backed away from the edge.

"We need to keep moving," Gates said. He motioned Valdez to follow him and they hurried back to their command Humvee.

"Gates is going to get us all killed," Jensen said quietly. He kicked a chunk of concrete into the hole. It landed with a plop. A shriek answered, the sound reverberating from deep within the tunnel.

"If we can secure that FOB, we might have a chance to hold those things off. It's our only chance," Beckham said. He followed Jensen back to the convoy. The sunset, bloody orange against a darkening sky, silhouetted the skyscrapers. It would have made the perfect postapocalyptic painting.

Meg was aware of the distant gunfire but wasn't sure if it was real. Her mind was a blank slate; she couldn't remember where she was or how she had gotten there. The darkness didn't help. She couldn't see much of anything. When she tried to move her numb body, it didn't respond.

There was no pain. Not at first. She focused on wiggling her fingers. They moved. That was a good sign: She wasn't paralyzed. Next she moved a toe, and then her right foot. It was caught on something—something coarse and sticky.

Twisting, she fought to move. Fear bit her like jagged teeth. She remembered now: The monsters had dragged her down into the water. Anger followed when she remembered Jed and Rex sealing her into the tunnel.

Those bastards, she thought. She hadn't trusted Rex, not since the outbreak. The man she'd followed into burning buildings had transformed into a coward. And Jed? The marine had proved that not all soldiers were brave. Now she knew why she had found Jed hiding under a Humvee. Heroes, so it seemed, were in short supply during the apocalypse.

If she could have moved her head, she would have shaken it in disgust. But whatever slimy substance she was stuck in made that impossible.

Meg focused on her surroundings, squinting in the

darkness as if it would help. She concentrated on the fuzzy, webbed shapes to her right. At first glance they looked kind of like tree branches, but they were wrapped around something. A bulb. Something curled up. She saw the same thing in her peripheral vision. And she could see one of them above her too. Everything was blurred, though, as if she was looking through a thick piece of glass.

Was she still inside the tunnels?

She had to be. But where were the monsters?

Afraid to take a breath, she listened for the clicking of joints and scratching of claws. Somewhere in the distance she heard the trickle of running water, but she saw no sign of her captors.

Her heart was beating hard now. Her body warmed as the blood started circulating again. When the numbness passed, she finally became aware of the substance covering her body. She was stuck to a wall, covered from her legs to head in some sort of sticky slime. Her left arm was plastered to her side. The only things she could move were her right hand and her feet.

Meg squirmed again, tearing a patch of skin on her forehead in the process. The result was a sharp jolt of pain that made her eyes well with tears. She held back a scream, breathing rapidly through a small hole in the filmy substance.

The pain passed, and the numbness returned. At least she could move her head now. Careful not to rip any more skin, she tried to see more of her surroundings.

Moonlight illuminated a pool of dark water below. She was in some sort of collection room, with waterfalls of sewage cascading out of tunnels on all sides of her. The walls and ceilings were lined with more of the same fuzzy shapes.

With no small amount of effort, she finally moved

her right hand and ripped her arm free. The pain was a small price to pay for the range of motion that allowed her to strip away the film over her face.

She pulled her hand away, studying the gel webbing across her fingers. That's when she saw the others. There were so many—hundreds of other human prisoners, plastered to the walls and ceiling with thick rose-colored vines that looked like tree branches.

It finally hit her. She was in some sort of lair.

A flash of motion made her heart leap. She froze, not daring to move an inch.

The bulging shape of one of the creatures skittered across the ceiling.

"No," she said, her lips quivering. "Please, no."

Another figure fell into line behind the first. A third and fourth joined in a moment later as the beasts awoke. Within moments, the ceiling and walls were crawling with pale, naked flesh.

This was no lair. This was a meat locker full of humans. The place where the monsters came to feed.

As the moonlight faded away, she let out a scream and closed her eyes, praying that her death would be quick and painless.

17

Kate awoke in the same leather chair she'd slept in for countless nights. She rubbed her temples, her mind held captive by a fog that wouldn't clear.

Kate wished that Reed was there to hold her and tell her everything would be okay, even if they both knew it was a lie. She couldn't think of him now. She had to keep focused, for the sake of her team and Horn's girls.

What time was it?

With a sigh, Kate rose from her chair. She moved like a zombie, slow and sluggish. If only the Variants were like the shambling undead creatures that pop culture had obsessed over. Then, maybe—just maybe—the military could defeat them.

Flipping open her laptop, she punched in her passcode and waited for the system to boot. She checked a wall clock as the computer loaded. It was after ten. Tasha and Jenny were probably fast asleep back in her personnel quarters. She would check on them in a few minutes. But first she had something else she needed to finish.

General Kennor had issued a request for all scientific outposts to compile reports detailing new information on the Variants. He wanted to know what their weaknesses were. The two-paragraph document on Kate's screen proved the creatures didn't have many. There wasn't some magical pill or treatment that would ever bring them back. And there was no easy way to kill them, besides a bullet to the head.

Sighing, Kate reached for a cup of cold coffee and slurped it down. The bitter taste made her cringe. She shivered, goose bumps rising on her arms. The room was *so* cold.

Her teeth chattered as she typed. She wanted to finish the report before going to bed. That way Cindy and Ellis could look it over in the morning. But when she got to the end of the document, she paused. The cursor blinked. She didn't know how to finish the memo. She read it over for the fourth time.

CDC Report #21

Location: Plum Island

Author: Dr. Kate Lovato

RE: Variant Research

<u>Overview</u>

Reports from across the country indicate approximately 10 percent of those infected with the hemorrhage virus are recovering from the virus after exposure to the biological weapon VariantX9H9. Scientists are calling these creatures Variants. The epigenetic changes caused by the VX-99 nanostructures from the hemorrhage virus have caused irreversible effects. The Variants continue to change, showing remarkable evolution.

Test Results:

- Glands are producing a consistent stream of hormones that in turn are causing stem cells to proliferate and circulate through the bloodstream. The result is faster-than-average healing.
- Remarkable concentrations of fibrocytes circulating in the bloodstream also allow for rapid healing of dermal layers.
- Improved vascular regeneration allows for expedited and improved growth of blood vessels to injured regions. This in turn restores physiologic nutrient and oxygen delivery as well as cell-waste removal.
- Microscopic setae, nails, and flexible joints allow for increased speed and agility.
- Eyes have developed more cones and rods for increased ability to see in dim lighting.
- Cochlear hair cell growth and regeneration allows for hearing loss reversal and improvement.

These epigenetic changes are all a result of the VX-99 nanostructures found in the hemorrhage virus. Amplified physical senses, rapid healing, and increased agility and strength are transforming the Variant population into excellent predators with traits expressed from multiple species.

Treatment:

There appears to be no treatment, and epigenetic changes demonstrate no evidence of reversibility. The only significant known weakness is a sensitivity to light.

Kate palmed her forehead. The report told Command nothing that they didn't already know, and the one weakness they had identified was embarrassing. Sensitivity to sunlight was hardly an Achilles' heel. The Medical Corps staff had performed grueling tests on the creatures, some bordering on torture, but none of them had revealed anything substantial. *It made sense*, Kate thought, considering the Variants could heal faster than humans and didn't seem to be bothered much by pain.

After spending her entire adult life studying medicine, it pained Kate to admit there wasn't anything science could do to save the human race. She bit her bottom lip and then finished typing the document.

Fitz paced around the small guardhouse marked L4 with a smile on his face. It felt good to have a rifle in his hands again, and the vantage point was spectacular. The eight-by-eight box had a view of the entire island. A cool spring breeze gusted through the windows. It was intoxicating: salty, fresh, clean. An amazing improvement from the putrid scents back at Bragg.

He took in a long breath and swung the muzzle of his new MK11 over the window to the east. Damn, it felt good to hold one again. The rifle came with a twenty-round box magazine of 7.62-millimeter rounds, advanced scope, twenty-inch barrel, and bipod. It wasn't capable of fully automatic fire, but that didn't matter. He was extremely accurate with the weapon, and gripping it made him feel whole again.

He directed it at a maze of barbwire fences that zigzagged across the beach. Yellow signs warning of electric shock hung every hundred yards or so.

No one was getting through that barrier without making a lot of noise and severely shredding themselves. He swept his rifle to the south, scoping the domed buildings.

Industrial-sized light poles lit up the center of the hexagonal post. He could see several Medical Corps guards patrolling the circular concrete path connecting the buildings. The entire place gave him the creeps. It reminded him of the Area 51 books he'd read as a kid.

Given the chance, he would have picked an alien invasion over a viral outbreak. But beggars couldn't be choosers. That's what his mother had always said, and he was simply glad to have a roof over his head that didn't stink of rotting flesh.

He turned away from the base and thoughts of his parents. They were gone now, but not because of the outbreak. They had died in a car accident several years before. A month later, his brother had taken friendly fire to the chest in Afghanistan. His flak jacket had done little to stop the 7.62-millimeter round. A closed-casket funeral followed. Then Fitz had lost his legs in Iraq.

He was a survivor, or as he liked to refer to himself, an anomaly. The doctors told him he should have died when the IED blew off his legs. And the truth was he had—flatlined four times before some medic brought him back. He'd never forgotten the look on the face of the kid who saved him. It was a mixture of shock and awe.

Fitz was the lone survivor that day; the bomb had killed everyone in his Humvee.

He had come home to a different world, and with his family gone, those first few months of recovery at Walter Reed National Military Medical Center had been mentally and physically grueling. He'd considered ending his life many late nights when the whiskey ran dry and he could no longer taste the cigarettes.

But he never gave up, and now he used his strength to help inspire others. When the outbreak hit, he had been giving a speech at Fort Bragg to wounded warriors just like himself.

Gripping the rifle tighter, he thought about the irony of his situation. He'd thought he was finished saving American lives after he lost his legs. Instead he was saving even more by preventing vets just like him from committing suicide. Now he once again found a weapon in his hand—a weapon he could operate better than 99 percent of the world's population.

He stood in the darkness, listening to the breeze and the lap of the surf. A seagull swooped down toward the waves, its gray body shimmering in the moonlight. For a beat he felt as if he was on vacation on some exotic island. Fitz caught a glimpse of a blinking red light on the horizon. He quickly shouldered his rifle and scanned the skyline using the scope. A chopper came into view. The bird was long and wide, with double rotors—a Chinook, by the looks of it. And it was in trouble. The military transport craft was flying at a low altitude, jerking from side to side.

Punching the comm, Fitz said, "Command, this is Tower Four. I have a bogey coming in hot."

"Copy that, Tower Four. Eagle Nine has permission to land."

Fitz magnified his optics. The nose of the chopper lurched toward the water and then corrected. Something wasn't right. He watched for several seconds, studying the bird's erratic behavior.

"Command, this is Tower Four."

Static crackled over the comm. He tried again.

"Command, this is Tower Four. Do you copy? Over."

A panicked male voice answered. “Eagle Nine reports hostiles. I repeat, pilot reports hostiles on board.” He sounded unsure, as though he didn’t quite believe what he was saying.

Had the Variants suddenly learned how to fly? “Come again, Command?”

“Eagle Nine is carrying a load of Variants for research. Pilot reports—” The line cut out, and Fitz dropped his jaw in shock as flashes of light lit up the porthole windows of the incoming Chinook. Bullets punched through the side of the craft.

“Oh my God,” Fitz whispered.

A new voice came online. “All towers, this is Major Smith. Eagle Nine has been compromised. Permission to engage target if they cross into home-turf air space.”

Fitz swallowed. Engage the target? Had he heard correctly?

“Command, this is Tower Four. Come again? I missed that last transmission.”

“Tower Four, if bogey crosses into air space, you *shoot them down*.”

Fitz ran a hand over his helmet. Now he knew why the FIM-92 Stinger was lying in a case on the ground. The impressive piece of machinery was designed as an antiaircraft weapon. It would take out a Chinook with ease.

Fitz hit the comm. “Copy that.” He watched the chopper. Its trajectory hadn’t changed. The craft was on a crash course with Plum Island.

Fitz cursed. His first night on the job, and he was dealing with a crisis. When Major Smith had handed him his assignment, he had been ecstatic, but shooting down a chopper—even if it had hostiles on board—made him sick. He thought of his brother and the friendly fire that had taken his life.

Friendly goddamn fire, he thought. Fitz didn't know if he could do it.

The bird swooped low and then pulled high, as though the pilot was trying to shake something. More gunfire tore through the side of the bird.

Fitz rested his MK11 against the wall and then reached for the case containing the Stinger. He'd only fired the weapon once, back in Iraq, when a suspected insurgent vehicle was racing toward their post. The Honda had burst into flame. It was overkill, but it ended up saving American and Iraqi lives.

Fitz remembered the promise he'd made to Beckham: He had to protect the island. Grabbing the launcher, he hefted it onto his shoulder. He was running out of time. The Chinook flew low over the water.

A missile streaked out of Tower 2. The shot arced across the night and went wide, narrowly missing the tail of the craft and curving out over the ocean.

The radio came to life a second later; Major Smith's tone was panicked and angry. "All towers, take out that fucking bird!"

Fitz aimed and waited for the sight to line up. He said a mental prayer and then pulled the trigger. The missile joined a trio of other shots that roared through the night. Dropping the launcher, he watched as two of the missiles hit the Chinook. The bird shook violently, orange explosions bursting from the nose and side of the helicopter.

Shielding his eyes, he braced himself against the wall of his tower as the chopper spun out of control. The rotors whined in protest. Fire rained from the shaking helicopter. By some miracle the pilot was able to crash-land on the tarmac. The belly hit the ground with a crunch and then the chopper rolled on its side, screeching across the airstrip. The rotor blades came apart, shooting off in all directions. One of the shards whizzed by Tower 4 just as Fitz dropped to the deck. The small tower shook as more explosions rocked the Chinook.

Fitz pulled himself up and watched in awe. The flaming mess of ruined metal skidded across the runway, sparks and fire trailing the bird, until it finally ground to a stop.

"Jesus," Fitz said as he took in the destruction. Grabbing his rifle, he glassed the ruined aircraft. Fire streamed out of the cockpit. One of the missiles had peeled the roof back like the skin of an orange, exposing the smoldering interior.

He lined the cross hairs up with the back of the craft. The cargo door was wide open. Another explosion sent a fireball into the air.

Something moved at the rear of the craft.

No one could have survived the crash, Fitz thought. But something was definitely moving. Silhouettes—three of them.

No, six. Fitz felt his heart racing. He zoomed in on the smoldering bodies piling out of the back of the Chinook.

And then he saw the others.

He hadn't seen them before, but they must have jumped out of the back when the bird was going down. A dozen of the creatures galloped down the runway toward the aircraft.

Fitz swung his rifle back toward the wreckage. Two of the creatures were still on fire, rolling on the concrete.

The screaming noise of an emergency siren wailed. Major Smith's voice spilled over the radio, barking orders. Fitz watched as the Variants formed a group and then took off in a mad dash toward the domed buildings. Their bodies jerked as they ran, silhouetted in the garish light of the burning chopper.

Three seconds passed before the shock wore off. And then Fitz did what he was best at: He raised his rifle and squeezed the trigger.

"Ten missing. Two confirmed KIA," Lieutenant Gates said with a groan from the passenger's seat. "And we're only halfway to the coordinates for our main attack."

Beckham and Jensen sat in the back seat of the lieutenant's Humvee, tense and nervous. Both men wanted to be out on the street with their teams, not sitting in the safety of the armored vehicle. But Gates had asked for a sitrep.

The longer Beckham sat inside the cramped, dark interior of the truck, the more he wondered if Gates was actually looking for reassurance. That was something Beckham couldn't give him. He stayed silent, keeping an eye on the street as Jensen and Gates spoke.

Jensen shifted in his seat. He made no attempt to conceal his irritation. "I told General Kennor myself that there were hundreds of thousands of those things unaccounted for. The man didn't listen."

The convoy was fucked. They were lucky to have survived the first Variant ambush. If Beckham were in charge, he would have ordered 1st Platoon to turn, run, and call in the air force to blow the shit out of the subways, the sewers, and every other dark hole beneath New York.

There was a vast network of tunnels snaking for hundreds of miles beneath the city. Like Rome, New York was built on top of old buildings and foundations. There was no way to know exactly where the Variants were without deploying teams. The best thing—the only thing—to do was burn it down and salt the earth.

A tremor rattled the Humvee, and Beckham watched through the filthy windshield as the Bradleys tag-teamed a CNN satellite truck. Steam Beast pushed the vehicle onto the sidewalk with grace, and Beckham smiled, overcome by a small sense of pride. He still couldn't believe the young track commander had made it by the tanker a few streets back.

Gates cleared his throat. "Are we sure the Variants are hiding underground?"

Jensen played with his mustache, plucking out pieces of dried blood and flicking them onto the floor. "What do you think, Master Sergeant?"

Beckham thought he wanted to smack Gates in the face. But no matter how hard he hit him, there was no knocking sense into an inexperienced commander. Battlefield smarts weren't something you could magically pull from a hat. Even worse were the fuckups behind Operation Liberty. General Kennor and his staff had jumped the gun. To make things even worse, the new president, a former senator named Nate Mitchell, was beyond desperate to take back the streets. He had gambled with what was left of the United States military and given General Kennor the green light to do whatever he wanted.

Gritting his teeth, Beckham said, "Sir, I have no doubts. Get Central Command on the horn. Request an extraction and an air strike. They need to drop bombs into every fucking hole in the city."

Gates shook his head incredulously. "I already told General Kennor. He isn't listening. He said the other platoons are working their way to their FOBs as we speak. Maybe the Variants are only using the tunnels in Manhattan."

"That's bullshit. *Sir.*" Grabbing the door handle, Beckham tapped the driver's seat of the Humvee. "Hold up."

The Humvee rolled to a stop.

Gates shot him a glare. "Where are you going?"

"If Kennor is going to get us all killed, then I'm going to die with my men, where I belong." He opened the door and got out.

18

The emergency alarm system at Plum Island wailed so loud that Kate had to clap her hands over her ears. It had started seconds after a massive explosion shook the entire facility. She had still been in the conference room, polishing up the report for Cindy and Ellis to look through in the morning, when the first detonation had rocked the post.

The alarm took her back to the evacuation of CDC headquarters in Atlanta. Plum Island no longer felt like the safe maximum-security facility Colonel Gibson had claimed it to be. Then again, she'd never really believed his bullshit.

The pop of gunfire snapped Kate into motion. She rushed into the hallway and toward the personnel quarters. Frightened and confused scientists poked their heads out of their rooms, their features accented by the red glow of emergency lights.

A technician from Chamber 3 stood in the hall. He grabbed Kate as she passed. "What the hell is happening?"

"I don't know!" Kate yelled. She pushed past a woman from Toxicology and swung open the door to her room. Tasha and Jenny were curled up in the corner.

"What's that sound?" Tasha cried.

She grabbed them by their hands and led them back into the corridor. She had no idea where she would take them or what was happening. But they couldn't stay here. It wasn't safe. They needed to find soldiers.

The distant crack of automatic gunfire deep in the base made her pause. The noises were getting louder and more frequent. A battle was raging outside.

Kate had never considered it before, but what if a hostile force had found their safe little island? Not Variants, but other survivors? The facility had food, water, and medicine—things people would kill for at the end of the world. The thought terrified her almost as much as the thought of Variants.

A familiar voice emerged from amidst the screams and the blaring of the alarm. "Kate!"

Ellis was waiting for her at the end of the hallway. He beckoned to her urgently. "This way!"

Another distant explosion reverberated through the post. Panicked scientists and other civilians cried out, some slamming the doors to their rooms while others crowded the hallway in a wild frenzy. Kate pulled the girls through the mass of people.

"What's happening?" she yelled when they reached Ellis.

"Follow me!"

He pushed open the door to the lobby, and they piled out onto the tile floor with a few other people from the hallway. Four soldiers waited near the front doors, their weapons aimed at the glass. Intermittent red light flickered over their stoic figures.

Outside, orange flames licked the night sky. They rose from what looked like the skeleton of a large helicopter. Darkened shapes rushed away from the wreckage.

She gasped when she saw one of them was on fire.

"Oh my God," Kate whispered. The figures ran forward, leaving the burning one behind when it dropped to the ground, writhing in agony.

Flashes from machine guns illuminated the armored fatigues of marines on the edge of the tarmac.

"Variants," Ellis whispered.

"Hold the line!" one of the marines guarding the door shouted into his headset.

Tasha let out a whimper, and the man turned in their direction. "Get back! Return to your rooms!"

Kate retreated a few steps, but Ellis stood his ground. His eyes were glued to the chaos.

Gunfire lit up the runway. Several of the creatures racing away from the chopper dropped to the ground. But more shapes appeared, charging at the gunfire.

The flashes from the rifles vanished one by one, like candles blown out by a strong breath. The Variants overwhelmed the line of soldiers and then pushed on into the darkness.

"Move!" shouted the marine at the front door. He waved his team back to the atrium's central desk. They shoved a computer monitor and stacks of paper onto the floor and set up their machine guns.

He turned to Kate. "I said get the *fuck* out of here!"

Kate bent down in front of Tasha and Jenny. "Remember that game you wanted to play earlier?"

"Hide-and-seek?"

"Yes," Kate said. "We're going to hide."

Fitz scoped the runway. He'd taken out three of the Variants himself, and the marines had dropped three more before they were overrun. That left another dozen—and they were on their way toward the civilian buildings. He had to stop the monsters before they reached Building 1.

"Why the fuck would they bring so many to the island?" Fitz muttered. It seemed stupid, but he figured the scientists had their reasons. Throwing the strap of his rifle over his shoulder, he grabbed the railing of the tower's stairs and climbed to the ground. Gunfire cracked in the distance. The reassuring sound told him there were still men and women left in the fight.

Fitz followed the trail back to the base, running as fast as he could on his metal blades. They clicked on the concrete as he moved, filling him with satisfaction. Years ago, when he'd arrived at Walter Reed, he'd thought he would never walk again. A couple months later he wasn't just walking, he was running.

Darkness shrouded him as he made his way across the island. He clung to the shadows and flipped his NVGs into place, probing the green-hued path for contacts. The street twisted around the north edge of the tarmac. He slowed to a trot as bodies and glistening pools of blood came into focus. He could feel the heat of the fire raging behind him, small explosions still rocking the downed Chinook.

Fitz didn't stop to check the bodies. He knew they were all dead; the Variants never left injured behind. They would be back, though, after they'd killed everyone on the base. They would return to feed and drag the bodies away. He couldn't do anything for the dead marines, but he could still save Dr. Lovato and Horn's girls. Fitz spat on the concrete and ran faster.

"Wait up!"

The guard from Tower 3 was jogging behind him. The man was heavyset and panted loudly as he ran. Fitz had met him just hours before but couldn't remember his name.

"Hurry up, man," Fitz shouted.

"Where are you going?"

"Building One. That's where those things were headed."

"Shit. No way those things get in."

Fitz shot the man a look as he ran. "Have you seen the way they move? They're not exactly easy to bring down either."

The Medical Corps guard wheezed. "No."

"Better prepare yourself," Fitz said.

The other man changed the subject. "What's your name?"

"Fitz."

"Cole."

Fitz filed it away, focusing on the night around them as they ran across the base.

A few minutes later, they arrived outside Building 1. One of the creatures lay on the concrete steps, clutching a bullet wound in its neck. Blood gurgled from its grotesque sucker mouth. The injured Variant swiped at them with its other hand.

Cole aimed his carbine at the monster's face, but Fitz pushed the muzzle away.

"No," he said. "We don't want to draw attention." Fitz pulled his knife and jammed it into the creature's skull with a crunch. Without hesitation, he continued on. Cole followed him up the steps into the building. The glass doors were blown out. The body of another dead marine lay slumped over the front desk, a pistol hanging loosely from a gloved hand. The lights were dim but still working.

"Clear," Fitz said, inching the door open. Inside, he swung his rifle over his shoulder and pulled out his pistol.

Together the two men covered the space, following a trail of blood leading to a dark intersection. The hallway to the left led to conference rooms and labs; the one to the right led to personnel quarters. That's where Dr. Lovato and the girls would be.

"Why the hell would someone turn off the lights?" Cole asked.

"Who knows?" Fitz said. "Keep moving."

A flashing red light flickered in the open doorway, a gateway to hell. "Keep quiet," he said, flipping on his night-vision goggles and pushing open the door.

They crept forward into the hallway, the sound of his metal blades clanking on the floor. He policed the hallway with his pistol, swinging it up and down, checking the ceiling and shadowy corners for the creatures. Instead he found dead scientists, their bodies battered and torn. Blood speckled the walls, the floor, and even the ceiling. Fitz gagged when he smelled rotting fruit. It was the awful perfume of the Variants.

The monsters were close.

Smoothly and slowly he led his overweight comrade through the carnage, clearing each room. By the time they got to the end of the hall, his heart had climbed into his throat. He felt every beat.

Fitz slipped into the final room with his pistol firm in his hands. The green optics revealed a small twin bed, desk, and closet.

Empty.

Exhaling, he lowered his weapon. Then he heard a crunch. Cole bumped into him, startled.

"What the hell was that?" the man asked.

Raising a finger to his lips, Fitz moved back into the hallway. He cautiously approached the door leading to the next hallway.

A clicking sound followed, and then the snap of bones. The noises came from the other side of the door. Fitz and Cole both took a step back, exchanging glances.

"On three," Fitz said, reaching for the handle and raising his pistol.

Cole's eyes hardened and he shook his head. "No, man, let's just stay here."

"You can stay, but I'm going in," Fitz replied. He'd made a promise to Beckham and he wasn't going to break it, no matter how terrified he was. Fitz was a marine, and marines didn't run from a fight.

"One.

"Two."

Cole backed away and shouldered his rifle.

"Three." Fitz yanked the door open and trained his pistol on a Variant. The creature's face was buried in the exposed stomach of a female scientist. Bodies clogged the hallway. He hesitated before pulling the trigger, hoping that he wasn't too late, hoping the woman wasn't Kate.

Night had fallen on New York City. Shrouded in darkness, the convoy rolled to a stop at the intersection of Fiftieth Street and Avenue of the Americas. The door to the command Humvee opened, and Lieutenant Gates stepped into the ash. He staggered away from the vehicle as if he was drunk.

With his NVGs active, Beckham could see Fiftieth Street was impassable. The former GE building and Rockefeller Center were reduced to stubs of metal and rebar. Stone, brick, and other debris formed a mountain that ended at the edge of the intersection. Remains of a Radio City Music Hall sign protruded from the rubble.

The view was horrifying and breathtaking at the same time. This was where Gates had said the convoy would experience the most resistance, but as Beckham scanned the area, he didn't see how anything, even the Variants, could have survived the blasts.

Then a voice cried out, "Contact!"

A pair of marines rushed over to the debris and aimed their weapons at the pile.

"Hold position," Gates yelled. Sergeant Valdez and the lieutenant approached carefully. Beckham hustled over to the marines. The crushed body of a Variant jutted out of the wreckage. The skin on its torso was burned away, exposing glistening muscle and fat. By some miracle it was still alive, twisting and lurching as it struggled to get free.

"Jesus," Valdez muttered. "Probably should put this one out of its misery before it alerts its friends."

"They already know we're here," Beckham replied. The creature reached up with mutated hands. Its nails were curled into sharp talons. They had to be four or five inches long. The creature pressed its swollen lips together and opened them again with a pop. It tried to let a scream fly, but only a faint gurgle escaped its mouth.

"Thing's not going to alert anyone," Gates said. He looked to the right. "Keep moving. We're almost to our final objective. I want to get this FOB set up ASAP."

Valdez nodded and whistled to the vehicle commanders. Then he flashed an advance signal. The men pulled the spotlights away from the crumbled buildings, and their bright white beams cut through the night.

Beckham remained near the wreckage, wondering what the Variants were waiting for. They had the advantage of darkness. His gut told him something was wrong, that the Variants were planning something.

The longer he waited for the convoy to start rolling, the more his sense of unease intensified. He thought of Kate, Riley, and Horn's girls. Had something happened on Plum Island? He gave his helmet a pat, quashing the concerns before they had a chance to take hold. From the moment he boarded the Black Hawk, he had promised himself he wouldn't think of Kate.

The beam from a spotlight caught him in the face. He flipped up his NVGs and shielded his eyes with a hand, squinting through his fingers.

"Let's roll," Valdez shouted from inside the turret of a Humvee. He gripped the M240 and trained it on the street. "Keep sharp!"

Black Reaper and Steam Beast screamed, their tracks reversing and then turning to the south. The Humvees drove after them.

"Six more blocks to go," Beckham muttered. Team Ghost fell into line and followed the platoon down Avenue of the Americas. The road was twice the size of Fiftieth Street and considerably less clogged. The Bradleys weaved around derelict vehicles and plowed others out of the way.

Beckham kept close to Horn. The last thing he wanted was to lose his brother in the chaos of the attack they all knew was coming. They walked in silence, glass crunching underfoot.

"How do you think the other platoons are doing?" Horn asked.

Beckham replied with a shrug. "Hopefully better than us." He hadn't heard a single gunshot or explosion for five hours.

He strained to hear something besides the hum of engines and the stomping of boots. He would have given anything to hear a radio transmission from one of the other platoons, or evidence that there were still marines out there fighting.

Horn stepped off the curb and glanced up at the skyscrapers. "Where the hell do you think all the other survivors are? Rex couldn't be the only one."

"Maybe there aren't any," said a voice behind them. It was Chow. Jinx followed him through the ash, leaving a trail of footprints behind as if they were walking through snow. There wasn't much to say after that.

Fifteen minutes passed, and the armored vehicles were pushing through a second intersection, with Forty-Eighth Street. Up ahead, the dark mouth of a subway entrance yawned. Beckham waited for the Variants, but none came. He lowered his weapon to give his arms a break and checked the Gap store on his left. He saw the scorched body of a headless female manikin. Her clothes were burned away. The other five models were all twisted from the heat of the firebombs. But there was one that looked relatively unscathed behind the others. At least it had a head. Beckham's hands found his weapon and focused on the figure.

It moved.

His heart rate rose along with the muzzle of his M4, but the creature disappeared before Beckham could pull the trigger.

"Contacts!" another marine yelled somewhere across the street.

Beckham backed away from the store and joined Horn.

"I don't see shit," Chow said from a few feet away. "Anyone got eyes?"

Jinx took a knee and angled his rifle toward the subway station. "There!" he yelled.

Suddenly, the street was alive with motion. The Variants streamed out of the subway entrance, climbing over one another and leaping toward the convoy. The grotesque snapping of their joints enraged Beckham. He was ready to fight. To kill.

Marines ran for cover behind the vehicles, but for one man it was too late. Two Variants tackled the marine and pulled him, screaming, into the thick of the growing horde.

Valdez swung his turret into position and opened fire with the M240. The bullets punched through the swarm, splattering the street with blood.

Beckham kept the Gap store in his peripheral vision as he fired. The flood of monsters continued coming from the depths of the subway station. He changed magazines as the Bradleys both maneuvered their turrets into position. Fire from their M242 chain guns erupted simultaneously. The wave of Variants disappeared in a cloud of crimson as the 25-millimeter rounds found targets.

Beckham held his palm facing out yelling, "Cease fire!" He wanted his team to conserve ammo, since it was obvious the Bradleys had the fight under control.

Soon, the ash-covered street was soaked with blood and covered in body parts. A marine to the side of the convoy fired a LAW rocket at the subway station as more of the creatures continued to pile out. The missile streaked across the road and detonated with a deafening explosion. A fireball rose from the stairway as the walls caved in on top of the horde and sealed the passage. Chunks of gore and cement flew. Pieces bounced off the ground and rolled to a stop in the scarlet ash.

"Cease fire!" Valdez shouted. "Check the man next to you. See if anyone's missing."

Heavy silence followed.

"They got McDonnell," a marine finally shouted.

"Anyone else?"

Somewhere down the street, a dying Variant let out a screech. A single shot ended its suffering.

Beckham checked his own team. Five helmets. Then he looked for the other strike teams. It looked as though they were all there.

He breathed a sigh of relief and mentally counted their remaining numbers. With ten marines missing and three confirmed KIA, 1st Platoon had forty-seven men left to fight. Not many to face an army numbering in the millions. Team Ghost wasn't new to shitty odds; the enemy always seemed to outnumber them. But this took it to an entirely new level.

19

Kate took a closer look at the marine who had helped them escape from Building 1. He'd said his name was Jackson. They'd stopped under a circle of light from an industrial pole as he swept his weapon over the concrete path ahead. The calm, confident sparkle in his eyes didn't reflect his age. He couldn't have been more than nineteen years old. *Just a boy*, Kate thought. But he had killed two of the Variants like a battle-hardened marine, with single shots to their heads.

After clearing the area, Jackson signaled for the small group to continue. Holding Jenny's and Tasha's hands, Kate trailed Ellis and a handful of other scientists. She counted heads as the light spilled over them. Only nine of them had made it out of the lab building.

Cindy wasn't one of them. Kate remembered seeing the Variant pounce on the young scientist. Her thrashing arms. Her screams. And then silence.

Kate bent over to throw up, dry-heaving on the ground.

Tasha and Jenny yanked on her sleeves. She wiped off her mouth with a sweep of her forearm and then grabbed their hands again. She still didn't quite believe this was all happening. The base was supposed to be secure.

Safe.

The word made her want to laugh. How could she have been so naïve? The Variants couldn't be caged like dogs. They were intelligent, powerful predators. Kate should have known they were too dangerous to keep locked up. She thought of Fitz and Riley, wondering if they were okay.

The girls were crying at her side as they ran. Footfalls pounded the concrete. There were other human sounds: labored breathing, coughing, and sobbing.

"Come on!" Jackson insisted. He ran past Building 2 and pointed at the third dome in the distance. He was leading them to the medical facility. Kate risked a glance over her shoulder. There was movement outside Building 1. She squinted, but the shapes melted away.

Another explosion lit up the sky. The Chinook that Kate was told had crash-landed was completely engulfed now, its full tank of gas burning out of control.

Everything seemed surreal. A dream.

A tug on her right hand forced her to turn back to the others. They were only a hundred yards from Building 3. Two silhouettes jogged down the steps. Kate's heart jumped again, but then she saw the rifles.

The soldiers moved into the dim light with their weapons shouldered.

"Get inside!" one of them shouted.

"Thank you," Kate whispered to Jackson as she led the girls into the building.

"Doing my job, ma'am." He paused and looked behind them. "I think that's it."

"There have to be more survivors," said the other soldier.

She lost track of their conversation as she followed Ellis and the others through the front doors. Riley was waiting in the atrium in his wheelchair, a pistol lying on his lap "What the hell's going on?" His eyes jumped from face to face.

"Kate," he said. "What the hell?"

Gripping the crying girls' hands tighter, she said, "The base has been overrun." She shook her head and looked back at the door. "I don't..."

Ellis took over. "A chopper full of Variants crash-landed. They're rampaging through the base, building by building."

Kate flinched when the doors opened. She backed away, pulling the girls with her. Jackson peered through the gap. "We're going to hold them here. You guys find a place to hide and lock the doors from inside."

"What?" Kate said, shocked. "You're not going to come with us?"

The marine narrowed his blue eyes and shook his head. "I'm going to do what I was ordered to do. I'm going to protect this base."

Kate marveled at the young man's heroism. The world needed men like him, men that were willing to make sacrifices. Men like Beckham.

"Thank you," she said again.

Jackson handed his side arm to Ellis. "Take this." Then he looked over at Riley. "Keep 'em safe."

"Good luck," Riley said. He checked the magazine in his pistol and then chambered a round.

More screams sounded in the distance.

"Jackson, get back out here," one of the soldiers shouted.

The marine exchanged one final look with Kate and then closed the door.

Ellis quickly locked it behind him. "We should go to the ICU and lock down every ward on our way. Those things will have a hell of a time getting through."

"Let's move," Riley said. He wheeled through the atrium and into the hallway connected to the medical wings. There were three total, and the ICU was housed at the end.

They heard gunfire before they were able to secure the first doors. It was over in seconds. The high-pitched shrieks of the Variants reclaimed the night.

Kate and Ellis exchanged a look. They both knew what the sound meant: Jackson and the others were already dead.

"Hurry!" Riley shouted.

Tasha and Jenny ran down the hall with Kate by their side. Dr. Holder and his nurse, Tina, came bursting around the corner.

"What the hell is happening?" Holder asked.

Kate slid to a stop. "No time to talk. Where are the other patients?"

The doctor ran a hand through his thinning white hair. "Colonel Gibson's it."

Kate grabbed the girls and continued down the hallway, their shoes beating against the tile. When they reached the final ward, the group stopped and huddled around the front desk. Ellis secured the doors and then raised his pistol, giving it a once-over as if he'd never seen a gun before. "Anyone know how to shoot this?"

A familiar face emerged from the group of strangers. It was Rod, from Toxicology, the tech who had helped them identify the nanostructures of VX-99 present in the hemorrhage virus. He held out a shaky hand. "I do."

"What the hell do we do now?" Holder asked.

Tina echoed the doctor's words. "Yeah, what are we supposed to do? Just sit here and wait for those *things*?"

Her tone reminded Kate why she didn't like the woman.

"Yeah. We wait," Riley said. "I mean, you could go find a place to hide if you want. But I'm going to camp out right here. He raised his pistol at the door. "And then, when those things come through, I'm going to kill every last one of 'em."

Tina looked at the man as though he was crazy and then took off running down the hall, disappearing into one of the vacant rooms. Dr. Holder shook his head and ran after her.

That left Rod, Kate, Ellis, the girls, and four other scientists she didn't know. Everyone but Riley was staring at her, looking to the "savior of the world" for strength. But just as so many times before, Kate didn't know what to do. Though she wouldn't say it out loud, she was convinced this was the end of the line.

Metal clanged distantly inside the facility. Kate tensed. The noise came again. Louder now. Closer.

"They're in," Riley said. He raised his pistol. "Stay behind me."

The monsters were finally coming. And this time Kate had no way to stop them.

The convoy slowed to a stop at the corner of West Forty-Second. Spotlights swept over the street, the beams cutting through the night like a scalpel. Beckham looked up at the Bank of America Tower. The air force had spared the area from the firebombs, but most of the windows were still shattered. As long as the frame was stable, he wasn't going to sweat it. The biggest concern was clearing the building and finding a place to set up sniping positions.

"All right, let's get this FOB set up," Gates said over the comm. He stepped out of the command Humvee and directed marines to the other two trucks. The remaining men unloaded equipment and weapons.

Beckham pulled off his gas mask and stuffed it in the bag on his hip. Ghost waited on the curb with the rest of the strike teams as the Bradleys worked on forming a perimeter around the street. They made a wall with the abandoned vehicles. The wall would slow down any Variants coming from the north, but it also blocked a potential escape route if 1st Platoon needed to get the hell out of Dodge.

What the fuck was Gates thinking? Any handbook would have told Gates to maintain an exit strategy. But the handbook didn't apply to end-of-the-world scenarios with monsters like this one.

Beckham studied the city, mentally mapping out the target zone of the New York Public Library and the forest of trees surrounding Bryant Park. Ash-covered branches swayed in a light breeze, the soot raining down like snow.

His legs felt numb from the hike. And he was filthy: Blood and soot covered him from boots to helmet. He wiped grime off his face and focused on the park. With the ash on the trees, the park looked as though it belonged on some Christmas card. He stood there, watching and waiting for orders, half expecting to see an army of Variants swinging through the branches as they had back at Fort Bragg. But besides the crunching of metal, all was quiet.

"Moving armor into position," Beckham heard through his headset. It was the voice of Sergeant Valdez.

Jensen walked over to Beckham. Even in the dim light, he could see the lieutenant colonel was furious. Beckham followed Jensen a little distance from the other teams.

"I'm considering pulling rank," he said. "Ordering in an extraction."

"Sir, I thought you would never say that," Beckham replied gingerly.

"Problem is, I don't think Kennor would approve the

order. I honestly think it's going to take a million of those fucking monsters for the general to realize the city can't be taken back by force."

Beckham nodded. "Kennor is a bullheaded asshole. Just like Gibson." He paused to take in a sidelong glance of their men and then said, "So what do we do?"

Jensen spat on the ground. "We set up shop and pray the Bradleys and Humvees can hold off the Variants when they decide to show their true strength. At that point, I'm hoping the flyboys finish the rest."

"I'm with you, sir. And my men are with you too," Beckham said.

Jensen put a hand on Beckham's shoulder. "To the end."

"To the end," Beckham repeated.

The comm channel came online a moment later. It was Gates. "Strike teams advance to Bank of America Tower. Command wants the FOB set up by dawn."

The tower loomed overhead. It was the perfect place for sniping positions, given the vantage it had over the park and the rest of the city. But what if there were Variants lurking inside?

It was going to be a long hike up. Taking in a measured breath, Beckham flashed an advance signal toward the shattered windows of the first floor. Team Ghost and the other strike teams hustled inside, broken glass crunching under the weight of their boots. Beckham took one last glance at 1st Platoon and said a mental prayer before following his men into the building.

"Clear," Horn yelled.

Beckham stopped in front of the elevators and scanned the two dozen Special Ops soldiers and marines. Weapons of all sizes and calibers were leveled at the ground, ready to rock and roll. Grenades and extra magazines hung from armored vests. NVG optics stared back at him.

"All right," Beckham said. He paused to wait for one

of the Bradleys to finish pushing a car into position outside. When the noise subsided, he said, "Our objective is to take out any Variants and support the FOB. I'm going to be honest with you—those things are waiting to strike. I can feel it. You watch yourself, and you watch your buddy. This may be the most important battle of our lives. There won't be any room for mistakes. Every bullet counts."

There were several nods from the group. Beckham decided to keep the talk short. "Who's got the building layout?"

The slender frame of Sergeant Peters stepped forward, followed by Sergeant Rodriguez, a man almost twice as thick. Peters pulled out the blueprints and spread them out on the floor. "The building is fifty-five stories tall, with fifty-two elevators, but obviously those aren't an option. I'm thinking we take stairwells here and here."

Beckham took a knee to scan the layout. "Are they secured passages?"

"Yup," Peters replied.

"I'll take care of that," Rodriguez said, swinging a M1014 twelve-gauge shotgun toward the floor.

"Alpha and Bravo, you take this stairwell to the twenty-fifth floor. Charlie and Delta, you're with me and Lieutenant Colonel Jensen. We'll take this other stairwell to floor twenty-six. If things get dicey, we're only a few beams of metal and drywall apart." Beckham rubbed his gloves together. "Keep your headsets on and your eyes open. Good luck."

Several of the marines clapped each other on the back and gave a muffled "Oorah!" before the teams separated and fanned out across the lobby.

One of Jensen's men was waiting for them at the stairwell, his shotgun leveled at the door. Beckham flashed a thumbs-up, and the man fired at the locking mechanism. Sparks and metal exploded from the door. It swung open. The marine stepped away, and a second marine darted up the stairs. A beat later he yelled, "Clear!"

Beckham fell into line behind Horn. He pulled his scarf over his nose the moment he smelled something rotting.

The teams filed up the steps slowly, clearing one corner at a time. On the third floor they came across a mangled corpse, crusted blood surrounding the body where the victim had bled out.

Poor bastard, Beckham thought. Alone and afraid was a really shitty way to die. He focused on the men in front of him. It was quiet—too fucking quiet.

Ten minutes into the climb, fatigue set in. He felt every step, the injuries from Fort Bragg dragging on him. He reached for his water bottle and popped a mild pain med into his mouth. Kate had given him a bottle before he left, but he'd held off using them as long as he could.

A sign for the twentieth floor rolled into view and recharged his muscles. Only a few more floors to go. He wondered if the Variants would show up in the park below before they were able to secure their sniping positions.

"Hold!" shouted one of the marines from Charlie team. He crouched on the landing.

Horn hunched in a defensive position. Beckham strained to get a view, but he couldn't see shit. Static crackled in his earpiece. The concrete stairwell was screwing with the transmissions. Beckham's hand crept toward his vest, and he ran a finger over the pocket where he kept the picture of his mother. The gesture quelled the anxiety building in his gut.

The marine on the landing finally stood and motioned the others forward. He disappeared around the corner.

A familiar sour smell filled Beckham's nostrils before he saw the dead Variant three floors up. The creature lay clutching a melon-sized hole in its chest. Its vertical pupils stared up blankly at the ceiling. Beckham halted when he thought he saw it blink.

Of course it hadn't blinked. Beckham wiped a hand across his face to clear the phantom vision. The creature was dead as a fucking doornail. He kicked it in the leg just to be sure and continued on.

The team came to a stop at the twenty-sixth floor. Beckham stretched his legs and then shoved his way through the pack to the front. Lieutenant Colonel Jensen was crouched outside the door next to the marine with the shotgun.

"On me," Beckham said.

Jensen nodded and backed away from the entrance. Beckham took his place and said, "Blow the lock."

The marine aimed and fired. He then pulled on the handle and swung the door open. Beckham rushed inside, his M4 sweeping over a carpeted hallway, clear of any signs of struggle. The opulent space looked as though it belonged in a fairy tale, but it smelled like hell. Then the lingering rot reached his nose, and he fumbled for his scarf. He pulled it up and breathed out a sigh when he saw the bodies at the end of the hallway.

"We got corpses," Beckham whispered into his mini-mic. "Lots of 'em."

He halted and balled his hand into a fist. Most of the dead were covered with tarps, but there were a few limbs exposed.

"Hold position," he said. He angled his weapon at a wall of cracked glass that looked over a floor of desks and cubicles. There were no contacts, no movement. Nothing. With his weapon at low ready, he moved slowly toward the pile of dead.

He took a knee when he was several feet away.

"God," he muttered, the reek burning his nasal passages. He clutched his M4 against his chest and held his breath as he reached forward.

He shifted the tarp and uncovered a hand. The fingers were stiff but straight, not twisted like those of a Variant. He peeled back the tarp all the way to reveal the face of a woman, an obvious victim of the hemorrhage virus. Crusted blood surrounded her lips and trickled from her eyes, nose, and ears.

He swiveled on his heels to scan the area with his M4. Someone had survived both the virus and the Variants long enough to stack the corpses.

A soft scuffling noise pulled him away from the pile. He slowly rose to his feet and aimed his weapon at the glass partition. He almost fired, but then he saw the wild, frightened eyes of a young boy staring back at him from the other side.

20

The ticking of a wall clock was a grim reminder that they were running out of time. The last of the gunshots had faded away minutes before. Now there was only silence and the tick-tock of their fate.

Kate jumped as a hollow pounding filled the air. Then a shriek of strained metal echoed through the building, sending Tasha and Jenny running for the nurses' station. The creatures had breached the first barricade.

Kate hurried after them. Bringing a finger to her mouth, she said, "Shh."

Tasha looked up, her eyes filling with tears. She whispered in Jenny's ear and then pulled her legs to her chest and buried her head.

"Where are they?" Ellis muttered. He stood behind the desk, his hair a disheveled mess. Kate peeked over the station and checked the door. Rod stood a few feet away, the gun shaking in his hands.

A metallic screech rang out in the distance once more.

Rod looked toward the ceiling. "Where's it coming from?"

For several minutes, no one said a word or moved. The banging reverberated as the creatures tore through the building. Kate clung desperately to any shred of sanity she had left, knowing it was only a matter of time before they were discovered.

Time crept by. The noises waxed and waned, making it impossible to determine where they were coming from.

And then they stopped. Kate stood. Had the Variants moved on?

Afraid to breathe, Kate crouched next to Tasha and Jenny. Glazed, swollen eyes stared back at her. Both girls were in shock. She corralled them to her chest, wishing she could do more to protect them.

Rod finally lowered the pistol to his side. In a low whisper he said, "Maybe they're gone."

"Wouldn't count on it," Riley said. He laid his gun in his lap and wheeled himself toward the desk. His features darkened, his jaw clenched. The fun-loving kid had vanished, replaced by a hardened Delta Force operator.

He locked eyes with Kate. "When those things come, you and the girls run."

There was strength there. The same strength she saw in Beckham.

"You got it, Doc?"

"Y-yes," Kate stuttered. She jumped as something rattled nearby. Riley scrambled for his pistol and aimed it at the ceiling. Rod hurried over and pointed his gun at the panels.

The clanging grew louder.

"They're right above us," Riley said. "Shit. They figured a way past the barricades. Up there."

He brought a finger to his lips with his other hand, and Kate turned to the girls to mimic his gesture. The thumping continued as the creature scuffled through the ductwork. The team followed the sounds as they passed overhead. The Variant was working its way to the back of the medical ward.

Riley jerked his chin toward the doors. "Now's our chance. We need to get out of here."

Rod protested with a violent shake of his head. "What if there are more out there?"

Ellis ran his hands through his hair for the hundredth time. "I'm with Riley. We need to get out of here."

The pounding from the ductwork stopped. An animalistic snuffling sound followed, like a dog trying to get a scent.

Kate froze, her eyes peering back down the hallway. Dr. Holder poked his head out of his hiding spot. He lipped something Kate couldn't make out. She shook her head and put a finger to her mouth.

A screech broke out above them, and then a desperate clawing as the creature struggled through the ductwork.

Ellis dropped to both knees by the desk to try to calm the girls. "It's okay," he said in a low and unconvincing voice.

Kate took a knee next to them and pulled them toward her, shielding them from the monster she knew would fall from the ceiling. She closed her eyes and prayed.

The scratching continued toward Dr. Holder's room. The rest of the rooms were empty, except...

Her eyes snapped open again when she remembered that Colonel Gibson lay hooked up to machines in the last room of the ward. The Variant was banging its way right toward him. His own creation was going to tear him apart. He was helpless, just as her brother had been helpless when he was infected with the hemorrhage virus back in Chicago. Conflicting emotions pulled at her.

Riley wheeled over to the door. "Help me," he said, reaching for the lock.

Rod hesitated. "What about the others?"

"They can come with us," Riley replied. "Let's go."

Jerking his chin toward the double doors, he unfastened the lock and inched it open with a hand.

Kate trusted the man. He'd helped save her in Atlanta, and he was their only chance of surviving now. "Come on," she said, reaching out for the girls. Grabbing both of their tiny hands within her own, she pulled the girls up and ran after Rod and Riley.

"You have to keep quiet," Ellis said. He held a finger to his lips as he looked at them.

Both girls nodded.

The flickering red lights guided them into the second corridor. They left the banging behind, and the terrifying scratching faded as they raced down the hall. Kate's heart rate slowed, but she didn't dare let herself relax. Not until they were safe.

She stole one glance over her shoulder, wondering if Colonel Gibson could hear his fate inching closer. In a blink, the ceiling collapsed in front of his room. Panels, ductwork, wires, and flakes of white ceiling tile streamed over the muscular frame of a man wearing nothing but frayed white trousers. Charred black skin ran from his right leg to his rib cage, muscles and flesh exposed to the elements. Tilting his chin, he sniffed the air and then dropped into a catlike position.

Everything froze. Distant voices told Kate to run. Dr. Holder and Tina poked their heads out of their room and then slammed their door shut.

There were more voices and a tug on Kate's arm. She wanted to move, she wanted to run, but she was petrified. Unblinking, she stared at the Variant. It whirled around to face her with arms extended outward and claws curled. A swollen tongue flicked out of bulging sucker lips. Kate could smell the sour rot of the creature from where she stood.

The creature's reptilian slits blinked, studying her.

"Kate!" Riley shouted, finally snapping her from her morbid trance.

"Help!" cried a voice. "Somebody help me!"

The creature twisted toward Gibson's room.

Tasha and Jenny squealed. Before Kate realized what she was doing, she dropped both girls' hands and rushed back to the doors. Tina and Holder had made their choice. She had children to think about.

Hating herself for doing it, Kate pushed the doors shut and locked the doctor, his nurse, and their patient inside.

The boy ran the moment Beckham moved. He took off through the maze of cubicles and then vanished.

Beckham swore under his breath. He flipped his mini-mic to his mouth and said, "We have a survivor. A kid."

Flashing an advance signal toward the office door, he traversed the hallway. Horn was waiting for him.

"You got eyes?" Beckham asked, taking a knee.

His earpiece crackled. It was Sergeant Peters. "Alpha and Bravo in position."

Lieutenant Gates replied a beat later. "Assembling FOB. Armor is in position. Charlie, Delta, sitrep."

Beckham flicked his mini-mic back to his lips and changed the channel so he could communicate with the entire platoon. "We have a survivor. Kid took off running."

White noised crackled in his earpiece long enough to make Beckham nervous. He knew what the officer was thinking on the other side. The objective was to set up a base and clear the area. Survivors were secondary, a liability to the mission.

Beckham brought two fingers to his eyes and then

pointed into the office. "Go get that kid," he whispered to Horn.

The man nodded his reply and reached for the handle. Beckham motioned for Ryan to follow as another order crackled across the comm.

"Set up position, but do *not* search for survivors. I need your men on those windows, Beckham," Gates said. His voice shook, but Beckham knew it wasn't really the lieutenant giving the order; it was the old fossil leading Operation Liberty—General fucking Kennor.

"Copy that," Beckham replied. Anger swirled through him at the thought of leaving a kid behind. *Fuck that*, Beckham thought. He wasn't leaving *anyone* behind again. He would never forgive himself for abandoning that family the last time he was in New York.

Beckham turned the channel back to Charlie and Delta. "Listen up. We got a survivor on this floor. We're going to clear the room, secure the kid, and then fall into position. Got it?"

Nine helmets nodded, including Lieutenant Colonel Jensen's. That was good; they all trusted him.

"I want two marines to hold security here," Beckham said. Then he signaled the strike teams to advance into the office. "Horn, you got eyes?"

"Negative."

Beckham pulled his scarf away from his mouth. "Ryan?"

"Negative."

Gripping his weapon, Beckham paused to map out the room. The cubicles were set up in rows of ten and went five deep. The glass that had overlooked Manhattan was mostly gone. Shards stuck out of a three-foot-high wall. That's where they would set up their rifles, he decided.

He looked for Horn next and found the man at the far right of the room.

"Clear," Ryan said over the comm.

Beckham swore again. The kid was probably long gone now. If he had survived this long, he likely had some secure hiding spot.

"Found something," Horn said.

Beckham pointed the rest of the strike teams toward the waist-high wall overlooking Bryant Park and the library. "Get into position."

He rushed through the row of cubicles to the window, catching a breathtaking glimpse of the city. The wind whistled, brushing against his armor. It was one hell of a long way down, like a break-every-bone-in-your-body long way down. He felt a flash of extreme vertigo and waited for it to pass.

He spied Horn's helmet jutting over a cubicle at the other end of the room. He broke into a run and found the man standing in the doorway of a small office. Filthy blankets and trash littered the floor.

"Looks like the kid was living here," Horn remarked.

There was rustling at the opposite end of the floor as the teams set up their weapons and gear.

Beckham shook his head. "Kid's gone."

"Maybe he'll come back when he realizes we aren't monsters."

Beckham stepped out of the space and checked the passage to the right. "Did you clear these?"

"Not yet."

"Let's go."

They cleared the last row of cubicles and stopped at the emergency exit. Beckham took a guarded step forward, reaching for the handle as Horn aimed his rifle at the door. They exchanged a glance, and then Beckham twisted the knob. Horn went first, with Beckham on his heels.

"Don't *fucking* move!" yelled a deep, panicked voice.

Beckham struggled to see around Horn's bulky frame.

"I said don't MOVE!" A bearded man with wild hair angled a mean-looking shotgun toward Horn. The boy Beckham had seen before cowered behind the man. It was then Beckham noticed the uniform.

He was a cop.

"We're friendly," Horn said. He lowered his rifle and raised his right hand. "We're not here to hurt you."

"Drop the shotgun, man," Beckham added, pointing his muzzle at the floor.

The bearded officer's hands shook, the barrel of the shotgun wavering. Beckham watched his trigger finger. It was dangerously close to squeezing off a round that would take off Horn's head.

"We're going to get you out of here," Beckham said. "Just lower your weapon." He realized what they must look like, with their NVGs and armored vests packed full of magazines. The passage was lit only by the moonlight streaming through the window behind them. Beckham imagined they looked a lot like something from the Terminator movies.

"You can't get us out of here," the man said. "There's no way out of the city."

Beckham wasn't sure how to respond. He was too worried about the guy firing a slug into Horn's dome.

"Listen," Beckham said in his calmest voice. "There is an entire platoon of marines on the street below. We're here to clear the area, set up a base, and then evacuate any survivors."

"You're not fucking listening!"

Beckham's earpiece flared to life. "What the hell is going on?" It was Jensen.

"Hold position," Beckham whispered into his minimic. If the other strike teams showed up now, the officer would either run or start shooting.

"I'm listening," Beckham said, trying to draw the man's attention.

He raised the shotgun and pointed it at Beckham. That was fine; it kept Horn out of the line of fire.

"Those things are everywhere, man. Everywhere. There is no way out of the city. Everyone that's tried has ended up in the nests." The man whimpered, the gun shaking again.

"That's not going to happen to you. We're going to get you out of here," Beckham said.

The man smirked, lowered his rifle, and slowly raised his chin toward the top of the stairwell. "You don't understand, do you? No one can save *you*. Those monsters..." He paused and wiped saliva from his lips before adding, "Those monsters own this city now. Every single inch."

Beckham wanted to reply, but they were running out of time. His earpiece came to life again. "In position. Where the hell are you, Beckham?"

Jensen again. He was agitated.

"Hold position," Beckham replied, trying to conceal his own frustration. He flipped the channel off and then took a step down the staircase.

"Maybe you're right," he said. "But either way, you have a better chance with us."

The kid peered out from behind him. "Maybe we should go with them, Dad?"

Beckham's heart leaped at the words.

"Fine," the officer said. "But I sure hope there are a shit-ton of you guys."

"There are," Horn lied.

Beckham moved out of the way and walked back down the wall of cubicles. The view of the destroyed city shocked him again every time he looked. It was remarkable that anyone had survived, let alone a father and his son. It was a true testament to what people could do when faced with daunting odds. Some ran for the hills. Others committed suicide. And there were a few, like these two, who fought to survive.

"What's your name, sir?" Beckham said as they walked.

"I'm Jake. This is my son, Timothy."

"Good to have you with us," Beckham said. "We're going to get you guys out of here." It was yet another promise he wasn't sure he could keep. But he was going to do everything in his power to make sure he didn't break it. Gripping the handle of his M4 tightly, he led the trio through the rows of cubicles back to where the members of Charlie and Delta were waiting, their rifles aimed at the park below.

21

They were trapped in the second medical wing. Kate wanted to cry. She wanted to break down and give up. But she'd come this far, and she had others to think about. She had Tasha and Jenny.

"Shit, shit, shit," Rod said. He jerked his pistol around frantically, searching for the source of the screeching. It was coming from everywhere: above, behind, even through the vents in the floor.

The Variant ripping through the ICU wasn't the only one in the building. There were others too.

An agonized scream broke out from the intensive care wing—human. A mixture of pain and terror so distorted that she couldn't place the voice.

Ellis paced back and forth. "So what do we do now?"

Riley shook his head. "There isn't anything to do but wait."

"Great, just great," Rod said.

"Would you rather have stayed in the ICU?" Kate asked.

He seemed to think for a moment. Before he could answer, another screech rang out. His eyes wild and wide, Rod swept the pistol over the hallway. The screams from the ICU had faded, replaced by the sporadic sounds of the other Variants deep inside the building.

Her heart racing, Kate hunched down to hold Tasha and Jenny. Both girls were in a state of shock, their eyes glazed, tears flowing freely down their rosy cheeks. Never before had Kate felt so alone. She'd lost almost everything in the past three weeks, and now Reed wasn't here to protect her. Instead he was out there somewhere, fighting, doing what he did best.

What did she do best? She'd created a weapon that had killed billions.

A thud pulled her back to reality. Something slammed into the doors to the ICU, leaving a deep dent in the metal.

Another thump came from the ceiling.

Furious scratching followed, like a dog digging for a bone.

"Stay close to me," Riley whispered. He waved Ellis, Kate, and the girls over with his free hand and kept his pistol aimed at the door. "Rod, you shoot anything that comes through that door."

A short nod from the toxicologist. But Kate could see he was hardly listening. The man was beyond his breaking point. She was starting to worry he would shoot one of them by accident.

"You with me, man?" Riley asked.

Another short nod.

Pounding rattled the door as the creature charged again and again, trying to reach them. The scratching above stopped, replaced by a cracking sound in the distance that could have been gunfire.

Kate looked up, filled with hope at the sound. There was still someone out there!

The door to the ICU shook again, tremors rippling through the floor from the force. The scratching in the vents amplified. The Variants were growing more desperate.

More gunshots. These were closer. The crack echoed through the building. Then there were footfalls in the medical ward. Heavy boots.

A soldier.

Kate's hope collapsed with the ceiling in front of her. Pulling them to her chest, she shielded the girls as panels and beams crashed down. Ellis joined them, wrapping his arms around them as best he could.

The pop of gunfire rang out in all directions.

There were screams. Indecipherable. Kate couldn't tell if they were human or Variant. She cracked an eyelid to see two of the creatures covered in dust and blood. Both of them were badly burned, just like the one in the ICU. Riley fired without hesitation. The bullets peppered the lead creature with holes, its chest jerking from each impact.

It let a screech fly and tilted its head toward Rod. A swollen tongue slipped out of its mouth as it lunged for the man. He didn't get off a single shot before it overwhelmed him, wrapping limbs around his waist and clamping down on his chest with its sucker.

"No!" Rod screamed. "Help me!" The clatter from the other door and the pop of gunshots shrouded his pleas.

Kate held the girls closer as the other Variant darted away. The monster leaped from the floor to the wall and crawled across the horizontal surface, joints clicking with every motion. Riley fired the rest of his magazine. Bullets tore into the creature's body, blood spraying across the white wall.

"Kill it!" Kate screamed.

The doors to the ICU shook again. Both girls clung to her. Their fingers dug into her back.

Riley snapped in a new magazine and fired at the injured Variant racing across the wall. A bullet took off the top of its skull and it fell to the ground, spasms shaking its body. Riley took careful aim and then fired one last shot into the creature's head. Then he twisted in his chair and fired at the monster that was busy bashing in Rod's head. The toxicologist had stopped moaning. His eyes were gone, lost in the sunken crater that had been his face.

Another tremor shook the locked doors to the ICU. Kate forced her gaze away from Rod's mangled body.

Riley fiddled with the pistol. "It's fucking jammed!"

The Variant growled, still perched over Rod. It looked at Riley, pursed its swollen lips, and then stood. Riley continued to work the jammed bullet out of the chamber as the creature walked toward him.

Kate couldn't believe her eyes. She'd never seen one move so slowly. But this one seemed relaxed. Confident, even. The creature knew Riley couldn't inflict any harm. It was like a cat playing with its food. Toying with them.

She couldn't look away from the bulging blue veins covering its pale, wrinkled skin or the thin strands of white hair hanging over its vertical yellow eyes. The Variant had undergone a complete transformation, from its talons to its sucker lips.

Blood oozed from a bullet wound in the creature's muscular chest. It stopped to examine Ellis, Kate, and the girls. It squeezed its lips together again and then opened its mouth to reveal jagged, broken teeth.

"Fuck," Riley said. Giving up, he hurled the pistol at the creature and raised his fists. "Come on, you piece of shit." He kept his eyes locked on the pale beast and yelled, "Run! Take the girls and—"

Before he could finish, the lock hardware to the door leading to the first medical ward exploded. The metal swung open, and a soldier wielding a rifle rushed inside. He was drenched in blood. He looked as if he'd taken a bath in it, and Kate couldn't see his face well enough to identify him. Then she noticed the metal blades attached to his knees, glistening scarlet.

Not a soldier.

A marine.

"Fitz!" Kate shouted.

The Variant's yellow eyes widened, as though it was trying to comprehend what had just happened.

"Get behind me!" Fitz yelled. He opened fire at the creature. The rounds ripped through its swollen chest and out the other side, painting the hallway with red. The monster shrieked, blood spraying from its mouth.

Fitz continued past Riley, who still held his fists in front of him. He fired again and again, but the Variant wouldn't go down. It stepped forward on blackened, burnt legs and held its ground.

Raising his muzzle ever so slightly, Fitz stopped three feet away from the monster and aimed for its head. It let out one final screech but was silenced by the gunshot. The creature's skull exploded like a piñata.

Fitz hovered over the corpse, fresh blood dripping from his body. Wiping an arm over his face, he reloaded and aimed his rifle at the dented door at the other end of the hallway. "Stay here," he said.

Ellis helped Kate to her feet and then ran over to grab Rod's gun. He handed it to Riley, and they huddled together in the middle of the hallway.

"Stop," Riley shouted, holding up a hand. Fitz shot him a glare that said, *I got this*. He aimed his rifle at the lock and watched as the crazed Variant continued to smash into the door.

Fitz waited for the creature to strike again. He reached forward, unlocked the door, and then backed away. A second later the burned creature came smashing through the right door, skidding face first across the floor. It scrambled and thrashed as it attempted to get back up. But Fitz was already firing. It was over in less than five seconds. The creature flopped and let out one final gasp.

"That's all of 'em in this building," Fitz said. "You guys okay?"

Kate nodded and then cupped a hand over her mouth when she saw the floor and walls of the ICU behind him. Tina's body lay in a puddle of her own blood, her hand only inches from the door.

"We better move," Fitz said. "There could be more outside."

Every man on Delta and Charlie teams looked to Beckham and his new company. The two teams were set up along the chest-high wall separating them from a twenty-six-floor drop. Ryan used his elbow pad to break out a final shard of glass and then hefted his MK11 onto the ledge.

"This is Jake and his son, Timothy," Beckham said as they approached the strike team. He moved his mini-mic back to his lips. "Charlie and Delta in position."

"Copy that," Lieutenant Gates replied. "FOB is established. I'll inform Command."

Jake grabbed his son's hand and stepped up to the window next to Beckham. The two men looked over the side, the wind rustling through their hair.

Several tents and a generator were set up below. The three Humvees were parked in a triangle, with the FOB shielded by the trucks. The M240s were angled in opposite directions, and the TOW launchers on the Bradleys were facing the park.

No matter how impressive the firepower was, Beckham knew there was no way in hell it would hold off an enemy numbering in the hundreds of thousands.

"Glad to see someone else made it," Jensen said, pulling Beckham's attention from the view below. He examined Jake and Timothy for a moment and said, "You're a cop?"

"Was a cop," Jake said. "The last of our group tried to leave the city a few days ago. We lost contact with them a few hours later. Those things have nests and—"

Ryan's raised voice cut the man off before he could explain further. "We got movement."

Beckham rushed back to the wall for a look. His stomach dropped. Was this it? Were the Variants finally attacking?

A gust of wind pushed Beckham back. He fought his way closer.

"I don't see shit," Horn said.

Ryan angled his MK11 toward the library. "Front steps."

Beckham scoped the grounds and zeroed in on the motion. Sure enough, dozens of Variants swarmed out of the building. The clanging of weapons vibrated through the room as the men shifted their rifles toward the motion.

"We need to get out of here," Jake said. "Those things know we're here now! You led them right to us!"

"Calm down," Horn said. "The Variants won't even get close. We're packing a ton of firepower up here and down there," he said, pointing to the armored vehicles.

Beckham flicked his mini-mic back to his mouth. "We have multiple contacts outside of the library."

"Copy that; stand by for orders," Gates replied, his voice deceivingly calm.

"Hold your fire," Beckham said to his men. "Wait for the lieutenant to give us the order. And conserve your ammo. Don't shoot until you have a target."

He watched dozens of the Variants flow out of the

building. They dashed under the tree cover of Bryant Park, most of them on all fours like the animals they were.

"Contacts incoming," Beckham said with disgust. This was just the beginning. He could feel it in his gut.

His earpiece filled with static, and then Gates said, "Engage the enemy. Fire when you have a target." His voice seemed gruff and tense.

At least you're not out in the open, Beckham thought, checking on the men below. Most of them were situated behind the armor, but a few stood in the street.

The Humvees' spotlights crisscrossed the concrete, and the vehicle commanders concentrated the beams on the east entrance to Bryant Park. Beckham clenched his jaw as more of the creatures piled out of the building, a never-ending flow of monsters. He'd lost count of their numbers now. There were well over a hundred—just a snapshot of their true strength.

"Stay focused," Beckham said. "Don't fire until you have one in your cross hairs." He felt like a commander at the Battle of Bunker Hill, ordering his line to hold their fire until they saw the whites of their enemy's eyes.

The sound of muffled breathing and the whistling of wind crowded around him. The teams waited patiently, every one of them knowing what was about to happen. Weapons were aimed tightly at the park.

Beckham flipped on his NVG optics and scoped the trees. The wind carried the inhumane screams of the Variants from the tree cover where they hid. The creatures were smarter now.

He wondered if they were taunting 1st Platoon. Nothing would surprise him at this point.

Beckham checked their rear guard. Two marines held security at the entrance to the floor, with their weapons aimed down the hallway. Everything was set.

Jake and Timothy waited in the shadows of a cubicle. The police officer held his trembling son. "We need to *leave*," he pleaded when he saw Beckham looking in his direction.

The chorus of shrieks, croaks, and high-pitched screams continued, making it difficult for Beckham to concentrate. His heart thumped. The battle for Manhattan was finally starting.

"Try to stay calm and cover your ears. This is going to be loud," he said.

"You're not listening!" the cop insisted. It seemed to be his favorite phrase.

Beckham moved back to the window. He didn't have time to argue. The armored shells of the Bradleys maneuvered their turrets.

"What the hell is Gates waiting for?" Horn whispered.

"For them to strike first," Jensen said.

The hungry wails of the creatures increased, and the convoy finally answered with the earsplitting 25-millimeter rounds. The chain guns belched fire. Trees disappeared in a cloud of wooden confetti.

"Hold your fire!" Beckham shouted. The Variants still weren't in view.

"Where the fuck are they?" Jensen yelled.

The marines in the Humvee turrets swept their spotlights over the destruction, searching for contacts.

Beckham's earpiece came to life with Gates's confused voice. "Does anyone have—" Then a brief pause. "Strike teams, do you have eyes?"

"We lost the Variants in the park," Beckham said. "Rodriguez, Peters, you got anything?"

"Negative," both marines replied simultaneously.

"Behind them! Behind them!" Timbo suddenly shouted.

Beckham pressed his body against the wall and out the window to scan the pile of cars at the rear guard of the convoy, but saw nothing. "Where? I don't see shit!"

"The manhole covers!" Ryan said.

Beckham's heart climbed into his throat. The Variants had laid the perfect trap.

They spilled out of the open manholes, breaking into a gallop as soon as they climbed onto the street.

"Check your six!" Beckham shouted into his minimic. But it was already too late. The creatures tackled a trio of marines before they could react.

"Open fire!" Beckham ordered as the monsters dragged the men across the concrete and into their lairs.

The marines in the turrets turned and fired at the Variants just as a wave more than a hundred strong streamed out of Bryant Park. The chain guns coughed and spewed rounds into the Variants, cutting them down with ease. But they kept coming.

Beckham focused on the marines. One of them stood on the rear of Steam Beast, firing his rifle wildly at the pack charging on the platoon's six. It was Sergeant Valdez.

"My God," Beckham whispered.

The crack of gunfire and the distant screams of dying marines activated Beckham's internal machine. His entire body went numb, his instinct taking over, and he started barking orders.

"Lieutenant, get your fucking men into the Bradley troop holds!" There was no response. He cursed. The officer was worthless now; he was probably cowering in the back seat of his armored chariot. He tried the sergeant. "Valdez, do you copy?"

"They're everywhere!" the man replied.

"Sergeant, get your men into the tracks!" Beckham shouted. The gunfire was so loud he couldn't even hear himself. He turned to the snipers. "Focus your fire on the Variants at the rear. Lay down covering fire for those marines."

Desperate men scrambled for the safety of the armored vehicles. Beckham paced back and forth behind the strike teams. They fired calculated shots into the melee. Empty magazines and bullet casings clanged on the floor.

A frantic voice spilled over the net. "More contacts to the northwest!"

Beckham squeezed his way between Horn and Jensen. He didn't need a scope to see the new flood of creatures climbing over the barricade of cars. First Platoon was surrounded.

"Can't hold 'em!" grunted Sergeant Valdez. He jumped off the track and herded a pair of marines into the back of the vehicle. Another two stood their ground a hundred yards away. In a blink, the men were gone. Swallowed by the horde, their screams were lost in the madness.

A second turret swiveled from the park and joined the fight to the rear guard. The two M240s cut through the creatures flowing from the manhole, buying Valdez a few extra seconds. Beckham scoped the street and watched a final marine pile into the back of Steam Beast. Valdez fired off another several shots before securing the hatch.

Only four of the marines on the street had made it.

Beckham cursed. He had to maintain control of his anger. Nothing he could do would change the fate of those lost. He had to think of the living, of the men still fighting.

The turret guns obliterated the final Variants that climbed from the manholes. Piles of the dead and dying creatures were hemorrhaging a lake of blood.

It was a small victory.

The vehicle commanders in the Humvees focused their fire on the approaching horde to the north as Black Reaper and Steam Beast kept their fire concentrated on the park. Packs of the creatures continued to charge out from the thick haze that lingered near the tree line.

Only a few made it through.

They dashed across the concrete, swerving and navigating around the gunfire. The creatures were making a run for the convoy.

"Keep them off the Bradleys!" Beckham yelled.

One of the Variants leaped onto Black Reaper and tugged on the hatch. A sniper bullet took off its head. Its body slumped over the hull and slid onto the street. Two more climbed onto the armor before more sniper fire erased them from the fight.

A beat later the battle to the east ended. Variants stumbled from the cloud of debris only to be dropped by the M240 fire from the third Humvee. Beckham couldn't believe his eyes. The massacre had quickly reversed sides. First Platoon had prevailed. Maybe Command was right after all—maybe bullets could win this war.

A voice spluttered over the channel, crackling with static. Beckham clenched his fists when he realized it was Lieutenant Gates. The man was babbling, incoherent.

Sergeant Valdez cut in. "Vehicle commanders, hold your fire. Strike teams, hold position."

"Delta, copy," Beckham replied. He exchanged a nervous glance with Jensen.

"Charlie, copy," the lieutenant colonel said, changing his magazine with a click.

"Alpha, copy," Peters replied.

Beckham waited for Rodriguez to respond. But the sergeant said nothing.

A small tremor suddenly rippled through the building.

"We need to leave!" Jake yelled. He pulled Timothy

from their cubicle and hurried toward the marines holding security at the exit.

"Wait!" Beckham ordered. But the man didn't look back.

Pushing his mini-mic back into position, Beckham said, "Rodriguez, do you copy? Over."

Another quake rattled the tower.

"Do you feel that?" Horn said.

"What the hell..." Jensen began to say.

The channel crackled, and Rodriguez came online. "Uh, copy, Delta." He paused and let out a weak cough. "You got to fucking see this to believe it."

"See what?" Beckham said.

"From the east. They're coming," Rodriguez replied, his voice shaking now.

Beckham hesitantly brought his scope to his NVG optics and glassed down Forty-Second Street.

"Holy fucking shit," Jensen whispered. "They're probably coming from the subways, from Grand Central Station. That's the only thing that makes sense."

Holy fucking shit was an adequate response, Beckham decided, watching as thousands of Variants flowed down the street. They fanned out in all directions, transforming the streets into a river of bodies. There had to be tens of thousands, if not more, and the number kept rising as more spilled from the station.

Now he knew why Jake had insisted on leaving. New York City no longer belonged to the human race. It belonged to the Variants. And 1st Platoon had awakened the hive.

Beckham snapped into motion. "Lieutenant Gates, do you copy? Over."

Static flickered over the net. He considered tearing the headset off and tossing it out the window. The fucking commander was worthless. Mastering his rage, he turned to the rest of his men waiting at the windows.

"Get to the street!" Beckham shouted. "We need to get the fuck out of here, ASAP. For all we know, that son of a bitch Gates is calling in an air strike!"

Jensen hopped to his feet. "I thought this location was supposed to be off-limits."

Beckham pointed to the Variant army. "They won't worry about some library when they can kill hundreds of thousands of Variants in one strike."

In seconds, the team was moving with unprecedented speed, scooping up gear and slinging straps over their shoulders. The doomsday clock was ticking.

Beckham caught up to Jake and Timothy. "You guys have to move fast, okay?"

Two nods.

Straightening his headset back into position, Beckham said, "Valdez, if you can hear me, hold tight. We're on our way."

22

The command center was guarded like Fort Knox. Radios crackled, buzzing with the voices of men at war. White lights flickered and spilled over the front entrance, blinking like a beacon calling a lost ship into harbor. Two marines on the steps frantically waved Kate and the others to safety. She squeezed Tasha's and Jenny's hands, trying to ignore the screams reverberating from the other buildings.

"Let's go! Get inside!" one of the men yelled.

She moved past him, catching a glimpse of his face. He was young, and she almost thought he was Jackson. But no, she knew Jackson was dead. The marine had sacrificed his life to buy them time to escape. They'd found his broken body a few feet away from the medical building. By some miracle, he'd still been alive, holding on for a final few seconds. When she'd reached down to help, he had let out his last breath.

Kate felt herself beginning to cry again as she walked into the command building. She let go of the children's hands and held up fingers glistening with blood. She wasn't even sure whose it was. Jackson's? Rod's? After watching the world hemorrhage, she thought she would be used to the sight. But the blood of strangers was different than that of people she knew. She hadn't known Rod well, but the image of his sunken face would be deeply rooted in her memory for the rest of her life. *However long that might be*, she thought.

Kate added Rod's and Jackson's deaths to the list of billions she felt responsible for. The burden ate at her, overwhelming her. An enraged voice pulled her back to the present. It was Major Smith's, and he stood in the middle of the atrium, surrounded by an entourage of marines.

"Somebody give me a sitrep!"

No one responded.

"You," Smith said, pointing to a marine who had followed Kate's group into the building. "How many of those things are still on the loose?"

"I'm not sure, sir," the man replied.

Fitz slung his rifle higher up over his shoulders. He spoke confidently. "Sir, I counted eighteen of the creatures. We killed six on the tarmac. Two were killed in Building Three, and another three went down in Building Two. I saw one other body in the concrete circle. So there could be another six out there."

Smith swore. He flicked his headset to his lips and barked out new orders. "Six more hostiles on the loose. All strike teams proceed with caution."

Kate followed his gaze around the room. Groups of frightened scientists and staff huddled in corners, some of them catatonic, others crying. There couldn't have been more than seventy-five people in the room.

"Where's everyone else?" Smith asked. When none of his staff replied, he looked to Fitz.

The marine straightened and said, "This *is* everyone, sir."

For the first time, Kate saw the major shocked into silence. He was truly overwhelmed by the loss.

And for good reason, Kate thought, focusing on the survivors. Half of Plum Island's scientists were dead, and an unknown number of soldiers had lost their lives in the fight. With six more creatures on the prowl, the future of the facility was at risk.

Smith twisted his wedding ring around his finger, his thoughts clearly still elsewhere. He turned to the marines and staff behind him. "Get all of these people to the end of the hallway and then secure the doors."

A marine with a Brooklyn accent motioned Kate and the others forward with two fingers. "This way, ma'am."

Ellis muttered as they walked, "I can't believe this is happening."

"Doctor Kate?" asked Jenny. "Where's my dad?"

"He's with Reed in New York, sweetheart."

When they got to the end of the hallway, the marines locked the door. Three of them remained with the group.

"What if he doesn't come back?" Tasha asked. "What if he dies, like Mommy?"

Kate kneeled in front of the girls. Releasing a deep sigh, she reached for her last reserves of strength and said, "Don't worry. Your dad and Reed are coming home soon. They're going to be just fine."

She hoped it wasn't a lie.

Fitz bolted out of the command center. The last time his body had hurt so much had been when he was still in rehab. Running like a madman across the island and killing Variants had taken a toll on him. But that's what marines did. They kept going.

To the end.

A hundred feet ahead, two Medical Corps soldiers stood guard under a light pole. Beams from tactical lights crossed the base as strike teams searched for the six missing creatures.

An evil shriek cut through the night. A rifle cracked. The shots stopped abruptly—another soldier, lost.

"Follow me," Fitz said.

"Our orders are to hold this position," one of the men protested.

Fitz snorted. "Did you hear that? We just lost another man."

The two guards exchanged a glance and then nodded.

"Let's go," Fitz said. He charged in the direction of the last gunshot with his weapon shouldered, his eyes probing the underbrush and trees for the creatures. A voice crackled in his earpiece as he ran.

"Command, Charlie. Four hostiles down. Repeat, four hostiles down."

Only two left, Fitz thought. He imagined the damage the creatures could do if they made it inside the command center. He and a handful of other men were all that stood in their way. Fighting the pain, he ran harder.

Budding tree branches whipped back and forth overhead as he rounded the corner of Building 4. Balling his hand into a fist, he stopped and took a knee next to the trunk of a tree. The other two men propped their backs against the side of the building, waiting for orders.

With the memory of Cole's death fresh on his mind, Fitz hesitated. The stocky Medical Corps soldier had died entering the first ward, his throat slashed by the claws of a Variant.

Fitz wasn't used to giving orders and finally understood the burden that came with leading men into battle. Exhaling, he rose and said, "Stay sharp."

After one final scan of the underbrush and the trees beyond, he pushed on. Thorns shredded his pants as he moved deeper into the bushes. Through the tree branches he should see the electrical fences and a guard tower.

He emerged from the brush and hurried over to the closest tree for cover. A scan of the beach revealed a mangled body on the ground in front of the tower, the soldier's neck twisted in a way that assured Fitz he was dead. He zoomed in with his scope and recoiled when the body was yanked into the bushes.

"Contact!" Fitz yelled. He managed to fire off three shots before something hit him from above, knocking him to the ground with such force that his lungs emptied in a huff. Red blossomed around the sides of his vision as the Variant he hadn't seen in the tree above beat his body. With each powerful blow, he imagined his organs liquefying.

A gunshot saved him before the creature could do too much damage. It slumped off his body and landed with a meaty thud in the dirt.

"You okay?" the Medical Corps guard who had saved his life said.

Fitz fought to refill his lungs, gasping for precious air. "Yeah," he said. "I think so… Thanks, man."

He rubbed the blurriness from his vision and then glanced down at the Variant. Its face was gone, nothing but a scramble of flesh and bone where the bullet had exited. Remembering the other Variant, Fitz crawled across the dirt and grabbed his rifle.

"Looks like it's dead," yelled the other soldier. Fitz watched the man drag a Variant corpse from the bushes.

"Nice shot," the soldier said.

Fitz collapsed with his back to the dirt. The stars in the cloudless sky sparkled with an intensity he hadn't seen. With the cities of the old world dark, the stars had a chance to truly shine. The beauty of the view was the perfect reward for their tiny victory.

Smiling, Fitz pushed his mini-mic to his lips and said, "Command, this is Fitzpatrick. All hostiles eliminated."

"Move!" Beckham shouted. His voice echoed through the concrete stairwell. He had taken point, leading the strike teams down twenty-six floors of the Bank of America Tower as fast as possible. He was flying down the steps, bounding two or three at a time. His muscles ached, but he ignored the pain. He had to get them the fuck out of here before the convoy took off without them.

It wasn't a question of whether Lieutenant Gates would leave; it was just a matter of when.

Beckham didn't have a single ounce of trust left in the man. Their only hope rested in Sergeant Valdez. He wasn't the type of leader to leave men behind, especially fellow marines.

The decaying body of the dead Variant lay across the next landing. He shoved the corpse to the side with a swift kick to the midsection.

Two marines brushed past him, the magazines tucked into their vests scraping against his own weapons. The sound of labored breathing and the pounding of heavy boots echoed through the narrow stairwell. Every man moved with urgency fueled by fear. The same fear raided Beckham's own thoughts.

He ground his teeth, praying and pleading they wouldn't emerge from the tower into a swarm of the ravenous creatures.

Beckham ran faster when he heard the faint crack of heavy gunfire outside the building.

Shit.

The Variant army was getting close.

A frantic voice called out from above, asking them to wait up. Beckham snorted and turned to look up the next stairwell, narrowly avoiding Timbo's massive frame crashing into him.

He signaled for Chow, Jinx, and Horn to proceed without him. Jensen and Ryan came next. Then a handful of marines. Finally he saw Jake and Timothy. With only a small flashlight to guide them, they were lagging an entire flight of stairs behind the group.

"Come on!" Beckham yelled.

Jake grabbed his son's hand. "We're doing our best! I told you this would happen, I freaking told you!"

Beckham wanted to offer reassurance, but what could he say? The man was right. The Variants were closing in.

His anger spiked as he led the police officer and his son down the stairs. How many soldiers had to die for Central Command to realize the creatures weren't mindless animals? This wasn't the same type of war generals like Kennor had spent their life fighting. This wasn't the same enemy. They didn't play by the same rules.

Beckham spied a sign for the fifth floor. They were almost there. He flipped his mini-mic back to his mouth as he ran and attempted another transmission. "Lieutenant Gates, Delta team. Do you copy? Over."

Static crackled in his earpiece.

"Shit! Come on!" Beckham shouted. He tried again. "Gates, goddamnit, if you can hear me, you better not fucking move that convoy!"

More white noise.

Beckham stifled another curse. There were so many people counting on him right now. Kate was waiting at

Plum Island—worried sick, he was sure. And Horn's daughters...

He wouldn't let them become orphans. Not today. Not ever.

Beckham pushed on. He strained to hear gunfire. It would mean the convoy was still waiting for them. He heard nothing but the stomp of boots as they raced down the stairs.

"Hurry!" Beckham yelled. He leaped down three stairs.

They piled to a halt at the second floor.

"What's going on?" Beckham asked. He moved through the teams forcefully, pushing them out of the way as he managed his way down the stairs. Horn and Jensen were waiting at the door leading to the atrium. It was propped open a hair, and Jensen peeked through.

Beckham squirmed past Horn and took a knee next to Jensen. The ground shook again. Broken glass rattled in the lobby.

"Where's the convoy?"

"I don't see 'em," Jensen said

"I'm going in," Beckham said. "We don't have time to wait here."

Horn grabbed his left arm. "I'm going with you."

Beckham didn't object. If they were going to die, he wanted to die by his best friend's side.

The ground continued trembling, a mini-earthquake that wouldn't stop. Beckham could feel the blood pumping through his veins. He wasn't sure what kind of reception they were going to receive outside, but there was nowhere else to run. If the convoy was really gone, then the only option was to fight.

He counted the seconds, knowing they were running out of time.

The two men slipped into the lobby. Beckham kept

track of Horn in his peripheral vision. They halted as broken glass rattled on the ground, the approaching horde so large that their footfalls shook the earth. It sounded as if a hundred M1 Abramses were charging through the city.

Beckham waved Horn toward the entrance. The street finally came into view. Not a single living thing moved.

Thirteen, fourteen, fifteen...

Beckham grabbed the broken door handle and pulled it open. Words sounded in his earpiece, but the rumbling was too loud to make them out. He placed his right boot outside, hanging halfway inside the building and halfway out on the sidewalk. Looking to the left up Forty-Second Street, he froze in place, not daring to move. His NVG optics provided him a vivid green field of view that would have petrified any veteran.

The mob of Variants was racing down the street, stirring up a cloud of dust and ash. Some leaped onto buildings, charging across their vertical surfaces.

There had to be thousands of them.

Twenty-eight, twenty-nine, thirty...

Forcing himself to look away, he checked the Avenue of Americas for the convoy. Steam Beast and a Humvee sat idling in the middle of the street. A man stood on the back of the Bradley, waving with his machine gun and screaming at the top of his lungs, the sound completely lost in the din of the Variants.

Beckham's chest heaved with relief when he saw it was Sergeant Valdez. He had waited after all. But the vehicle was built only to hold eight, and the Humvee would only hold another eight, max. They had over twenty-four men between the four strike teams, not to mention Jake and Timothy.

"Let's go!" he said, motioning Horn to pass on the message to the team.

Soon the teams were sprinting down the street. Beckham considered his options as they ran. There weren't many. Only half of them would be able to squeeze into the vehicles. Unless some rode on top, but if the Variants caught up...

The army screaming down Forty-Second and Forty-Third Streets was closing in fast. Only a block separated the teams from countless hungry mouths.

Valdez jumped off the fighting vehicle. "Get your men inside! Eight in the Humvee and eight in the track! Hurry! Gates called in an air strike!" The sergeant looked down at his watch. "We have two minutes to get out of here before we're barbecued!"

The ground shook from the pounding of Variant feet. Beckham strained to focus his rattled brain. His eyes roved from the vehicles and then back to the team.

"Get Jake and Timothy in the Bradley!" he shouted. "That leaves room for another fourteen of us. Ten will have to stay behind, unless you want to take your chances riding on top of the track." He spoke rapidly, watching the Variants hit Bryant Park, their twisted bodies exploding through the haze.

Horn grabbed Beckham's arm again. "Boss, we can all make it—"

"Get inside the track," Beckham said sternly. "That's an order. Your girls need their father."

Horn hesitated. His gaze shifted to the monsters for a fraction of a second, just enough time for Beckham to see the overwhelming pain in his friend's features. They both knew the chances of surviving if they stayed behind were slim.

But the decision was already made. Horn eased his grip on Beckham's arm and embraced him instead. "Love ya, bro. Watch your ass, and good luck."

"You too, Big Horn. Take care of those girls, and tell

Kate I'll see her soon," Beckham said. Then he shouted, "For those staying, let's move!"

The vehicle commander of the remaining Humvee swung his M240 into position and opened fire. A missile from the Bradley's TOW launcher streaked overhead.

The chaos bent time, warping every second into minutes. Crimson explosions burst in the park where the missiles found targets, showering the battleground with meaty chunks of the enemy.

"Come on!" Beckham yelled. His words were lost in the crushing sound of gunfire. He spun away from the Variant horde, ready to shove shell-shocked troops into the vehicles. But the men were already moving. Horn and Jake hefted Timothy into the Bradley, and marines piled in behind them.

A handful of soldiers had crowded around Beckham, their weapons forming a perimeter. He recognized every face: Timbo, Ryan, Valdez, Chow, Jinx, and Jensen.

"No time to argue. Smith's more than capable of leading while I'm away," Jensen said when he saw Beckham's confusion. He spat on the ground and yelled, "*Move!*"

The M240 barked overhead. Shells clicked off the pavement as the team ran for the nearest manhole cover, the only place they had a chance of surviving the bombs about to be dropped over the city. Another missile popped from the TOW.

"Help me with this!" Beckham said. "Those jets are en route!"

Timbo took a knee, and together they slid the heavy cover away from the hole. The team funneled down the ladder as the Humvee raced away. Steam Beast remained behind, Matthews clearly hell-bent on providing Beckham and the others a chance to escape.

"Get out of here," Beckham shouted.

Matthews glanced down at Beckham. The look of

fear on the young man's face had been replaced with courage.

"Good luck!" Matthews yelled.

Beckham nodded and began the descent, pausing momentarily to watch the Bradley lurch away. The tracks crunched over the broken bodies of dead Variants. Behind them, the swollen mass of creatures charged from Bryant Park.

He knew then that Operation Liberty had likely failed in every major city. What little hope humanity had was gone. The Variants were now the dominant species.

"Let's go, Beckham!" came a voice inside the tunnel below.

Beckham started climbing into the darkness when another sound came, a screaming louder than a hundred thousand Variants combined. He eyed the skyline and saw a squadron of jets flying low to the east. Ducking inside the hole, he slid the cover over the top, sealing them in.

He climbed down and then dropped into knee-high water. The team was already moving west through the muck. Beckham hesitated. He had saved half of his men, but he had only delayed the inevitable for the loyal soldiers who had joined him. They were now in Variant-controlled territory. And God only knew what they would find in the dark tunnels.

Beckham took off running as fast as he could through the stagnant sewage. Somewhere in the distance, a massive explosion rocked the street. Dust and rock rained from the ceiling. The entire passage shook as the bombs dropped above. With every blast, he hoped and prayed that Horn and the others had made it out of the kill zone.

Epilogue

Kate hated leaving Tasha and Jenny, but Major Smith had requested her presence in the command center. An hour had passed since the soldiers had cleared the base, and now the major said he had news.

She wiped her hands on her pants and then bent down in front of the girls. Both sat against the wall, their shirts stained scarlet. Jenny had her head buried into Tasha's armpit, sobbing uncontrollably.

Taking one knee, Kate said, "I have to go for a bit, but I'll be right back, okay?"

"But what if the monsters come back?"

"The monsters are gone. It's okay. You're safe now."

Tasha glanced up with glossy eyes. "My daddy was wrong."

"What do you mean?" Kate asked.

"Those sick people," Tasha said, wiping away a tear. "They *are* monsters. He told us monsters weren't real."

Kate thought about swallowing her response but decided it was better to tell the truth. "Yes, they are real, but they can't hurt you now. You're safe here. Riley will make sure nothing happens to you," Kate said, glancing over at the man.

The operator wheeled his chair closer and smiled. "She's right. Everything's going to be okay. I promise."

Tasha patted her sister's back and nodded weakly, as though she didn't believe Kate.

"I'll watch 'em," Riley said. "Go, and bring back good news."

Kate, her heart aching, forced herself away. She followed a Medical Corps guard down the hallway to the command center and walked through the doors. Chaos greeted her. Soldiers she didn't recognize huddled around the war table, frustration and fear present in their raised voices.

Smith paced behind the wall of radio equipment, stopping every few seconds to ask the operators what they were hearing. Chatter flowed from the speakers. Kate took a seat and waited, anxious to hear word of Operation Liberty. The news trickled in from across the country. Central Command was reporting heavy losses in every major city. The Variants had overwhelmed each unit, just as she had argued they would.

She wanted to cry, knowing Beckham was likely amongst the dead. Instead she listened for more radio transmissions.

"Sir, First Platoon is reporting sixty-five casualties," one of the soldiers at the table shouted.

Smith bowed his head, shaking it from side to side. When he looked up, he locked eyes with Kate.

" Doctor Lovato. I'm sorry, I didn't hear you come in," he said.

Kate stood and walked over to him, her stomach in knots.

"Thought you'd like to know First Platoon is being extracted from Pier Eighty-Six shortly," he said, checking his watch. "They suffered heavy losses. Less than half of the team made it."

"Did Reed...?"

Smith looked at the ground solemnly. "He stayed behind with several other men, including Lieutenant Colonel Jensen. There wasn't enough room in the vehicles to get them out before the bombs dropped."

Kate cupped her hands over her mouth. Hot tears blurred her vision.

Goddamn you, Reed. Why did you have to be the hero? You promised you'd come back...

"I'm sorry," Smith said, placing a hand on her shoulder. "But if anyone can survive out there, it's Beckham. I'll let you know the moment we hear anything."

When the shock passed, Kate suddenly remembered her promise to Tasha and Jenny. "What about Horn?" she asked, biting her lip in anticipation.

"He's on his way back," Smith replied.

Kate nodded, dazed and numb. Folding her arms across her chest, she trembled as she walked slowly across the room, pausing to stare out the observation window. The waves sparkled under the moonlight. She swept a strand of hair from her eyes and looked out on the endless beauty of the ocean.

The military couldn't stop the Variants. They were evolving at an unprecedented rate, transforming into faster, smarter, and deadlier predators. Bombs and bullets couldn't kill them all. And now there weren't even enough soldiers left to carry out orders. Humanity was no longer on the edge of extinction—they had plummeted over the side.

Dr. Allen's final words repeated in her mind as she stared blankly over the shimmering water.

In order to kill a monster, you'll have to create one.

Rising from beneath her pain and despair grew the seed of an idea. She had been wrong before. Science could still save the human race.

If you want to hear more about Nicholas Sansbury Smith's upcoming books, join his newsletter or follow him on social media. He just might keep you from the brink of extinction!

Newsletter: www.eepurl.com/bggNg9

Twitter: www.twitter.com/greatwaveink

Facebook: www.facebook.com/Nicholas-Sansbury-Smith-124009881117534

Website: www.nicholassansbury.com

For those who'd like to personally contact Nicholas, he would love to hear from you.

Greatwaveink@gmail.com

Acknowledgments

It's always hard for me to write this section for fear of leaving someone out. So many people had a hand in the creation of the Extinction Cycle and I know these stories would not be worth reading if I didn't have the overwhelming support of family, friends, and readers.

Before I thank those people, I wanted to give a bit of background on how the Extinction Cycle was conceived and the journey it has been on since I started writing. The story began more than five years ago, when I was still working as a planner for the state of Iowa and also during my time as a project officer for Iowa Homeland Security and Emergency Management. I had several duties throughout my tenure with the state, but my primary focus was protecting infrastructure and working on the state hazard mitigation plan. After several years of working in the disaster mitigation field, I learned of countless threats: from natural disasters to manmade weapons, and one of the most horrifying threats of all—a lab-created biological weapon.

Fast-forward to 2014, when my writing career started to take off. I was working on the Orbs series and brainstorming my next science fiction adventure. Back then, the genre was saturated with zombie books. I wanted to write something unique and different, a story that explained, scientifically, how a virus could turn men into monsters. During this time, the Ebola virus was raging through western Africa and several cases showed up in the continental United States for the first time.

After talking with my biomedical-engineer friend, Tony Melchiorri, an idea formed for a book that played on the risk the Ebola virus posed. That idea blossomed after I started researching chemical and biological weapons, many of which dated back to the Cold War. In March of 2014, I sat down to pen the first pages of *Extinction Horizon*, the first book in what would become the Extinction Cycle. Using real science and the terrifying premise of a government-made bioweapon, I set out to tell my story.

The Extinction Cycle quickly found an audience. The first three novels came out in rapid succession and seemed to spark life back into the zombie craze. The audiobook, narrated by the award-winning Bronson Pinchot climbed the charts, hitting the top spot on Audible. As I released books four and five, more readers discovered the Extinction Cycle—more than three hundred thousand to date. The German translation was released in November 2016 and Amazon's Kindle Worlds has opened the Extinction universe to other authors.

Even more exciting, two years after I published *Extinction Horizon*, Orbit decided to purchase and rerelease the series. The copy you are reading is the newly edited and polished version. I hope you've enjoyed it. I want to thank everyone who helped me create the Extinction Cycle.

I couldn't have done it without the help of a small army of editors, beta readers, and the support of my family and friends. I also owe a great deal of gratitude to my initial editors, Aaron Sikes and Erin Elizabeth Long, as well as my good author-friend Tony Melchiorri. The trio spent countless hours on the Extinction Cycle books. Without them these stories would not be what they are.

Erin also helped edit *Orbs* and *Hell Divers*. She's been with me pretty much since day one, and I appreciate her more than she knows. So, thanks Erin, Tony, and Aaron.

A special thanks goes to David Fugate, my agent, who provided valuable feedback on the early version of *Extinction Horizon* and the entire Extinction Cycle series. I'm grateful for his support and guidance.

Another special thanks goes to Blackstone Audio for their support of the audio version. Narrator Bronson Pinchot also played, and continues to play, a vital role in bringing the story to life.

I'm also extremely honored for the support I have received from the military community over the course of the series. I've heard from countless veterans, many of them wounded warriors who grew to love Corporal Joe Fitzpatrick and Team Ghost. I even heard from a few Delta Force operators. Many of these readers went on to serve as beta readers, and I'm forever grateful for their support and feedback.

They say a person is only as good as those that they surround themselves with. I've been fortunate to surround myself with talented people much smarter than myself. I've also had the support from excellent publishers like Blackstone and Orbit.

I would be remiss if I didn't also thank the people for whom I write: the readers. I've been blessed to have my work read in countries around the world by wonderful people. If you are reading this, know that I truly appreciate you for trying my stories.

To my family, friends, and everyone else who has supported me on this journey, I thank you.

extras

meet the author

Maria Diaz

Nicholas Sansbury Smith is the *USA Today* best-selling author of *Hell Divers*, the Orbs trilogy, and the Extinction Cycle. He worked for Iowa Homeland Security and Emergency Management in disaster mitigation before switching careers to focus on his one true passion: writing. When he isn't writing or daydreaming about the apocalypse, he enjoys running, biking, spending time with his family, and traveling the world. He is an Ironman triathlete and lives in Iowa with his fiancée, their dogs, and a houseful of books.

if you enjoyed

EXTINCTION EDGE

look out for

EXTINCTION AGE

The Extinction Cycle

by

Nicholas Sansbury Smith

In the fight for humanity's survival, one final hope remains....

Humans are losing the war. Master Sergeant Reed Beckham and the survivors of 1st Platoon must battle through the tunnels—where they make a grisly discovery.

Dr. Kate Lovato is working on a new bioweapon to destroy the Variants when a derelict navy destroyer crashes into the Connecticut shoreline, carrying yet another threat.

As the doomsday clock ticks down and military bases fall across the country, the human race enters the age of extinction. Will they prevail—or will mankind vanish off the face of the planet?

May 7, 2015
New York City

The tunnels below Manhattan reeked of death, but Master Sergeant Reed Beckham blocked out the stench of decay in the sultry air. Injured, rattled, and down to only his side arm, his focus was on keeping his men alive.

He pulled his shemagh scarf up to cover his nose and burst around another corner, following the sound of clanking gear and labored breathing through the underground sewer system. Light danced across the green-hued view of his night-vision goggles and bent eerily in the darkness. The graffiti-covered walls seemed to narrow as he ran, the artwork distorting as if he was in some sort of carnival fun house.

Breathe, Beckham ordered himself. *Breathe.*

He ignored the burn in his lungs and concentrated on the six helmets that bobbed up and down ahead. The loyal soldiers had followed him into the tunnels to escape the firebombs and the Variants, but Beckham feared he had only delayed the inevitable for these brave men.

"Keep moving!" Staff Sergeant Chow shouted. The Delta Force operator turned and waved Beckham forward.

An inhuman shriek answered, amplified by the enclosed space. The rapid clicking of joints followed as the Variants homed in on Team Ghost's location.

Beckham brushed against the side of a wall and threw a glance over his shoulder. The creatures clung to the shadows, their diseased flesh glowing in the moonlight streaming through partially open manhole covers. They skittered horizontally across the walls, just close enough to keep his team in view.

The monsters had transformed into perfect predators that could see in dim lighting, heal remarkably fast, and move like insects. Dr. Kate Lovato called it evolution. Beckham called it natural selection. And with every passing second, the Variants grew stronger while the human population dwindled.

Beckham had been there from day one, back in Building 8, from whence the virus that turned men into monsters first escaped. But even now, the sight of the Variants flooded him with raw fear. Adrenaline emptied into his system like a fast-release pill as he ran.

The creatures were testing him, seeing how far they could approach before Team Ghost opened fire. He responded with a shot from his M9. Rock and dust exploded from a wall. The warning would buy them only a precious minute or two.

A sudden tremor rumbled through the tunnel. Fragments of concrete poured from the ceiling, showering the team with debris. The jets were making a second pass on Manhattan, firebombing Midtown.

Beckham thought of his brothers-in-arms and of Timothy and Jake, hoping to God they were all out of the kill zone. He shook the thought away as he bolted through a cloud of dust and ash, one hand shielding his face. He slopped through ankle-deep sewage and turned every hundred feet to fire off another shot.

A frantic voice broke through the chaos.

"Which way?"

"Left!" came a second voice.

"Right!" shouted another a second later.

Beckham could barely see the junction ahead. None of them had any idea where they were or where they were going. Entering the tunnels had been a last resort. Now, deep beneath the streets, Beckham's only plan was to keep moving.

"Left! Go left!" he yelled, just as a second torrent of dull thuds hit the streets above. These explosions were closer, and the aftershock sent Beckham crashing into a wall. He braced himself with an elbow and whirled to fire at a trio of Variants darting across the ceiling. Two of them melted into the darkness, squawking in anger, but the third and largest creature dropped to all fours, its muscular limbs pounding the water.

Beckham fired another shot and took off running. By the time he passed the next corner, his team was fifty feet ahead. Timbo's bulky frame loomed in the darkness.

"Come on!" the Ranger huffed.

"I'm with you!" Beckham replied between raspy breaths. His earpiece crackled with static as he made up lost ground.

"You got a *plan?*" Lieutenant Colonel Jensen asked, putting deliberate emphasis on the final word.

Beckham couldn't lie. He was still trying to come up with a Plan B. So far, running around in the maze of tunnels wasn't working.

"We're going to need to make a stand! Get these Variants off our ass!" Beckham finally shouted. "Ammo count!"

The replies trickled over the comm channel. Amongst the seven of them, they had a handful of mags for their primary weapons and only a couple of frag grenades. Several of his men were also down to side arms.

Beckham probed the green oblivion of the tunnel as he considered their options. This wasn't the first time he'd had his back to a wall. At Fort Bragg, Beckham and Horn had been down to their knives before Chow had showed up with the cavalry. But this time no one was going to ride in and save him. Team Ghost was on its own.

A guttural croak echoed through the passage. Two more answered the call. The evil cries rattled his senses.

He examined his vest for something useful, anything that might buy them some more time to escape. Two smoke bombs hung next to his remaining M67 grenade.

Out of desperation, he plucked one off and tossed it as far as he could. It landed in the water about a hundred feet away with a faint plop. Smoke hissed out of it a moment later.

"I'm right behind you," Beckham said into his mini-mic. The ceiling rumbled as jets swooped overhead for a third pass, drowning out his voice.

Command was hitting the Variants hard. After 1st Platoon had drawn them out of their lairs, General Kennor had likely ordered every available pilot in range to mount up. The flyboys were showering New York with hellfire and death. Beckham clenched his jaw—Kennor had used him, his men, and thousands of other soldiers as bait.

A shard of concrete slashed Beckham's arm, tearing him from his thoughts. A second piece clanked off his helmet so hard it threw him off balance. He dropped to a knee and raised his pistol toward the smoke. Moonlight from an open manhole bathed him in light. He flipped up his NVGs and squinted at the smoke.

"Move!" Timbo shouted.

"I'll catch up!" Beckham yelled back. He held his position and continued searching for the monsters. The swirling cloud quickly spread over the corridor. His heart thumped as he waited. Seconds ticked by. Five. Ten. The footfalls of his team splashed through the water, gradually fading.

A flash of motion broke inside the curtain of smoke. The single shape of the colossal Variant lingered at the edge of the barrier. It tilted its head, yellow eyes blinking rapidly as it searched for Beckham.

He fired on reflex, his trigger finger responding to the

stab of fear with three shots. The rounds punched into the thick Variant's sweaty chest, jerking it from side to side. It let out a roar and leaped to the wall.

Beckham fired off two more shots. One clipped the Variant's cranium, blowing off an ear and a piece of skull. That only enraged the monster. It clambered across the bricks, closing the gap between it and Beckham. He could smell it now. The sour stench of rotting fruit carried over the putrid sewage.

"What the hell are you—" Chow started to say over the comm as Beckham's gunfire silenced him. He fired again and again, but the monster's thick muscles seemed to absorb the bullets. The high-pitched screeches and the popping joints of other Variants echoed through the tunnel in the break of his gunshots.

Beckham knew what came next.

Fatigue had screwed with his senses. He should have known the smoke wouldn't cover their escape—should have known his bullets wouldn't stop them. Without thinking, he reached for his last grenade, bit off the pin, and tossed it at the beast of a Variant that was now only fifty feet away.

"Frag out!" Beckham shouted.

He turned to run when a meaty body knocked him onto his back in the water. There was no time to react, no time to call for help or curse the fact he hadn't seen the other Variant stalking him through the manhole above. There was only a fraction of a second to whip his head away from the Variant's maw.

The beast pushed against Beckham's chest, forcing him below the rancid water. Stars broke across his vision as he battled his way to the surface. A realization hit him then. He had four, maybe five seconds before the grenade exploded. The timer counted down in his mind as he fought.

Five seconds.

Beckham clamped a hand around the creature's thick neck while flailing for his pistol with the other. He came up empty, the weapon lost in the muck.

Another second passed. He panicked, knowing he was well within the kill radius of the grenade. In a final, desperate attempt to escape the monster, he reached for his knife. He jammed the blade into the open mouth of the Variant. Teeth shattered as he plunged the tip into its brain with a wet *thunk*.

A gurgling croak escaped the monster's swollen lips before it went limp. The deadweight pushed down, forcing Beckham beneath the water again. He heard a muddled voice as he struggled back to the surface.

"Beckham! Hold on! I'm com—"

The words vanished in an explosion. Shrapnel whistled through the tunnel, tearing into the flesh of the corpse on top of him. A piece bit into Beckham's exposed right shoulder. He winced from the raw heat that instantly turned his right arm numb. Pinned down, he was forced to watch helplessly as fissures broke across the ceiling. Chunks fell from the network of cracks into the foul water.

He squirmed under the dead Variant, but his right arm was out of commission. The corpse had saved him from the blast only to suffocate him beneath the water.

Red flooded his vision, and a memory of the night he spent with Kate floated into his mind. It disappeared into a flashback of Building 8 and the members of Team Ghost who had never made it out.

The memories gnawed at his mind as his lungs groped for oxygen. Darkness slowly replaced the red. His body was numb now, so numb he could hardly feel the weight of the Variant roll off him. His eyes snapped open as someone grabbed his flak jacket and hauled him from the water.

A voice, distorted by the dull ringing in Beckham's ears, called out for him.

"Beckham! You with me, man?"

"Yeah," Beckham managed to say. He was still alive, but he knew he was in bad shape. His shoulder burned as if someone had dumped battery acid on it, and his lungs felt like they'd been crushed. He squinted to focus on the face hovering over him.

Fingers snapped in front of Beckham's eyes. His vision slowly cleared to the sight of Chow looking him up and down for injuries.

Beckham took in deep breaths filled with the scent of seared flesh and the rotten water. The burn of stomach acid ate at his throat. He ran his tongue over slimy teeth and spat into the muck.

"You okay?" someone else asked.

Beckham could hardly hear anything over the rush of blood in his ears. He sat there for a few minutes as the world slowly returned to normal.

"We need to get moving," another voice said.

Beckham flipped his NVGs back into position. Smoke and dust whirled through the tunnel behind Chow, Jensen, and Timbo. He twisted to see Jinx, Ryan, and Valdez holding security on their rear guard.

"You good, man?" Chow asked.

"Everything but my right shoulder," Beckham said. "Got nicked by some shrapnel."

"Help him up," Chow ordered. "And be careful."

Beckham grimaced as Timbo bent down, grabbed him under the armpits, and hoisted him to his feet. The other men formed a perimeter around him, like a legion of knights protecting a fallen warrior.

"You're one crazy son of a bitch," Jensen said as he stared at the destruction.

"Had to hold them," Beckham said.

"Yeah," Jensen said. "Looks like you did."

"For now," Beckham added. He applied pressure to his wound and scanned the dissipating smoke one more time for movement. Nothing stirred. The Variants had been reduced to scattered chunks of gore.

"Let's move out," Beckham said. He was light-headed, but they had to keep moving.

"Hold up, man. Let me look at your shoulder," Chow said.

"It can wait," Beckham said. "Someone give me a gun. I lost mine in the blast."

Jensen handed him a revolver. Beckham flipped open the cylinder of the Colt .45 and counted the six hollow-tipped cartridges.

"That's my girl," Jensen said. "I want her back."

Although the NVGs were covering his eyes, Beckham knew the lieutenant colonel was sizing him up. If he were in Jensen's shoes, he would be doing the same thing.

"On me," Beckham said. He didn't give his men a chance to protest. He strode through the group and led them away from the carnage, blood still dripping from his shoulder.

Ringing followed him through the tunnels, singing in his ears. He lost track of time in the rancid, damp network of storm drains and sewers.

The next corridor widened and curved into a larger passage with brick platforms on both sides. Beckham jumped onto the right ledge and hugged the wall, happy to be out of the shit. Jensen and Jinx hurried across the platform on the left, Timbo close on their six.

Beckham pressed down on his wound. If he made it out of this, he was going to need stitches and some powerful antibiotics to combat sepsis. The injury blazed from the bacteria that had already entered his system.

"You got eyes?" Chow asked.

"Looks clear," Beckham replied.

There was no sign of Variants or other threats in the tunnel. For the first time in hours, Beckham could make out the trickle of water. The ringing from the grenade was still fading, but the air force had finally finished its bombardment.

As the team worked forward, the trickle intensified into a steady stream. Falls cascaded in the distance. The shades of green folded into darkness, the end of the tunnel transforming into a black portal of a cavern. Beckham slowed as he approached a waterfall of sewage spilling over the edge into the massive room.

He formed a fist with his hand and then pointed to his eyes and then at the drop-off. Jensen and Timbo acknowledged with nods and eased into a stealthy formation on the left platform.

"Let me bandage you up," Chow whispered. He squeezed by Beckham and crouched in front of him. "How you feeling, man?"

"Dizzy," Beckham replied. A random star floated across his vision.

"You've lost some blood," Chow said. He reached into his pack and pulled out a small medical box. Then he leaned in and flipped his NVGs, using what little light the tunnel behind them provided for a better view.

"Looks deep," Chow said.

"Feels…" Beckham shook his head. He caught a glimpse of Timbo walking closer to the ledge.

Chow cut away a piece of Beckham's shirt and dressed the wound with antiseptic. The cold gel burned its way into his shoulder, and Beckham gritted his teeth. He closed his eyes and waited for the agony to pass. Chow applied a bandage over the injury.

"Should stop the bleeding," Chow said. "But we need—"

Timbo's voice flickered over the comm, cutting Chow off.

"Holy...holy *fuck*!"

Beckham's eyes flipped open. The Ranger was crouched at the end of the left platform, peering over the side. In a blink of an eye, he stumbled away and fell on his ass, scrambling backward with his beefy arms.

"Contacts?" Beckham said, his heart kicking. He pulled away from Chow and walked slowly to the edge of the tunnel.

Timbo didn't immediately reply. His gasping breaths crackled across the comm channel as he scrambled away.

"What the fuck did you see?" Beckham asked.

"I...I..." The shock in Timbo's voice gave Beckham pause. He'd never heard the man so terrified.

Beckham inched closer to the ledge, with Chow as a shadow. Together they crouched and looked over the side. A moment passed, a second frozen in time. The image his eyes relayed to his brain went unprocessed. It had to be a trick of the light, a mirage. An illusion fired off by his overtired brain. Or, at least, that's what he wanted it to be.

But this was no illusion.

This was real.

A half dozen other tunnels dumped into a central chamber, feeding a pool of sewage below. The walls and ceiling of the massive room were covered with hundreds of human prisoners, their bodies plastered to the walls with thick vines of webbing that crisscrossed their flesh like bloated veins. Some were mutilated beyond recognition. Others were missing limbs.

Variants crawled across the walls, their backs hunched, clinging to the bricks with talons and the hairlike fibers Kate's team had discovered. One of them clawed its way through the sticky film covering an unconscious man.

His eyes shot open when the creature clamped down on his stomach and ripped into his flesh. He screamed, but his voice was quickly lost in the roar of the waterfall.

"Let's go," Chow whispered.

Beckham swallowed, unable to formulate a response. He backed away from the ledge, only to see a woman in a CBRN suit attached to the wall on his right. Her eyes met his, and she reached out with a trembling hand.

"Please. Please help me," she whispered, her lips trembling.

Beckham brought a finger to his mouth, but it was already too late. Their whispers had attracted the nearest creature. It let out a high-pitched roar that made Beckham's heart kick. The clicking of joints and the scratching of claws followed as the sleeping Variants stirred and searched the darkness.

"We need to move," Chow said. "Now, man."

Footfalls pounded the platforms as the team retreated, but Beckham hesitated. His eyes shifted from the prisoner to the Variants racing across the ceiling.

"Please," the woman cried. "Please don't leave me."

Beckham threw a glance over his shoulder. The other men were halfway down the hall. Only Chow remained.

"Come on," he said, waving frantically.

"No," Beckham said. "Help me." He wasn't going to leave someone behind. Not when she was in arm's reach.

Chow hustled over without further hesitation. "You're fucking crazy."

"Hold my belt," Beckham said. He drew his knife and crouched, using the blade to cut away the sticky vines across the woman's feet and legs. When those were free, he slit through the webbing across her stomach and chest. Her body sagged forward, but Chow grabbed her before she plummeted into the water below. He pulled her to safety and she collapsed to the ground. Beckham bent down to help her and saw the deep gashes on her legs beneath the torn suit.

"You're going to be okay," Beckham assured her, hoping it wasn't a lie. He caught a glimpse of the pack charging across the ceiling and walls. They were close now. Seconds away.

"Beckham, Chow, where the hell are you?" Jensen said over the comm.

"On our way," Beckham replied. He grabbed the two grenades off Chow's vest and considered what he was about to do. The decision only took a split second. If he couldn't save the mutilated captives, he was going to make sure they didn't suffer any longer.

"Get her out of here," Beckham said. "I'm right behind you."

Chow looked at him and nodded. The woman moaned in agony as he bent down and scooped her up.

Beckham cradled the grenades in one arm and fired off a flurry of well-aimed shots with the .45 to buy him a few seconds. When the Variants scattered, he jammed the pistol into his belt and plucked the pin off one of the grenades with his teeth. He launched it into the air with his good arm and watched it stick to the webbing of a prisoner. Then he pulled the pin off the second grenade and tossed it over his shoulder as he ran, like so many times before, away from the monsters.